Fire Point

A Ryan Lock Novel

Sean Black

Praise for Sean Black

'This series is ace. There are deservedly strong Lee Child comparisons as the author is also a Brit, his novels US-based, his character appealing, and his publisher the same' – Sarah Broadhurst, *Bookseller*

'This is a writer, and a hero, to watch' – Geoffrey Wansell, *Daily Mail*

'Black's style is supremely slick' – Jeremy Jehu, *Daily Telegraph*

'The pace of Lee Child, and the heart of Harlan Coben' – Joseph Finder, *New York Times* Bestseller (*Paranoia, Buried Secrets*)

'The heir apparent to Lee Child' – Ken Bruen, internationally bestselling author of *The Guards*

'Ryan Lock is a protagonist tough enough to take on the Jacks of this world (that's Bauer and Reacher)' – Russel McLean

'Black's star just keeps on rising' – *Evening Telegraph*

Copyright Sean Black 2014

All Rights Reserved

This book is a work of fiction, and except in the case of historical fact, any resemblance to actual persons, living or dead, is coincidental

www.seanblackbooks.com

PART ONE

Fire Point: *the temperature at which a flammable substance continues to burn after being ignited, even after the source of ignition is removed.*

1

Blood in, blood out. That was the deal. To join them, you had to take someone's life. To leave you had to surrender your own, or expect to have it taken from you. Not that anyone had ever left. Or even hinted that they wanted to. Why would they?

Leaving would be an admission of defeat. It would involve returning to the life they'd had before, and that was no life at all.

To go back to being a beta male? To return to the life of an AFC (average frustrated chump)?

No. That wasn't even a possibility. Once you had taken the red pill, and embraced your inner alpha male, there was no going back. You saw the world differently. You saw it for what it was rather than what you had been conditioned to believe it was.

But seeing wasn't enough. Not for Krank, anyway. Knowledge without action was worthless. Perhaps if he'd been selfish it might have been. After the San Diego lair, he'd had everything that most men desired – even if they weren't honest enough to admit it. Money, status, so many women it actually became a chore. But, like the other the men who had come before him, men who bent the world to their design, he had soon tired of the material, the external. He wanted to leave his mark. He knew that he had to embrace his destiny.

To do that, he set out on a new course of study. He left the lair. He traveled to Europe, staying first in London, then moving south and east. From London he moved to Paris, then Rome and Prague and Budapest. All the while he read, devouring two, sometimes three books in a single day. History, politics, science, anthropology. A lot of anthropology. Before he'd left, Gretchen had given him a reading list culled from her study of feminism and gender studies. He had studied them with rigor, all the better to understand the enemy.

He saw how the world had shifted. He identified the damage the shift had done. He identified those responsible. He began to formulate a plan of how balance might be restored. Not that he would be able to do it alone, or even with help. But, thought Krank, he could begin the change that was needed. He could light a flare of hope for the others who would undoubtedly follow.

More time passed. His reading inched back toward more contemporary matters. That was when he stumbled upon the idea of blood initiation as practiced by street gangs in Los Angeles. Of course, this rite of passage had much deeper roots, any idiot knew that, but it could serve a higher calling than controlling foot soldiers who would sling dope. It could provide a strong, permanent bond.

What Krank had in mind wasn't a criminal enterprise, even though that was how it would be regarded by this feminized society. No, thought Krank, he had a much nobler goal – the return of the natural order as it had been for thousands of years.

Tonight was another initiation. Blood in. The third such ceremony since he had come home.

Krank shifted a little in the driver's seat of the black 5-series BMW as they cruised through the midnight-blue streets of downtown Los Angeles. It was a little after three in the morning. The clubs were starting to empty.

That was when he saw her. White. Blonde. Staggering a little uncertainly on high heels. Most important of all, alone, a calf separated from the herd.

She reached down to tug at her skirt, and almost lost her balance. Her hand went up to the wall as she steadied herself. She opened her purse, took out her iPhone, no doubt ready to conjure up a cab using Uber or one of the competing apps that were driving taxi companies out of business.

Krank pulled the BMW over to the curb. He took out his cell phone. He hit the call button. 'You see her?' he said into the phone. 'That's the one.'

'I see her,' came the reply. Tension in the voice. Nerves. It was one thing to talk about this stuff, and quite another when it came to game time. Not that Krank minded. Nerves were good. Nerves meant you were alive.

'Okay,' said Krank. 'Over to you. But don't be too obvious. Give it like a minute. Forty-five seconds minimum.'

'I know.'

Krank smiled at the tetchiness in the reply. No, he thought, you don't know shit. You're a virgin when it comes to this. Everyone is. You only know afterward. Nothing prepares you for your first. It's like taking that red pill for the first time but multiplied by a hundred. With the rush comes the horror. Like how someone taking heroin for the first time usually gets sick.

Blood in.

2

All Kristina Valeris wanted to do was get home, climb into bed and go to sleep. She swiped at the screen of her iPhone and pulled up the app she was looking for. Like Uber, SafeHome used the GPS location technology in her iPhone to send out a request for a driver in the area to pick her up. The difference with SafeHome was that it tried to match female passengers with female drivers, especially when it was this late. You paid a little more, but it was worth it.

A few seconds later, her iPhone vibrated. She opened the message saying a car was on its way, along with the fee it would charge to take her home. She hit accept and slouched against the wall to wait. She could feel the pounding bass line from inside the club. Dehydrated from one too many cocktails, she had the start of a headache, and her feet were sore. Worse than that, she'd had the fight to end all fights with her girlfriend over this guy they'd met at the bar. *So dumb*.

As the sweat cooled on her body, and the wind picked up, she shivered. Down the street, there was a black sedan. It had been there since she had come out of the club.

She was pretty sure there was someone in the driver's seat, and it was creeping her out.

Uh, hurry up, stupid cab.

She narrowed her eyes a little in the gloom and tried to get a look at the guy in the BMW. She could see him now, his hands high on the steering wheel, staring at her.

Creep.

She had a good mind to march over, tap on his window and ask him what the hell he was staring at. She checked her watch – a gift from her father on her eighteenth birthday. A Cartier. Money making up for the fact he was never around.

Kristina turned at the sound of a car engine coming from the other end of the street. *Thank God.* She just hoped that the driver didn't want to chat.

She walked over to the car, a dark blue Honda. She stopped as she realized that the driver was a man. A young man, barely out of high school, with thick, curly black hair and oily, pimply skin. He lowered his window. 'You ordered a car?'

'You're from SafeHome? I thought it would be a woman.'

He looked away from her with a little shrug of his shoulders. 'I'm who you got. If you don't want to use me, it'll be at least twenty minutes more to wait.'

Screw it, she thought. He didn't look like a threat. Hell, she had more muscles than him, and in any case she always carried pepper spray. Plus, all the drivers were police checked and their journeys logged – who they picked up, where they collected them, and where they dropped them off. That probably made it safer than hailing a cab in the street with no one knowing which cab you had taken and where to.

Down the street, the BMW driver was still staring at her. She opened the rear door of the Honda and got in. Settling herself on the back seat, she unzipped her purse and rifled through all the crap for her tiny canister of pepper spray. She moved it to the top so that it was in easy reach, and zipped the purse back up.

The driver was sitting there, like a dummy. She could feel his eyes on her in the rearview mirror. She was starting to wonder if maybe one of her boobs had popped out or something. Not that guys didn't stare, but this was weird.

The driver half turned in his seat. He looked scared. His pupils were wide, and his face flushed. He turned back round. 'I can't do this. I'm sorry,' he said, his voice barely rising above a whisper.

At first she wasn't sure she had heard him correctly.

Then he said it again.

'I'm sorry. You'll have to get out.'

Now she was pissed. 'Look, I need to get home, and standing out there was creeping me out. There was some guy back there sitting in his car— Never mind. But look, I need to get home so can you hurry the fuck up and drive?' She could have left it at that. But she really was cranky. He was looking at her wide-eyed, like he hadn't heard her. She whispered under her breath, 'Just drive would you, asshole?'

3

He was saving her life, and all she could do was bitch at him and call him an asshole. Well, he told himself, he would show her what an asshole was. He reached down, shoved the car into drive and hit the gas. He peeled away so fast that she was thrown back in her seat.

'I said drive. Not break my neck.'

He ignored her. He got to the end of the narrow street and swung out onto Olive, heading for the 110. Krank was coming up behind in the BMW, thrown off by his fast getaway. He saw the van that Loser was driving fall in behind.

He tore down Olive. The girl in back grabbed his headrest and pulled herself forward. 'Take it easy, okay? I didn't mean to shout at you. I've had a bad night.'

He ignored her, his hands tight around the wheel, his shoulders tight with tension born of the knowledge that he was going to take her life. He felt ready for it now. The rage was building in him. He ran through all the rejections, all the times that girls had blown him off, or humiliated him, or treated him like dirt. He held his wrath tight, gathering it up, getting it ready to unleash on her.

'Why are you going this way?' she asked. She sounded on edge, unsure.

It felt good to hear the uncertainty in her voice. 'It's faster,' he said.

There was a ping from her phone. She reached down and plucked it from her bag. He guessed it would be the driver who should have picked her up messaging to ask where she was. He half turned to see her staring at the screen. If the look on her face was anything to go by, he had guessed right.

Once the shock passed, she would start making calls, and he couldn't have that. He pulled down hard on the steering wheel. Behind him Krank slowed, flashing the BMW's headlights.

The sudden change of direction sent her flying and the phone flipped out of her hand. She started scrambling around under his seat for it. He slowed, took one hand off the wheel and reached under his seat, feeling for it at the same time she was searching. He felt its edge and used his fingers to inch it forward. He grabbed it.

'Give me that!' she screamed.

He hit the button to lower the window and tossed the phone out onto the street. She lunged for him. Her nails scraped at his face. It stung. She jabbed for his eyes. He reached back and grabbed her wrist, twisting it hard enough to make her cry out in pain.

The sound excited him in a way he hadn't expected. This was control. This was what being in charge felt like. He wanted more of it. Being ultra-alpha was what Krank called it. There was alpha and ultra-alpha, and the bridge between them was violence.

He twisted her wrist more, and she let out another yelp. This was easier than he'd imagined. She was weaker. He was stronger. His nerves were gone.

A second later he heard the hiss, felt the spray splash across the side of his face and felt the intense burn in his eyes. He struggled for breath. He let go of her so he could rub at his face. The pain only grew.

He couldn't see. He jabbed down on the brake pedal. The Honda slowed. The car hadn't stopped, but he heard the rear passenger door open. He looked round, grabbed for her trailing leg as she threw herself from the still moving car. But she was gone. Out onto the early-morning deserted streets of downtown Los Angeles.

4

Krank could only watch as the Honda braked hard and, seconds before it came to a complete stop, the girl bailed. She landed hard on one knee. For a second she didn't move, and he had hope. The van was right behind. They could scoop her up and spirit her away before anyone saw what was happening.

She rose, one hand clutching her knee. She moved toward the sidewalk, shaking off the pain, adrenalin finally kicking in. She broke into a run that was half jog half hobble.

Krank pulled up directly behind the Honda. If the cops showed now, he could make out like it was a fender bender. The girl wasn't going to hang around to contradict him. She was already a hundred yards away. Still catchable but he needed to check something first.

He got to the driver's door. 'What happened?' he demanded.

The driver looked up, hands balled into fists that rubbed furiously at his eyes, a toddler fighting sleep. 'She pepper-sprayed me. The bitch pepper-sprayed me.'

'Can you drive?' Krank asked him.

'Maybe,' the driver said, blinking.

Krank waved at the van. Loser got out, looking, as he always did, like a slightly better-dressed version of Shaggy from the *Scooby Doo* cartoons. 'We need to find her. We'll give it fifteen minutes. If we haven't found her by then, we'll split,' he said to Loser.

Krank climbed back into the BMW. The engine turned over. He closed his eyes for a moment and tried to visualize the girl in his mind's eye.

He had a sense that she would try to hide. A bad strategy. The worst. Her best chance at escape was distance from them and staying where she might be seen by others. Hiders tended to find the nearest spot they could and stay there, out of their pursuers' gaze but out of everyone else's too.

5

She was still so shaken from what had just happened that she almost missed it. She had never heard of the place. She had thought that the two guys standing next to the door were dealers who had found a doorway to ply their trade. It was only when the door they were standing in front of opened, and two men stumbled out, arms around each other's waists, that she realized what it was.

Oh, thank God.

She slowed to a walk, and tried to catch her breath. It had all happened so fast. One minute she was getting into a car to be driven home, the next . . . Being kidnapped? Raped? Killed?

And they were still out there. Looking for her.

Meanwhile the two doormen were staring at her, arms folded. Doing her best to appear calm and composed, Kristina walked over to them, took a deep breath, trying to find the words that best described what had just happened. It didn't work. The words tumbled out of her.

'I need your help. I just almost got killed. I ordered a cab and the guy that turned up, well, he wasn't a cab. I got in, and he was going to drive me off.'

The slightly shorter of the two doormen smirked. 'You ordered a cab, and he drove you off. That's usually what cabs do, honey.'

'No – I mean he was kidnapping me. He grabbed my phone and threw it out the window and I had to—'

She stopped. They were both looking at her like she was crazy. She needed to row back. Spare them the details. 'Do you have a phone I could use to call someone?' she asked.

The bigger guy made a big show of patting himself down. 'Must have left it at home. Now, keep walking. We got enough crazies inside,' he said, hooking a thumb toward the door.

'Didn't you listen to what I just said? I was attacked.'

The shorter one stepped toward her. She could feel the menace as he flexed his biceps. 'Look, sweetie, we're not the cops. Now, you walk one block that way it puts you on Verdugo. LAPD usually have a patrol in that area. Go tell them your story. We don't get paid for this kind of shit.'

Just her luck to find the most asshole-ish nightclub doormen in downtown. The way they were staring at her, she knew they wouldn't help. But as long as she could see them she didn't think anyone would try to snatch her off the street. If she walked toward Verdugo, there would likely be people. She could flag down a patrol car. They would have to help her.

'Thanks for nothing.'

The short doorman with the big biceps gave her a fey little wave that was all fingers. 'Bye-bye.'

She started walking.

6

Engine dead, headlights switched off, Krank watched the girl walk away from the nightclub door. He tapped the screen of his phone, waited for the others to pick up.

'She's heading your way. Soon as she turns the corner, do it. Fast and rough as it takes. RV back at the usual place.'

The usual place was a small, beaten-up wood-framed house on two acres near Mulholland Drive in the Hollywood Hills, a short distance from the 101 freeway. It had belonged to Krank's grandfather, who had left it to him as part of a trust. It came with the condition that it could not be sold for at least thirty years after transfer. As far as Krank was concerned, it was a classic move that typified his relationship with his family. Leave him something that was worth enough money to change his life, but make sure that he couldn't actually use it to do that. Turn a windfall into a millstone. Yeah, that was his family, all right.

Using it like this was Krank's way of subverting his grandpa's wishes. *You want me to keep the house? Okay,*

Pops. I will. But I'll make sure that by the time I'm done no one will ever want to live there.

As a place to bring people like the girl, it was perfect: tucked in close to the freeway, with easy access to the Sunset Strip, but still secluded; plenty of room out the rear that didn't back onto any other homes. Krank had added extra height to the wall at the front and put in electric gates but those were the only changes he'd made.

He hit the clicker, and the BMW slid through, then up the winding, weed-infested driveway. He parked in back. The others were already there. The Honda was at an angle, and the white van was tucked in tight next to the external steps that led down into the barn his grandfather had used to store his collection of classic cars.

Krank crossed to the main house. The door that led into the kitchen was open. MG was there, head over the sink, dousing his eyes with water. Krank pulled open the refrigerator door and took out a carton of milk. 'Water just makes it worse. Use this.'

He had to place the carton in MG's hand. He'd be amazed if he didn't have to wipe the kid's ass some day. He wondered why he bothered. Then he reminded himself that he had been like MG. It was just that he was further ahead on his journey than the kid.

'Thanks,' MG said, cupping some milk in hands that still trembled from the adrenalin dump of his screwed-up abduction. He splashed his eyes, which were like red slits that had been carved into his face.

Krank had to hand it to her: she'd got MG good. It was something he would use later with MG as a teachable moment. Showing mercy, hesitating in the fight, could only end badly for everyone. Now what would have been a quick death had been prolonged.

He leaned against the kitchen island, with its knife block and red granite top, and watched MG get cleaned up. Finally, he said: 'You ready?'

MG looked at him, or as best he could with his eyes like that. 'I don't know.'

Krank advanced on him. He reached across and tapped MG's left temple with his knuckle. 'You're thinking too much. Thinking time's over.' He dug out a Nietzsche quote he'd used before in this kind of situation. '"When faced by unpleasant consequences, one is too ready to abandon the proper standpoint from which an action ought to be considered."'

MG ran a hand through his dense mop of hair and gave a little nod. Krank slapped him on the back. 'First one's the hardest. It gets easier after that.'

PART TWO

7

Even though he wasn't a father, Ryan Lock understood the power of children to change people. Some of the biggest idiots he'd met – and, in his line of work, he'd met plenty – could often set aside their own self-obsession and egomania, albeit temporarily, when they became parents. Around their children, they were different people. Sometimes for the better, other times for the worse.

Becoming a parent increased your surface area, and made you more vulnerable. A child's pain was yours. Its failings tracked back in many parents' minds to some failure on their part. Was there something you could have done differently? Had you been too harsh when a softer approach would have worked better? Had you been too soft when a little discipline was needed?

There were no easy answers. People did their best. It was just that sometimes their best wasn't enough. Tarian Griffiths was just a mom trying to do her best. When the dust settled, and the body count had been tallied, that fact would be lost. But it was the truth.

Ryan Lock handed the keys of his new car, a custom up-armored, metallic grey Audi S6, to the valet parking attendant standing outside Café Del Rey. Along with the keys he also palmed the man his usual hefty gratuity, along with the instructions that went with the cash: 'Keep my car up front, parked facing out and ready to go.'

The valet accepted the cash with a smile. 'Certainly, sir.'

Lock walked into the restaurant that looked out over the marina. It was early evening on a Tuesday. The place was quiet. This was a meeting he had agreed to with reluctance. From the initial conversation it had sounded a lot like babysitting. Not that a babysitting gig was unusual, far from it. Much of the time bodyguarding could be described as babysitting, but with guns.

Over his years working high-end private security, Ryan Lock had realized that it was a hell of a lot easier to save someone from an external threat than from themselves. Stalkers, kidnappers, blackmailers could all be dealt with. Headed off. Arrested. Scared. If it came down to the wire, and they presented a clear and present danger to life, they could be killed. But a principal who was determined to screw up their life? Or to place themselves in a bad situation? That was a whole other deal.

The challenge of the job was managing the individual you were charged with protecting, your principal, whether they be a politician who liked to plunge into the crowd or a rock star with a taste for the low-life. Then you had to factor in the wishes of the client – the person or organization who was picking up the tab.

At the restaurant reservations desk, Lock informed the hostess whom he was there to meet. She led him toward a table at the front of the long dining room that looked out over the boats in the marina. Tarian Griffiths was already seated, a glass of mineral water on the table in front of her. She tapped away at the screen of her iPhone with perfectly manicured fingers.

'Ms Griffiths,' said Lock, waving away the offer of a menu. 'No, thank you,' he said to the hostess. 'Just some water, please.'

Tarian Griffiths didn't get up but she did extend her hand. Lock shook it. With auburn hair, bright blue eyes, high cheekbones and a perfect smile, Tarian had been a successful soap actress back in New York, before she had met and married wealthy tech entrepreneur Peter Blake. They'd had one son together, Marcus, before divorcing a few years later. Peter Blake must have fallen hard because he'd married Tarian without a pre-nuptial agreement.

She had married again a few years ago, a fellow multi-millionaire she had met via her charity work. Teddy Griffiths came from Texas oil money, and to keep her happy he had re-located to LA, where she had continued to pursue her acting career, with mixed success. They'd had two children together – a boy and a girl, both under ten – and were a regular feature on the LA philanthropy circuit. But she was there to talk to Lock about Marcus.

When Lock had spoken to her the previous day, she had been deliberately vague about the specific problem. All he knew was that twenty-year-old Marcus Griffiths was having problems, and his mom didn't want to go to the cops. If he'd had to guess, he'd have put his money on drugs. Maybe money owed to someone heavy, or a blackmail attempt that she wanted him to shut down.

Lock sat across from her. Outside on the dock an elderly guy was parking a sky blue Maserati next to one of the half-dozen wooden docks.

'Thank you for seeing me, Mr Lock,' said Tarian. She made strong eye contact. He understood why men fell for her. Not only was she beautiful but there seemed to be a real person there too, beneath the sheen of glamor.

With all that said, this wasn't a date and Lock wanted to get down to business. 'How can I help you?'

'It's my son, Marcus. He's going through a difficult time at the moment, and . . .' She sighed. 'Well, I'm sure you know what kids are like when it comes to talking to their parents. I need someone to keep an eye on him for me.'

Lock flattened his hands palm down on the bright white linen tablecloth as a waiter brought his water. 'Okay, first things first. Is there something specific you're concerned about? Do you believe your son is being threatened by someone? Is he involved with drugs? Has he fallen in with a bad crowd? All easily done in this town.'

She swallowed hard. 'No, nothing like that. No one is threatening him that I know of, and I very much doubt he'd be involved with drugs. It's difficult to explain. He's living on his own here in the Marina, and I'm just worried about him.'

Lock decided to change tack. Clearly something was wrong but she couldn't, or wouldn't, articulate it. When he first met a client it was often the case that they didn't want to say flat out what the problem actually was. Some kind of trust had to be established first. 'Okay. When you say keep an eye on him, are you thinking surveillance or security?'

She gave him a puzzled look. 'I'm not sure.'

'Well,' Lock said, 'do you need someone to track him without him knowing? That kind of keeping an eye on? Or do you think he needs someone with him, offering close protection? Because if it's the former, you'd save a lot of money just using a regular private detective rather than myself or my partner.'

Her eyes widened. 'Oh, yes, I see. No, the latter. I want you to provide security. Be his bodyguard.'

They were finally getting somewhere. 'And he needs a bodyguard, because . . .' prompted Lock.

'I can more than afford to pay your fee, Mr Lock,' said Tarian.

Lock didn't doubt it. 'I'm sure you can. But that wasn't what I was asking you. Why does your son need protection?'

'I don't know that he does,' she said.

In future, for meetings like this, Lock was going to ask potential clients for money up front – some kind of consultation fee to offset time wasted. He took a breath. 'Mrs Griffiths, if Marcus is caught up in something that you might not be comfortable telling, say, law enforcement, well, I'm not law enforcement so it goes no further. If he's being blackmailed, and you don't want information to become public—'

'No, it's nothing like that,' she said, and lapsed back into silence.

Lock didn't say anything for a good ten seconds. After that, he started to get up. She motioned for him to sit down. She was struggling with this. Perfect white teeth bit down on a plump lower lip. 'I'm concerned that my son is either going to hurt himself or someone else.'

Lock wanted to be clear on what she was saying. 'By hurt you mean physically harm?'

Tarian looked away. 'Yes.'

8

Sunlight sparkled on the water as Lock strolled with Tarian Griffiths by his side. He had suggested they take a walk for two reasons. First, there would be less chance of their conversation being overheard, and second, walking made conversations like this easier. There was something about physical activity that helped people unburden themselves. And while Tarian Griffiths had what seemed like the perfect life, the reality was different. In Lock's experience, it usually was.

According to Tarian, even though Marcus had been barely five when she had left his father, he had never recovered from his parents' split. He was a quiet child, introverted, and had found it difficult to make friends. Later, when his behavior had become more difficult a psychologist had diagnosed Asperger's, but Teddy Griffiths had flown into a rage at the very idea. He was old school. Didn't believe in putting labels on kids. He definitely didn't want people thinking his stepson was some kind of a (his words) 'loony tune'.

For her part, Tarian had hoped that her first-born son was simply a late developer. That he would find his feet and place in the world at college. He was bright and attended the University of Southern California. But barely three months after starting in the fall, he had dropped out and moved to a place in Marina Del Rey. No amount of coaxing from Tarian or bluster from Teddy would get him to go back to college. His biological father, Peter, blamed Tarian.

A breeze picked up from the Pacific, sweeping Tarian's long auburn hair back over her face. 'So,' Lock asked, 'why don't you speak to a mental-health professional?'

'Marcus flips out if I even mention the idea. I thought that perhaps this way I'd have someone close to him who could keep an eye without any of that stigma. And, if I'm honest, I don't think it would hurt to have a male role model around him who isn't constantly telling him he's a failure.'

'You think that's how Marcus will see it? Or do you think he'll believe you're interfering?'

'He won't think I'm interfering if there's a reason for us to have called in private security.'

'But there's not,' said Lock, not liking where this was going.

Tarian stopped and stared out across the marina to the ocean beyond. 'A white lie, Mr Lock. And, given the unusual circumstances, I'd be happy to pay double your usual fee. If you can get Marcus back on track, perhaps even re-enrolled at USC, I'll pay you an additional fifty thousand dollars.'

'Fifty thousand dollars?' Lock said, not entirely sure he'd heard her correctly.

'If that's too small an amount . . . I'd have to talk to Teddy, but I'm sure that I can—'

Lock cut her off: 'First, let me talk to my business partner. If we think we can help, we will. But I don't want to take your money without a good reason.'

Something approaching a smirk flashed across her face. 'Well, Mr Lock, for someone like me, that'd be a first.'

9

Sitting in traffic on Ocean Avenue, Lock called Tyrone 'Ty' Johnson. They had crossed paths while serving in the military, and quickly established an unlikely friendship that had turned into a lucrative high-end private security business after they had both moved to civilian life. Lock took Ty briefly through his meeting with Tarian Griffiths, getting no great response until he reached her offer. Ty cleared his throat. 'Double our usual fee? What's there to think about, brother?'

'The money's good, but it hardly qualifies as a job. I mean, what are we gonna be doing apart from making sure he eats his Wheaties and wipes his ass? That's the beauty of it, know what I'm saying? And the mom's smoking hot too, Ryan. I Googled her. Goddamn, that's one good-looking woman.'

Lock flipped on his turn signal to take the Channel Road down to Pacific Coast Highway. He was heading back to the condo he was renting in Pacific Palisades. 'Number one, she's married. Number two, clients are off limits.'

'Just saying. Listen, I'm driving up from Long Beach in the morning. Don't turn it down before I get there.'

'I wasn't planning on it,' said Lock, as the lights flipped and he joined the jostle of beach traffic and people heading back to the Valley from jobs on the West Side; the ocean shimmered to darkness on his left as the sun crashed hard into the Pacific Ocean.

As he pulled into a parking spot outside his condo, Lock's cell phone rang. It was one of the ex-cops he'd tasked with checking out Marcus. He listened to what the guy had to say, asked a few questions and killed the call. If he'd been curious before, now he was worried.

He ditched his plan to head back to his condo, switched lanes, then headed through the McClure Tunnel and onto the 10 freeway, heading for the main campus of the University of Southern California near Westwood.

10

Next morning, Lock took a seat on the hotel terrace where he had agreed to meet Tarian. It was a table in the far corner. His seat backed onto a wall and gave him a view not only of his fellow guests but the deep stretch of beach. Unfeasibly tanned and healthy-looking folks biked or rollerbladed past on the concrete path. Further down, a group of young men who looked like they'd stepped off the cover of *GQ* magazine were getting ready to play beach volleyball.

Lock glanced at the file he'd begun to assemble on Marcus Griffiths, then up at the perfect blue sky. Everywhere he looked all he could see were beautiful people busy being beautiful. He had a sense of why this young man might have felt he didn't fit.

Ty strode toward Lock's table, pulled out a seat and sat down. Boot-cut jeans, a grey-marled T-shirt that revealed tree-trunk arms, and Oakley sunglasses that only a six-foot-five-inch African-American Marine could pull off without looking like he was trying too hard.

The two men fist-bumped as a waiter appeared. 'Ice water's fine,' said Ty, his elbows resting on the table. He glared at Lock from behind his Oakleys. 'Trying to e-con-o-mize.'

The waiter left them to it. 'You need a loan, Tyrone?' said Lock.

'No need of a loan when we got a primo gig ahead of us. Right?'

Lock slid the file over the table to his partner. Ty took off his sunglasses, opened the folder and began to flick through the pages.

'This is an upscale place, so try to read without moving your lips,' said Lock.

Ty flipped him off by way of reply.

'How's Malik?' Lock asked. Malik was the friend Ty had been visiting with in Long Beach.

'About how you'd expect a man to be after what went down,' said Ty, flipping to a fresh page. Malik's family had been killed after Malik had uncovered a case of serial child sex abuse at the college where he worked as basketball coach in Minnesota. Ty and Lock had come to his aid, but too late to save Malik's wife and kids.

'He knows he can call me anytime,' said Lock.

Ty gave a curt nod. 'I told him. He appreciates it.' He paused as he flipped another page. 'How you doing?' He shrugged his massive shoulders. 'Y'know, being here.'

'I'm okay.'

'Uh-huh,' said Ty, as he got to the section of the hastily assembled file where things got interesting. The letterhead read: 'County Court of Los Angeles'.

Ty's ice water was delivered with the flourish befitting an eight-hundred-dollars-a-night beachfront hotel. He took a sip, put it to one side and went back to reading the court document. After a time, he looked up. 'Who's the girl?' 'Don't know for sure, apart from what it says there. Freshman at USC. Grew up in Orange County. Kappa Alpha Theta sorority. Had some of the same classes as our boy. Guess that's where he ran into her.'

Ty rubbed at his face. 'If they were in the same classes and he has a restraining order that prohibits him being within two hundred yards of her, that might explain him dropping out. You think the mom knows?'

Lock glanced past Ty to the white-painted french doors that led out onto the terrace. 'I don't know. Let's ask her.'

11

More than a few male guests, including those seated with wives and girlfriends, checked Tarian out as she crossed the terrace toward them. Lock guessed that, behind his Oakleys, Ty was one of them. If she was fazed by the male attention, she didn't show it. Lock guessed she was used to that kind of reaction to the point where it barely registered.

He and Ty stood as she reached them. Lock did the introductions. Tarian sat down. The waiter was dismissed with the back of her hand and a curt 'In a moment.

'So?' she began. 'Do we have an agreement that you'll help my son?'

Lock picked up the folder and tossed it across the table at her. 'We did. But I can't work for someone who lies to me.'

'It was stupid of me not to tell you,' said Tarian, her eyes fixed on Lock. 'I thought that if you knew you might not be prepared to help. I didn't think you'd be amenable to helping someone who'd been accused of stalking.'

'A little more than accused,' said Lock, tapping a finger down on the folder. 'Judges don't hand those out for nothing.'

'And I'm taking it seriously, Mr Lock. Though I do have to say that . . . Well, Marcus gets obsessional about things. And sometimes he doesn't realize the effect that can have on other people. He never actually threatened this young woman. He was just overly persistent.'

Ty was looking at Lock. 'That so?'

Lock nodded. 'I went out and spoke to her last night. He never threatened her, but she still felt threatened. Not sure how useful a distinction that is, Mrs Griffiths.'

'What else did she say?' Tarian said. 'Only we're trying to sort something out with the administration at USC to see if Marcus might be able to return in the spring.'

'And I hope you do,' said Lock. 'But I'm afraid we can't help you.'

'Can't?' asked Tarian. 'Or won't?'

'We protect people from others, not from themselves,' said Lock. 'You need a mental-health professional, not private security. And I don't say that to be unkind.'

Tarian leaned forward, lowering her voice. 'Teddy's spoken about that. About having Marcus . . .' She hesitated. Lock had noticed that, unlike cancer or heart disease, when people spoke about mental illness they tended to be more careful about their choice of words. It was as if, even after all this time, the stigma wouldn't go away. 'Well,' she continued, 'my husband thinks Marcus might be better off if he was placed in some kind of secure facility. For his own good. But until he does something . . .'

Right now, Lock couldn't shake off his unease. The girl he'd spoken to at USC, the one who had been stalked by Marcus Griffiths, had told him way more than he was going to share with Tarian.

'By which time it will be too late,' said Lock.

'I don't want that to happen,' said Tarian. 'Please, if you would just meet with my son. Perhaps if someone such as yourselves were to recommend that Marcus needs residential care it might be taken more seriously.'

12

Ty got into the passenger seat of Lock's R6 and closed the door. They were waiting for Tarian. They would follow her car the short distance to her son's apartment in Marina Del Rey.

It was hot. High eighties. That was well above average for Santa Monica, where the ocean breeze tended to keep things nice and pleasant. A heatwave was predicted. It would get up to the nineties here on the coast and the hundreds out in the Valley.

A grey Mercedes with tinted windows appeared. Tarian had the driver's window lowered so they could see it was her. She cruised past them. Lock pulled out behind her and into the traffic on Ocean Avenue.

'So we assess him like we would any other external threat to a principal?' said Ty, one arm dangling out of the window as they drove past a couple of young women in denim shorts and crop tops rollerblading down the sidewalk.

Lock buried the gas pedal to make a light and stay with Tarian's Mercedes. 'Something like that,' he said.

'What's going on here, Ryan? Is there something you're not telling me about this?' What did that co-ed at USC tell you?'

Lock's eyes flicked to the rearview mirror and the black BMW sedan that had been following them since they'd left the hotel. He glanced at his partner. 'It's more what she didn't say than what she did.'

13

Lock pulled in behind Tarian's Mercedes as she talked to the lone security guard manning the entrance to the apartment complex. Every non-resident visitor had to be signed in. They had to give details of who they were, and whom they were there to see. Their vehicle details were recorded too.

Thirty seconds later it was Lock's turn. The security guard was Hispanic, in his late forties, with an easy smile and a professional manner. It was a feature of Marina Del Rey that if you saw someone who wasn't white they were likely working rather than living there. Lock nudged the Audi past him and followed the Mercedes past a series of boat docks and jetties. The BMW had fallen away.

The Mercedes turned right, and disappeared down a ramp into an underground parking lot. Lock followed, pulling into a visitor's spot as Tarian got out.

He and Ty walked her to the elevator. 'Does your son know we're coming?' he asked.

'I called ahead to tell him,' she answered.

'And what did you say about who we are and why we're here?'

She snapped off her sunglasses as the elevator doors opened. 'He knows who you are, but I said the family'd had some kidnapping threats and that you were here to talk about that.'

Lock didn't like it. He wasn't opposed to telling a white lie once in a while, but in general he believed in being honest with people. For a start, the truth was a whole lot easier to remember. And if Marcus had issues, trust would be key. Lying to a volatile person meant you were taking a risk.

He put a hand across the elevator door, preventing it from closing. Tarian had already stepped inside and was waiting for him and Ty.

'That's not gonna do it. You tell your son the truth or we're out of here,' he said to her.

She looked like she was about to argue, but decided against it. Her eyes narrowed. 'I'll tell him I'm worried about him, and you're here to make sure he stays safe. How about that?'

Lock let the door go and stepped into the elevator with Ty. Tarian hit the button for the third floor. The doors closed.

'And the kidnapping threats?' Ty asked. 'You already mentioned those, correct?'

'A family like ours always has some level of threat.'

'Okay, that works. But from now on in, the truth?' said Lock.

'Absolutely,' said Tarian, as the elevator stopped, the doors opened – and somewhere down the corridor a gunshot rang out from behind an apartment door.

14

For a woman wearing heels, Tarian Griffiths could run. She sprinted down the corridor toward her son's apartment.

'Which one's he in?' Lock shouted, as he raced to catch up with her. Ty was already out in front of both of them, his SIG Sauer 226 drawn, his broad chest providing Tarian with body cover.

The reverb of the gunshot had faded. Lock counted off seven doors down this stretch of corridors.

'Which number?' he demanded again.

'Seven. Three zero seven,' Tarian said

Lock counted off the numbers: 307 was the apartment at the very end. He stepped level with Tarian and grabbed her wrist.

So far, what he knew didn't point to anything good being behind the door. Marcus was, at best, emotionally volatile. He knew his mother was on her way up to see him, and for all Lock knew, he might have figured out that she wasn't alone. If he was in a paranoid state and had seen his mom arriving with two heavy-built men, he might have put two and two together and come up with five. Maybe he'd decided it was some kind of tough-love intervention that would end with an injection and a strait-jacket.

More worrying was that they had heard a lone gunshot. Then silence.

If Marcus had just taken his own life, Lock didn't want Tarian walking in on it, client or not.

'Stay out here with Ty,' Lock said to her, then turned to his partner. 'Call nine-one-one. Tell them we have a suspected shot fired inside.'

Tarian began to struggle, trying to get past Ty to the door. It was no contest: doing his best to keep her calm, Ty ended up lifting her up and moving her back.

Lock stepped to the side of the door and knocked. 'Marcus? I need to make sure you're okay so open up. If you can't or won't open up, I'm going to have come in anyway.'

They could wait for security to appear with a master key, but Lock figured it would take too much time. He also knew from experience that the number of people who tried to take their life with a gun and ended up wounding but not killing themselves was surprisingly high.

Tarian began to shout her son's name.

Ty leaned in close to her, his cell phone to his ear as he waited to reach a police dispatcher. 'You're not helping us here, Mrs Griffiths,' he said to Tarian. 'Ryan needs quiet so he can listen. Now let's move back down here. Okay?'

He guided her along the corridor. A door opened, and an older man popped his head out. He was wearing a bathrobe. 'What the hell's going on?'

Ty turned to him. 'Go back inside, sir. The police are on their way.'

The neighbor looked like he was about to argue, until he took in Ty's full frame and decided against it. He disappeared back inside his apartment and closed the door as Ty gave the dispatcher the details the responding officers would need. He turned back to Tarian. 'Does your son have firearms or access to firearms?'

She shook her head. 'Not that I'm aware of.'

Ty fed that information back to the dispatcher.

Lock still hadn't got a response from inside the apartment. Not good. He took a step back and got ready to take a kick at the door.

'Marcus? It's okay. I just want to know you're safe.' Not a sound.

There was nothing else for it. Lock raised his left foot and kicked the door open. Allowing his momentum to carry him forward, he barreled through, his own weapon drawn.

He stood in a narrow corridor. There was no sign of blood or injury.

The air in the apartment was stale and fetid. There was the faint hint of stale cannabis.

'Marcus?'

His question was met with silence.

He stepped through into the main living area. There was a couch, an armchair, a TV mounted on one wall and a games console. A bag of popcorn disgorged its contents across the grey carpet.

Lock bent down, checking under the couch for a weapon. As he did so, he felt a breeze on his back. He looked over at the slatted white blinds and the glass sliding doors that led out to a small balcony. A section of one blind was torn, and a hole punched in the pane. Fragments of glass lay on the carpet. Lock followed the path of the bullet to a hole in the wall.

Someone had been playing with a gun – more than playing by the look of it – but it likely hadn't been Marcus Griffiths, or anyone inside the apartment. With five quick steps, Lock reached the glass doors and forced them open.

His gun drawn, he duck-walked out onto the balcony, staying low.

He took a peek. Down below was a grassy area, and beyond that the next apartment block. It was quiet. He scanned the apartments opposite. Nothing.

Lock walked back into the corridor. Tarian broke past Ty and ran toward him. 'Is he . . .?'

Lock put a hand on her shoulder. 'He's not there. He's gone. There's no blood, no sign of a struggle.'

'Sheriff's Department are on their way,' said Ty. 'You want me to cancel that ambulance?'

'No, leave it for now. We may still have a shooter.'

As Lock turned back to the open apartment door, Ty fell in behind him. Lock prodded the door open with his foot, and both men, guns drawn, pressed forward through the living room toward the balcony.

A breeze picked its way through the hole in the glass door, sweeping up the pages of a paperback book that lay on the coffee-table, next to a laptop computer. Lock motioned for Ty to follow him out onto the balcony. Together they scanned the apartments opposite for any sign of a sniper. Nothing. The only person they could see was a middle-aged man on an exercise bike. He appeared not to have registered that a shot had been fired. Then Lock picked out the white earbuds of his iPod.

To the left was the road that led down to the other blocks in the complex. Beyond the road, gangways led down to the boats. There was no sign of movement on the road or the boats, not that Lock had much of a view of either. Ty was on his cell to the security office. They hadn't seen anyone. Nor had anyone left.

It could be that the shooter was on one of the boats. Either that or they were holed up somewhere else in the complex. In one of the underground parking structures or an apartment.

Finding them would be next to impossible without a lot of boots on the ground. A single shot fired with no one injured and the only damage being a broken door was hardly going to get a huge response from law enforcement. Even in somewhere as usually quiet as the Marina.

More importantly, there was no sign of Marcus Griffiths. There was no blood, no indication that anyone had been injured. Given that his mother had spoken to him not long before, when he had seemed fine, Marcus Griffiths couldn't even be considered a missing person.

The two men looked at the drop from the balcony to the ground. 'What you think?' Lock asked his partner. 'He hears the shot and jumps?'

'It's grass, so it's doable. He hears the shot, followed by someone yelling outside in the corridor and decides to split by the fastest route available,' said Ty.

Lock's eyes narrowed. 'But if he does that he's running toward the shooter.' Glancing back over his shoulder, he saw Tarian walk into the apartment.

'Where is he?'

She kept walking toward them. 'He's not here, but that's not a bad thing. Look, you'd be better waiting in the corridor. We still have someone out there with a gun, and they've already taken one shot at this place.'

Tarian took in the broken glass. 'I need to find my son.'

She started to move again, heading for Lock and Ty. Side on to her, out of the corner of his eye, Lock caught the speck of movement down below. He turned to see someone move behind a metal ventilation grate at the very bottom of the apartment block opposite.

15

'Threat!'

As Lock shouted, he made a dive for Tarian, throwing himself toward her, pushing her back through the open door. He tackled her at the knees, like a rugby player. His shoulder caught the back of her legs – the fastest way he knew to collapse someone and get them on the ground. She yelped with surprise, and shrieked with pain as her knee banged against the floor. Lock was on top of her, his body covering hers. If a shot came through the doors, he would take it first.

His reaction and the speed with which he moved were the result of years of training, and endless repetition. It took hour upon boring hour of walking drills and debus/embus procedures, as well as more static security drills, to shave tenths of a second from your reaction time – to go from being the quiet man to a raging bull.

Less than five seconds after he had spotted the threat, Lock glanced back across to the balcony. Crouched low, Ty had drawn his SIG Sauer 226 from his holster and was taking aim.

There was the crack of a shot from down below. Another round whistled through the open glass door, and embedded itself in the wall.

'Ty!' Lock said. 'You see the shooter?'

'I see them.' Ty's answer came by way of a squeeze of the trigger as he fired at the metal grate. There was a clang as his shot hit metal followed by a moment of silence. Then he growled, 'Missed the motherfucker. He's on the move.'

Lock could feel Tarian's breathing, smell her perfume, feel the heat coming off her body. He eased off her. 'You okay?'

'I think I might have broken my ankle.'

Lock crouched next to her as she rolled onto her side. She didn't seem like a woman accustomed to physical pain, which meant he was fairly sure her ankle was likely sprained. If you broke a bone, you knew about it. Unless you were on drugs or drunk there was very little 'might have' involved.

'Stay down,' barked Lock, rolling off Tarian, who was clutching at her ankle. 'Cops will be here soon.'

'They're moving,' Ty shouted, one long leg over the balcony, ready to make the drop.

'I'm coming,' said Lock, springing to the balcony, and following Ty over the edge. The grass below made the drop of sixteen feet manageable.

Ty was already off and moving, gun drawn, toward the opposite apartment block. Lock dropped into a modified Weaver stance, his SIG punched out ahead of him, and scanned the territory, ready to provide covering fire.

Ty made it to the edge of the apartment block, and Lock sprinted to join him. He ran in a slightly irregular zigzag pattern to make the shooter's job harder, but they were nowhere to be seen.

They reached the metal grille where the shots had come from. Beyond it was the parking structure. A couple of car alarms wailed in protest, no doubt triggered by the fleeing gunman.

They skirted around the edge of the building. Steps down to a door that opened into the garage. Lock pulled the door open. Ty spun through first, and gun-faced the empty space. Lock followed. He kicked out his heel to slow the closing door. It closed with a gentle click. They stood in the semi-gloom and listened. There were four rows of cars, each row two-thirds occupied by vehicles. Facing them was an elevator for residents who didn't want to take the stairs.

Slowly, Lock and Ty moved through the vehicles. There was no sign of anyone. On the other side of the parking lot, there was another set of stairs, and another door that led out to the other side of the block. The shooter would have had plenty of time to make it there before they arrived.

They walked toward it. Took the steps, opened the door and stepped out into bright sunshine. Azure blue water lapped gently against the boats tied up in the marina. Nothing and no one stirred. Besides the wail of sirens in the near-distance, everything was perfectly quiet.

16

Although two shots had been fired, including one that looked like it had been aimed at Tarian Griffiths's head, the Los Angeles County Sheriff's Department didn't seem all that interested. The two officers who had responded went through the motions, but that was about it. Extra units arrived to search the complex for the gunman; they interviewed everyone present and took pictures. When that was done, they hooked their thumbs into their belts and began to study the carpet.

Lock wasn't entirely surprised. The empty apartment was a crime scene without a victim. There was no blood, no sign that anyone had been so much as injured, never mind killed. The only damage had been to the glass doors, the wall, and Tarian's ankle, which appeared to be sprained rather than fractured.

The possible involvement or whereabouts of Marcus Griffiths didn't seem to trouble them much either. Given that his mother had spoken to him not so long ago, he couldn't be considered a missing person. When it came to someone who had reached the age of majority, a certain amount of time had to elapse before the police would even register them as missing. As far as law enforcement was concerned, it added up to a bunch of not very much. If they'd found Marcus dead, or Lock hadn't taken Tarian to the floor and she'd been shot, it would have been a very different story. But he wasn't dead, and she hadn't been shot, and cops didn't get overly excited with things that might have happened. Hypothetical mayhem wasn't popular with prosecutors and thus tended to be unworthy of court time.

Lock, on the other hand, had a whole world of concerns that he hadn't had when he'd first responded to Tarian's request for help. They went nicely with his growing sense of unease. Not just about Marcus, his state of mind, where he might be and what he might be thinking, but about the whole deal. Tarian had contacted him to keep an eye on her son, he'd been reluctant to help and then this had happened. The son missing, a couple of gunshots, and someone trying to take her out.

It was all way too coincidental. And Lock didn't believe in coincidences. Not the convenient kind anyway. Not the kind that worked in your favor. The kind that messed you up, those he believed, but the type that got you what you wanted? Not so much.

With what had just gone down, it was pretty certain that he and Ty were going to be unable to do a one-eighty and walk away. Now Tarian and her husband needed his and Ty's close-protection services. And they still had a missing son out there. If Tarian Griffiths's mission had been to get him onboard, it had been accomplished. Not that he believed she was connected to the shooter who had tried to blow her Botoxed head clean off her shoulders. But he couldn't help wondering.

His mind flashed back to the vehicle that had followed them earlier. Minutes later, someone had been taking pot shots at them from below. Could it have been the same two? The timing suggested it couldn't. They had been behind Lock, Ty and Tarian on the way from the restaurant to the apartment complex. To get ahead of them, and in place to fire the first shot through the apartment window, would have taken speed and planning.

Then again, Lock thought, the two men who had fled the scene of the shooting clearly knew a fast way of leaving the complex. If they had slipped in the same way while Tarian and then Lock were dealing with complex security at the guard booth it was conceivable that they could have been in place by the time Lock was walking toward the apartment.

But why a shot into an empty apartment? The second shot had been professional, and a professional didn't fire without a target in their sights. The only thing that Lock could think was that it had been some kind of a come-on. A single shot that was intended to draw someone in. If the shooter knew Tarian was looking for her son, was worried about him, then a shot into the apartment would likely draw her in to see if he'd been hurt. Maybe they just hadn't factored in that Lock and Ty would be making first entry.

Lock took another look around the apartment. Too many questions. Too many imponderables. In the kitchen that lay just off the hallway, Ty had Tarian sat down at the two-person table and was taking her through some breathing exercises, trying to get her to calm down without resorting to the pills she'd immediately dug out of her Chanel bag when she'd finished talking to the Sheriff's Department. Lock and Ty needed her present and correct, rather than whacked out on Xanax, if they were going to figure out what the hell was going on. But even without drugs, Lock had to concede that she wasn't making much sense. Coming within an inch of getting your head blown off could do that to you.

Stepping into the kitchen, Lock was struck by how clean and tidy it was. It was not the type of scene he would readily have associated with a kid of that age who was living alone. The sink was devoid of dishes, dirty or otherwise. The counters were spotless. Even the floor was free of the usual detritus. Lock started to open cabinets. Clean, everything neatly stacked. He crossed to the refrigerator. As the light blinked on, he was confronted with something that was almost more surprising than the two gunshots. Not only did the interior sparkle, it was filled with fresh produce. Kale, spinach, tomatoes, peppers, kiwis, strawberries, and all manner of other fruit and vegetables, along with coconut water and soya milk. Lock had seen some messed-up stuff in his time, but a twenty-year-old college kid who ate like Gwyneth Paltrow?

Holding the refrigerator door open, he glanced over his shoulder at Tarian. 'You did something right anyway. At this age, I was living on a diet of ramen noodles and Twinkies.'

Tarian stared at the contents and shook her head. 'That's new. I've never seen Marcus so much as eat a banana without me having to nag him.'

'Well,' said Lock, 'at least you know he's been looking after himself.'

Her face fell. Lock immediately felt bad about saying it. It had come out glib and uncaring when he'd intended to sound positive. If one of the worries was that Tarian's son was a suicide risk, Lock had wanted to highlight the fact that people contemplating ending their lives tended not to take care of their diet and nutrition.

'I'm sorry,' he said.

She shook her head again, a little too quickly, like she had bees buzzing about inside that she was trying to dislodge. 'It's okay. I know what you mean.' She raised her head a little, and the sun from the small kitchen window caught the side of her face. 'He started working out a few months ago. Running. Cycling. I think he may even have started going to a gym somewhere down near Sunset.'

Across the table from her, Lock noticed Ty perk up. 'You know what it was called?' Ty asked.

'I don't,' said Tarian. 'He mentioned it in passing.'

'Maybe if we got a list you'd be able to pick it out,' Lock pressed.

'Maybe,' said Tarian, as they heard a knock at the apartment door. Ty rose from his seat. Lock closed the refrigerator and raised his hand to indicate to Ty that he would get it. Perhaps the prodigal son had finally returned.

Or maybe it was the gunman, come back to finish the job now that the LA County Sheriff's Department were no longer on the scene.

Drawing his SIG Sauer 226, Lock stepped out of the kitchen into the corridor. His back flat to the wall on the hinge side of the door, he said quietly, 'It's open. Come on in.'

He raised his SIG as the handle turned slowly, the door opened, and a man walked in. His face drained of blood as he stared at Lock.

'Who the fuck are you, and where's my wife?' said Teddy Griffiths.

17

As far as Lock was concerned, Teddy Griffiths had arrived with a question mark hanging over his head. After the attempted shooting and attendant mayhem, Tarian had finally thought to contact him. The delay itself was telling in terms of family dynamics, but that wasn't what had troubled Lock.

What niggled at him was the trouble they'd had contacting Teddy, who had told his wife he was playing golf at the Riviera Country Club in Pacific Palisades. The manager in the pro shop had informed Tarian that Mr Griffiths was out on the course and that they would try to get a message to him, but that it might take some time. So far, so ho-hum. A lot of married men played golf. Not always for the love of trying to propel a small white ball around a park with tiny holes, but precisely because it allowed them time away from their domestic duties. Being uncontactable was the point. So Tarian being unable to get in touch with him meant nothing.

But then, about a half-hour later, he had called Tarian's cell phone. Lock could hear him bellowing at her and caught almost every word of the conversation. Teddy had told his wife he had just finished up and was walking off the eighteenth hole. He was coming straight there.

Again, all very normal. The part that was hard to explain came about fifteen minutes later when Teddy had knocked at the apartment door.

Even with light traffic, which was almost unheard of in Los Angeles, where the freeways ran close to capacity during daylight, the drive from Riviera to this part of the Marina would take a minimum of a half-hour.

The man either had a time machine, a very fast helicopter or hadn't actually been on the golf course at Riviera when his wife had called. And even if he had been able to get there that fast, Lock was fairly sure that a country-club-type course like Riviera didn't allow members to tee off in Bermuda shorts, sneakers and a T-shirt. Teddy Griffiths might have been spending the afternoon enjoying himself, but Lock was fairly certain it hadn't involved golf.

Whether guilt was a factor in his pushing Lock aside, rushing to his wife and throwing his arms around her, Lock couldn't be sure, but he wouldn't have ruled it out. As Teddy made noises of comfort and Tarian burst into tears, Lock waved Ty back out into the corridor.

'You think he was playing golf?' Lock asked his partner.

Ty gave a languid shrug. 'Might have involved balls and holes, but taking ten minutes to get from the Palisades to the Marina?'

Lock shot his partner a 'You have to go there?' look.

It was met with yet another languid shrug. 'All I'm saying is, Teddy boy may have a hobby, but it ain't golf.'

The wind had picked up outside. Fractured window blinds fluttered through the hole left in the glass door by the gunshot. Yeah, thought Lock, a guy facing a costly divorce? It was an old, old story.

Teddy Griffiths appeared from the kitchen. His cheeks were still flushed, and sweat trickled down from a mop of dishwater blond hair. At five ten, he was carrying an extra hundred pounds. What Lock guessed was his usual bluff good-old-boy demeanor seemed to have been stripped away.

When he spoke, his voice was remarkably soft.

'Mr Lock, can I speak with you a moment?'

18

Teddy placed a hand on Lock's shoulder as they walked down the corridor. Lock stopped walking and looked at the hand. It dropped back to Teddy's side. He could still smell the waft of stale sweat oozing from the man's skin. Wherever Teddy's hands had been, Lock didn't want them near him.

'So, what do you want to say to me?' he asked the man.

Teddy sucked in some air and puffed out his cheeks. He did a slow exhale. 'I'm worried about my wife.'

Lock kept a straight face. It took no little effort. 'I'm sure. That was a close call. Do you have any idea who might want to harm her or your stepson?'

Teddy shook his head. 'This is way beyond anything.' He drew another deep breath. He was trying for the air of a man who had reached the boundary of what he understood about life. To someone less cynical than Lock, it might have worked. But all Lock could think was, Cut the bull crap and save us all some time, would you? Instead he said, 'Mr Griffiths?'

'I don't know. You know that kid of hers. I mean, I've tried. The Lord only knows I've tried. Tried talking to him, not talking to him, taking him out with me, leaving him alone.' Teddy leaned in, giving Lock another burst of body odor, and lowered his voice to a whisper. 'He's just effing weird. He gets this look in his eyes sometimes. Maybe he took a shot at his mom.'

Lock didn't respond. Teddy stared down at the faded hall carpet. 'I shouldn't have said that. He loves his mom. It's just that look he has. I got a hundred fifty pounds on him, but that kid, I think he could just snap.'

From the open apartment door, Lock could hear Ty and Tarian Griffiths talking. She appeared to have recovered from her shock and was now bombarding him with questions. Now was not the time for Lock to be having this particular talk with Teddy Griffiths.

'I'll tell you what I can do. I was already talking to your wife about helping you with this situation,' said Lock, though he didn't have much of a clue what the situation was, apart from being a hot mess with extra hot mess thrown on top and a whole load of trouble garnish on the side. 'If someone is threatening your family, it doesn't matter yet that I don't know the who and whys of it. Ty and I can provide close-security protection. Make sure you're safe. And while we're setting that up for you, we can go look for Marcus. Maybe if we find him, we'll figure out what all this is about.'

Teddy's sweaty paw took another swipe at Lock's shoulder. For a terrible second, Lock thought he was going to try to hug him. He took a precautionary step away. Teddy settled for a vigorous handshake. 'I can't thank you enough. Not enough.'

'Shall we go collect your wife and get you folks home?' said Lock, ushering Teddy Griffiths ahead of him. He dug in his pocket for some hand sanitizer, squirted some onto his palms and rubbed them together.

Back inside the apartment, Ty was standing with Tarian. He had picked up the laptop computer that had been lying on the table. 'Mrs Griffiths wanted us to take a look at this,' he said to Lock. 'I'd already suggested it wasn't a good idea to leave a computer in an unsecured apartment.'

Lock looked at Tarian. They were riding a line by taking the computer – even with Tarian's permission. Marcus Griffiths was her son, but he was also an adult. He had a right to privacy. Technically the laptop was his property. 'You sure?' Lock asked her.

'I'm sure,' she said.

19

Tarian and Teddy Griffiths lived on a quiet street in up-scale Brentwood, along with the two kids they'd had together. The Griffiths home, which had just about the required land to be considered an estate, was a few doors down from where O. J. Simpson had lived at the time of his wife's murder on North Rockingham Avenue.

Lock pulled into the long, meandering driveway, a tinge of apprehension clinging to him, along with the odor of Teddy's funk. He was hoping the ghost of one of LA's most infamous former residents wasn't some kind of omen for what lay ahead of him and Ty. He was still thinking about the Oedipal nightmare Teddy had hinted at. Was it misdirection or something more sinister? If you'd ended up as a person who struggled with the world as an adult, many people chose to lay the blame at a parent's door.

Lock had always regarded such thinking as an easy out. When you grew up, or even if you didn't but your age ticked over to eighteen, then you took responsibility for what you did, if not wholly for who you were. Nobody could fully control who they were, but they could at least attempt to behave like a decent person.

He reversed his Audi into a space between Tarian's car, which Ty had driven back with Tarian as passenger, and Teddy Griffiths's mid-life-crisis automobile, a canary yellow Ferrari California. Ty was already escorting the couple through the front door where they had been met by an attentive Hispanic housekeeper. The kids were nowhere to be seen.

Stepping out of the Audi, Lock snapped a few pictures of the house's exterior with his iPhone. He also noted the security features, which he picked out with ease, something that was significant in itself. Easily noted cameras and alarms operated as a general deterrent. When there existed a real, credible threat, they tended to be more discreet. If you wanted to be aware someone was coming, you didn't always want them to know you knew.

The house was mock-Tudor in style, a fairly common theme in LA's privileged enclaves where, by the standards of old Europe, the money was new. Walking along a single street in Brentwood, you could go from ultra-modern contemporary to Tuscan villa and on to olde-English cottage in a single block. LA was the be-who-you-want-to-be town. The only problem, as Lock could see it, was the number of people who had chosen to reinvent themselves as assholes.

Leaving his exterior recce for the time being, Lock walked through the front door and into a large open hallway with a sweeping staircase. Off to one side there was a vast living room that faced out over the front gardens. At a wet bar near the back of the room, Teddy Griffiths was fixing himself a Scotch and soda that was nine parts Scotch to one part soda. He looked up. 'Where are my manners? You guys want a belt of the good stuff?' he asked Lock.

'No, thank you,' said Lock, curtly.

Heading back out of the room, Lock found Ty in the kitchen with Tarian. She had clearly found a stash of Xanax and was palming two pills while filling a glass from a stand-alone water dispenser. She threw them back with some water and sighed with relief. Lock had the feeling that Teddy's drink and his wife's pill-popping weren't self-medication strategies they reserved for extreme situations.

A commotion on the stairs announced the arrival of the two Griffiths children. They seemed to part run, part wrestle their way into the kitchen.

'Mom,' said a cute blond boy, who, Lock guessed, was seven-year-old Fletcher, 'she won't let me in her room. She says it's girls only.'

His sister, equally cute and blonde, nine-year-old Carrie, stuck her hands on her hips and struck a defiant pose. 'Girls rule. Boys drool.'

Ty pursed his lips. 'She's kinda got a point. We do drool.'

The two children looked up at the huge former Marine, and said, in perfect sync, 'Who are you?'

'This is Mr Johnson and that is Mr Lock. They're going to be around for a little while helping Mommy and Daddy out with some stuff.'

'What kind of stuff?' asked Carrie, hands still on hips, her laser-like blue eyes moving from Lock to Ty and back. She'd make one hell of an interrogator, Lock thought.

'Hey, is that a real gun? Cool!' said Fletcher, hopping onto a kitchen stool as he eyed Ty's shoulder holster with wide-eyed excitement.

The little boy's question prompted Lock to catch Tarian's eye. 'I'm going to need to run through a few things with you and Mr Griffiths.'

The Xanax kicking in, Tarian nodded while her facial expression indicated that she'd not actually processed what Lock had just said.

'It's better if the kids aren't present,' said Lock, trying to keep it light.

'Oh, yes,' said Tarian, turning to the housekeeper. 'Rosa, could you?'

As the kids protested – 'Hey, I wanna know what's going on!', 'Not fair. We always miss the real fun' – Rosa hustled them out and Tarian followed Lock and Ty into the living room. Teddy had already done some serious damage to his first highball. Another couple and Lock would have to leave asking any more questions until the morning.

He cut to the chase. 'Firearms,' he began. 'Do you have any in the house? I'll need type and location.'

Teddy shook his head. 'Take Tarian to the range sometimes, but won't have a gun in the house.'

He must have read Lock's and Ty's somewhat puzzled expressions because he immediately followed up with 'Texan, right? You think I'd be driving round in a pick-up with a gun rack and a moose head on the hood?'

He was right: that was what Lock had assumed. But he wasn't going to admit it. 'A lot of high-net-worth individuals have at least one firearm in their home for protection.'

'See?' said Tarian.

Clearly Lock had touched upon another fault line between them.

'Really?' said Teddy, belligerence creeping into his voice. 'You want a gun in the house with Marcus running around, and the kids upstairs?'

Lock opened both palms. 'If you can both stay with me here, this won't take long. We'll get to Marcus in a moment.'

Lock ran through a quick set of standard questions, and the Griffithses did their best to answer with only a couple of minor detours into areas of marital discord. How long had the housekeeper worked for them and had she been background checked? Did anyone else work for them or regularly visit? A gardener? Pool boy? What about their neighbors? What was the family's daily routine?

At one point Teddy seemed frustrated by the questioning. He looked up from mixing his second drink and said as much.

'Patterns are important in our line of work,' Lock explained. 'If someone wants to hurt you, then one of our first tip-offs is something that's out of the ordinary so we have to establish what ordinary is in your day-to-day lives.'

Teddy stirred his drink as Tarian threw herself onto a white couch next to a huge marble fireplace that was weighed down with family photos. Lock noted the absence of Marcus in the images, which were mostly from vacations in various exotic locales.

'I understand,' said Teddy.

Lock moved through what they knew about the security system they had in place. It was, as he had expected, fairly standard. Sufficient to push a prospective break-in artist toward a softer touch, but nothing that would offer any real resistance to someone who was determined to do the family harm. If they were to stay in the house, Lock would have to improvise some kind of a panic room.

The checklist complete, he circled back toward Marcus. He had already heard Tarian's take. Now he wanted to hear what Teddy thought but he didn't want it to escalate into a blazing row, which he had a feeling was almost inevitable.

'Mrs Griffiths,' he said, 'would you mind showing Tyrone the alarm system? And also, Ty, if you could recce upstairs, see if we have a space that would fill the gap as a temporary safe area.' Lock had learned a while back that the term 'panic room' tended, unsurprisingly, to instill panic in clients.

'Certainly,' said Tarian. Ty followed her out.

Lock waited until they were out of earshot.

'Sure I can't get you one, Mr Lock?' asked Teddy.

'How old was Marcus when you two met?' Lock asked.

Teddy closed his eyes, his head lolling a little from the booze, his face flushed. 'Let me see, he would have been about twelve.' His eyes opened. He shot Lock a defensive look. 'He was already seeing a therapist when I got together with Tarian. I tried my best, y'know, but . . . Our two are great, just normal kids so it's not like it's . . .'

Teddy trailed off. The more he talked, the more Lock was beginning to feel some sympathy for Marcus, a young man he hadn't even met. To go through a marriage split was hard enough on most kids, then to see your mother have kids with another man, that wasn't easy either. But for those kids to be regarded as 'normal' while you were the freak . . . And Lock had the feeling that Teddy made his feelings plenty clear, even if he hadn't necessarily said it out loud.

'It's not like it was your fault?' Lock said.

'I don't mean it like that. But, yeah, I guess. I mean, his dad is kind of high strung. Geeky type. And you've seen Tarain gobble down those pills like they were M&Ms.' He rattled the ice in his glass. 'I'm rambling on here. Tell me to shut up or something.'

'Talk to me about Marcus over the past year or so. Something's changed, from what your wife said. He's become more aggressive. Threatening? Walk me through it.'

The bottle of Johnnie Walker Blue clanked hard against the rim of the highball glass. Teddy flinched, a drunk who didn't like to make it too obvious. 'It started off with Marcus spending all his time on that computer of his. That was what he always did. But it really got obsessive. We tried talking to him about it, but he wouldn't open up, not even to Dr Levi.'

'That's his therapist?' Lock asked.

'The one before his current one, yeah. His current shrink is a guy named Stentz,' said Teddy. 'Anyway, about eighteen months ago, Marcus suddenly started going out. Y' know down to the Sunset Strip. Hollywood. Downtown. He asked his mom for new clothes. It was like some kind of a miracle. It was like this was a new Marcus. He was clean. He was even coming to the club with me to play a little golf. Working out. Being a regular kid his age.'

'What happened?' Lock asked. 'People usually don't change that suddenly.'

Teddy shook his head and splashed some soda onto the marble counter of the bar before adjusting his aim back toward his glass. 'I gotta be honest with you, Lock, Tarian and I were so freaking relieved that we didn't want to ask too many questions.'

'So everything's going great?' prompted Lock.

'I think we maybe got our hopes up too soon. Tarian was pushing for him to enroll at USC. He always had the grades for it. It wasn't like I had to write any checks. Academically he was always an A student. That's when the problems started. It was like it was too much for him. He started bothering that girl and it all went to shit from there. Anytime either of us tried to talk to him, he'd just get crazy. Cuss in front of the kids. Cuss out his mom. Storm out of the house. That was when I suggested I get him his own place. I just couldn't take it anymore, and I was worried he might go too far when he got angry. Or that I would. That someone would get hurt. And now this . . .'

Lock wanted to ask about moving therapists but stuck a pin in that subject and circled back to the period when Marcus the moth became Marcus the butterfly. 'When he started going out, who was he hanging with?'

Teddy's eyes narrowed as he struggled to access that part of his memory, the booze twisting the passage of time. 'There was a bunch of 'em. They all kind of blended together. Real nice kids, though. Really fun. They even joked about taking me with them to chase tail on the Strip.'

Lock's face must have betrayed something because Teddy straightened up. 'Not that I would. I mean, I'm married – we were joking around.'

'Remember any names?' Lock pressed.

'Not really. Kids that age, it's all "bro" and "dude". They kind of had their own little language going on. Man, I must be really out of touch because most of it went way over my head. "Negging". "AFCs". "LMR". Like all this inside baseball jargon.'

'Anyone from the group that stood out from the pack?'

Something clicked finally. Lock could see it in Teddy's shift of expression and the smile that crept across his face. 'I think the leader, if you will, was this Asian kid. I always assumed they were kind of geeky but this young man . . . Party animal. Real charming too. Think he had his eye on Tarian.'

Lock noted the 'they'. 'How'd that go down with Marcus?'

Teddy kept smiling. 'Usually it wouldn't have. Hell, the kid never liked me even holding his mom's hand. But it was like Marcus was in thrall. Is that the expression?'

Lock nodded.

'Yeah,' Teddy went on. 'It was like Marcus hero-worshipped that kid.'

'And you never caught a name?'

'Not unless "bro" counts as a name, no.'

20

They worked their way down the channel in the darkness. Krank led the way. Discovering the route into the complex where Marcus lived had been part of a game. One day, instead of driving in, like he usually did, Krank had decided to try something different. A big part of the lifestyle he'd discovered through pick-up had been about approaching things differently. There was a playfulness to it. So, rather than knocking on the front door, when Krank visited someone, he would find a different way of arriving.

One afternoon he'd been sarging – a term in the community for trying to pick up – cute tourist girls on the Venice boardwalk when Marcus had called. His car was in the shop so he'd walked all the way down along the beach and canals to the Marina. That was when he'd found the route into the complex from the ocean side. It wasn't even hard. It was just that people in LA didn't walk so no one thought to use this way. When he'd shimmied up onto Marcus's balcony he'd thought the kid was going to have a heart attack.

There was another side to his prowling, though. One that, at first, he hadn't been proud of but which he had come to accept as part of who he was – as part of his inner hunter-gatherer man. He had begun to prowl at night, without the rest of the group.

It had begun semi-randomly with a girl who had blown him off after one date. He realized later that she had only agreed to go out with him as a joke with her friends. She had known from the jump that he was a pick-up artist. She was curious, but immune to all the game he threw at her. After the date, when she had spent fifteen minutes making fun of him and he'd finally lost his cool and stormed off, he found that he couldn't help thinking about her. It was stupid. It went against the code. But there it was.

He had tracked down the house where she still lived with her parents out in La Canada on Google Maps. One night he had parked his car a few streets away and gone on the prowl, through backyards and past shimmering dark blue swimming-pools lit from underneath in the darkness.

How could he describe the thrill of that night? It was like the first time he had gone out sarging and it had worked. Prowling through the early-morning streets of La Canada had been a rush beyond even that. He had felt special, like the only man who was truly alive at that hour.

From time to time a motion-activated outside light would snap on. Or a yappy dog would bark. He would start, feeling a surge of fear at the possibility of discovery. He would step out of the pool of light, or the dog would quiet, and he would be at peace again.

After a time he started carrying treats for any dogs, and was adept at spotting lights, sensors and other security features. But standing outside the girl's bedroom that first night had been like a junkie's first hit, magical and sick-making at the same time. He hadn't done anything to her. That had never been the intention. It had been enough, back then, to know that he could.

Tonight was a little different. He had MG and Loser with him and they were heading to Marcus's apartment to get some stuff.

Krank held up his right hand so that the moonlight from the ocean caught his fingertips. Nearby, a boat strained against its ropes as a swell tugged it back from the dock. Krank and the other two faded back into the shadows as a lone security man walked by.

They gave him time to pass and started moving again. In under two minutes they reached the green space under MG's balcony. It was enough of a climb to focus the mind. They stared up at the balcony. Krank knew that both he and MG had to be thinking the same thing. He looked over at MG. 'How could you have missed her?' he asked.

MG shook his head. 'I didn't. It was that guy pushing her out of the way.'

Krank choked back a laugh. 'Fucking with you, dude. You did good. Now, are we gonna do this thing or not?'

With Loser acting as a look-out, Krank gave MG a boost and he began the climb, hand over hand, toward the edge of the balcony. Loser gave Krank a boost and soon he and MG were pulling back the board that had been placed across the shot-out glass door.

They ducked through into the apartment. There was enough light from outside that they didn't need the Maglite Krank was carrying. He stood in the living room while MG went to find it.

A few moments later, MG was back from his bedroom. 'It's gone,' he said.

'You're sure?' said Krank, panic rising in his chest.

'I know where I left it, and it's not there,' said MG, running a hand through his curly mop of hair.

'Maybe someone moved it,' said Krank.

MG shook his head. 'I bet my mom took it. You know, so it wouldn't be stolen or something.'

'Then,' said Krank, 'you'll have to go get it.'

'How?' asked MG. 'It's not like coming here. They have cameras, alarms.'

MG was so dumb sometimes, thought Krank. He always overreacted. Made things bigger than they were. 'Who said anything about breaking in? It's your home, too, right?'

'Now?'

This time Krank did laugh. He held up his wrist so that MG could see the luminous dial of his watch. 'No, not now. It's too late. In the morning.'

'We heading back to the house?'

Krank glanced down at his wrist. It was a little after eleven thirty. The Strip would just have started to get moving. It had been a day filled with tension. It was time to party.

21

In the half light of the Griffiths family residence, Lock walked into the living room to find Ty standing by the window, peering out into the garden. Ty glanced round, though he barely needed to: both men could pick out the sound of the other's footfall from some distance.

'We good?' Ty asked.

'Kids are asleep. Tarian will probably sleep till midday and hubby's got a serious whisky snore going on,' said Lock, joining Tyrone by the window. 'You?'

'Did a full circuit outside. Quiet neighborhood. Not even midnight and I think everyone within two blocks is in bed asleep.'

'Early to bed, early to rise so they can stay focused on making money,' said Lock.

Ty stepped away from the window, and took a seat next to the fireplace. The last embers of a fire Lock had started earlier were glowing among the ashes. 'Guess that money's all well and good until something like this comes along. What'd Teddy say?'

Lock stayed by the window. He traced the shadows in the garden, trying to map them in his mind. 'Seems like

Marcus fell in with a party crowd a little while back. Teddy thought it was the beginning of the end of their problems but not so much.'

'Kid doesn't seem like a party guy. Not from what everyone's saying anyway,' said Ty. 'But if he fell in with kids who were partying real hard that could explain some of this.'

'Explain what?' Lock asked.

'Well, partying in LA usually means drugs. Say Marcus is bi-polar or some shit. He starts dropping whatever these kids are taking. Wrong drug for a kid with mental-health issues? That's like throwing a hand grenade into the middle of a fire. Shit's gonna get messy real quick.'

Lock hadn't thought of the drug angle, yet it made perfect sense. Marcus is withdrawn. He falls in with what they used to call a 'fast' crowd. He starts using and pretty soon he has some serious psychological problems. With all the designer drugs floating around, who knew how it would affect someone like him? Ty was right. There was stuff out there now that was lab-engineered and able to part your hair straight down the middle with the first sniff, snort or pill. It would easily explain the mood swings and aggression that both Tarian and Teddy had talked about.

'We need to find this kid, Ty.'

'Don't worry. We will. Teddy say anything else?'

'That jumped out at me?' said Lock. 'No, not really. He doesn't think that either he or his wife have any enemies that dislike them to the extent that they'd try to kill them. Apart from Marcus, everything is domestic bliss.'

'Domestic bliss, huh?' said Ty, with a wry smile.

Lock shrugged. 'You know how it goes. People tell themselves the stories they want to believe. Anyway, that's none of our business. Tomorrow I'm gonna go looking for Marcus and I want you to stay back here at the ranch. Go get some sleep. I'll wake you in three hours.'

Ty crossed the room and reached out a huge fist toward Lock. They bumped knuckles. 'Later.' He nodded out toward the wall that fronted onto the street. 'You see anyone come over the top of that, blow their goddamn head off.'

22

A bad night was getting worse. Krank stood with his boys at the red rope as the two bouncers stared them down. On any other night, they would already be inside, chilling in the VIP area, but this club had changed hands recently. New owners had brought in new staff, and the new staff didn't want the place turning into a sausage fest of horny single males so a group of three guys in their twenties wasn't getting inside.

Krank stayed courteous and polite and moved to the back of the line. A group of six women were about to join it. They were older, in their thirties, and, from their clothes, were from out of town, way out of town. 'Like Indiana out of town,' Krank joked to his boys.

The three guys set to work. Loser pulled out a deck of cards and started doing magic tricks, while Krank and Marcus split two of the women away from the others and started chatting to them. The women, initially resistant, soon began talking, even if it was to poke fun at Krank. He rolled with their jibes, firing them back with interest but all the while with a smile.

Marcus, who had been understandably quiet, managed to go through some old canned routines, asking one woman to imagine a cube in an empty room. Then when she had described it in detail he ran through what her choices meant. A large cube meant she was very sexual. He fine-tuned the meanings by gauging her responses and soon she was talking up a storm. The Cube was so ancient in pick-up artist terms that it qualified as retro but, between the routine, some magic tricks and Krank's natural cocky approach, the women agreed to accompany them to a nightclub two blocks down.

This time, with a mixed group that had slightly more women than men, they walked straight to the front of the line and inside. Once inside, Krank and the others quickly ditched the women they'd work so hard to befriend. They took a table near the back while the women shot them evil looks from the bar. Krank ordered drinks.

While they waited for them to arrive, they scoped out the interior. In their world, women were ranked on a scale of one to ten. The women they had come in with were strictly threes and fours – older, out of shape, trying too hard with their make-up and outfits. Krank had explained to Marcus early on that there was no shame in sleeping with a three or a four. It was a good confidence-builder. From there you could make your way up to the sixes and sevens, and beyond. The holy grail was a ten. Tens were girls with the look of a Victoria's Secrets model, beautiful, sexy, and fundamentally unattainable. They were hard to find, and rarely single. Krank obsessed over any tens he met. To him they were the ultimate prize, like a lion to a big-game hunter. But that was all they were. Not people. Prizes. A notch.

The three young men sat at their table, sipped their drinks and argued over where various women in the bar fell on the scale. The waitress who'd served them was, by general agreement, a solid six. Loser, the hipster of the group, argued for a seven rating but was quickly shouted down. Even MG joined in: 'She has the body-fat ratio of a four. She's lucky we're giving her a six.'

Krank had noticed early on that MG was the most eager to run women down in situations like this. The kid had so much hostility, so much repressed rage, that Krank had found it funny at first. Later, he'd realized that it was a natural resource, there to be tapped. Except, when it came down to it, he wasn't sure if MG's rage could be channeled into swift, decisive action. Anger was fuel, but it needed direction. That was what he'd been working on. Seeing if he could channel MG. Seeing if he could turn him into a killer.

The guys were still running down the women in the bar when Krank spotted Devon Malcolm standing by the bar. Krank grabbed his beer and headed over to say hi. Devon had been part of the San Diego lair but he claimed to have 'outgrown' the pick-up lifestyle. What that meant, as far as Krank could see, was that, having sponged off the community, Devon had finally hit the age when he had access to his family's trust fund. A few days later he had moved into a palatial party pad high up in the Hollywood Hills.

To be fair to Devon, he'd allowed Krank and the guys use of the place. They'd had some great times there. Crazy parties that went on for days. But Devon had hooked up with an LA Lakers cheerleader, who had convinced him to propose to her. She was a blonde WASP from somewhere back east, a solid eight, maybe even a nine. She hated Krank with a passion, and to keep her happy Devon had distanced himself from his old friends. It went against the code. Devon had never been part of the new inner circle. He had never had to live by the new code of blood in. But as far as Krank was concerned, Devon still owed him.

Krank noticed that Devon had seen him coming over. He hoisted his drink in salute and tried to disappear further into the crowd but Krank cut him off, circling round toward the door. He bumped Devon with his shoulder. 'Hey! Thought it was you. What's new, player?'

Devon's girlfriend hated that Krank still called Devon a player, which only made Krank do it all the more. Her dislike of the term must have transferred to Devon because Krank noticed him grimace. 'Where's Lauren?'

'Back east. Visiting her family,' said Devon.

Krank grinned. 'Snuck out while she's away, huh?' He clinked his bottle of beer against Devon's glass. 'Nice.'

'I couldn't sleep.'

Krank thought about busting his balls for coming out with such a lame excuse but decided against it. Glancing back over his shoulder, he could see that Loser and MG had opened an all female five-set of sixes and sevens. They were still getting daggers from the women they'd arrived with, which amused Krank no end. It gave him an idea, though. He nodded at his boys, then said to Devon, 'What about us heading back to your place to party? Maybe we can get these girls to call some friends. I mean, Lauren's away, right?'

The very suggestion seemed to cause Devon pain. He scrunched up his face. 'She really doesn't like me having people over. I mean, guys is one thing.'

Krank clenched his fists, digging his nails into his palms. Devon would never have managed to get a seven, never mind an eight like Lauren, to speak to him without Krank's help, and now he had, it was like Krank was some kind of inconvenience.

'Hey,' said Krank, 'Remember the time that little honey at the Lizard Lounge threw a drink over you? Remember how I helped you with her?'

Devon flushed at the reminder of that night. Some of the guys from the San Diego lair had been out looking for girls when they'd run into one at a bar whom Devon had taken a shine to. But she was way out of his league and he just didn't have the game yet to bridge the gap. Krank picked her up instead, took her back to their apartment. Then in the middle of the night, while she was half asleep, he snuck out of the bed he was sharing with her, woke Devon and offered to trade beds. 'Just keep the lights off. She's kinda drunk. She'll never know.'

If the situation had been reversed, Krank would never have gone for it like that. It would have been an insult. And it was rape. Krank knew it, and so did Devon. But Devon craved sex more than power so, like the asshole he was, he slipped out of his bed and into Krank's with the girl.

About half an hour later there was one hell of a commotion and the girl was sprinting down the hall, calling Devon all the names under the sun. She was screaming about getting the cops on all of them.

Krank intervened. It got ugly. Really ugly.

In the morning, as dawn was breaking, Devon helped Krank move the body. Although killing her had freaked Krank out, it meant that, as far as he saw it, lame-ass trust fund Devon owed him. And if you owed Krank he never tired of reminding you.

Devon was still stuttering, his face flushed to a deep crimson. 'Maybe another night, Krank.'

Krank put an open hand on Devon's chest. 'No, not another night. Tonight. Lauren's away. She'll never know.'

Devon started to protest, but Krank cut him off: 'It's not much of a favor, bro. Not in the grand scheme of things.'

Of course Devon knew exactly what he was talking about.

'That was a long time ago,' Devon pleaded.

Krank hadn't wanted to play his next card, but Devon wasn't leaving him with much choice. 'Just as well I captured the moment, then, huh?'

All the bedrooms in the San Diego lair had been fitted with cameras. They could operate in low light as well as daylight. It gave the footage a green tinge but you could still make out who was doing what to whom. The one in Krank's room had captured Devon sneaking into bed with the girl, right up until the moment she had realized who he was and flipped out. The footage had been Krank's insurance policy. It implicated him, too, but even at that early stage he had done things that were just as bad.

Devon sighed. 'I'll see you guys up there.' He slammed his glass back down on the bar, pushed past Krank and headed for the exit.

Over at the table, MG and Loser were in full flow. Krank felt good to see it. He pushed his way through the crowd and launched himself into the middle of the merry throng at the table. 'We got ourselves the best party house up in the Hills. Friends of ours. Big-time movie guy. Pool. Wet bar. Hot tub. What say we get out of here, go have ourselves some real fun?'

23

Krank was woken by a woman screaming. In his world it wasn't that unusual. There was always drama. He grabbed a pillow from under the head of the blonde six in bed next to him, and shoved it over his head. The blonde girl woke and made a grab to get it back. 'Asshole!'

The screaming went on. It was coming from the hallway. It was a scream of anger, rather than fear. He wondered if it was MG. He had a habit of saying weird shit to girls, or asking them to do stuff that set them off. It was a running joke among the guys. Krank figured it was down to MG's lost teenage years when girls had never even looked at him, never mind anything else. MG was a kid making up for lost time in a hurry. He only had to hear about some messed-up fetish and he got all one-track about trying it out. Which would have been fine if he didn't then immediately spring it on some poor unsuspecting woman he'd just met.

Krank threw the pillow at the girl lying next to him. 'Here!' He got up from the bed, an early-morning erection tenting his boxers. He had to step over Loser, who was crashed out on the floor next to a redhead five. Redheads, by Krank's estimation, were usually fives or below, though he had met some exceptions. The floor was a mess of clothes, red plastic Solo cups, half-empty glasses and beer bottles. He almost tripped over a glass ashtray overflowing with cigarette butts.

Through the window, he could see a fully clothed couple crashed out on a lounger next to the infinity pool that looked out over the Sunset Strip. MG raised his head from the lounger, looked at him, then turned over and went back to sleep.

Now Krank could hear Devon meekly trying to defend himself as Lauren tore him to shreds.

'What are they doing here, Devon?'

This was followed by some mumbled effort at appeasement before Lauren started up again: 'We discussed this. You are not to go anywhere near these losers. Hey, did you go out and meet them?'

Devon offered up some half-hearted denial.

'You did, didn't you? I knew it. You can't be trusted on your own for one night.'

Krank tuned out, although he did get the sense that Lauren was busy waking one of the female guests none too gently to ask whether she had slept with her fiancée. He found his pants among the detritus on the floor, and pulled them on. He figured he wouldn't waste the time required to find his socks. He grabbed the rest of what he could see and finished getting dressed.

Stepping out of the bedroom, Krank looked left. Lauren had a short, freckly brunette pinned against the wall. Her right hand was around the girl's neck. Her left hand was pulled back and bunched into a fist.

'Honey, no!' shouted Devon, as he went to grab Lauren's arm.

'Don't honey me, you asshole. To think I was back home with my mom so I could plan our wedding.'

'Hey, Devon, great night, man. Thanks for inviting us over,' said Krank, sliding past.

Devon and Lauren looked to him. The girl with the freckles took her chance and squirmed from Lauren's grip. Lauren let her go and turned to Krank, hands on her hips, lips thinned to a razor's edge, ready for war. His old buddy Devon wasn't looking too happy either, thought Krank.

'I knew you'd be involved,' said Lauren, still staring at him. Her voice was calm, which worried Krank.

'Lauren, you look great. Me and the guys are going to head now,' said Krank. 'Sorry if we caused any friction between you two. It was really my idea anyway. I talked Devon into it.'

'He did. He totally did,' said Devon, eager to grab hold of a lifeline.

'Yeah, you're leaving,' shrieked Lauren, 'because I've called the cops.'

Krank froze. He wasn't sure he'd heard her correctly. Devon seemed to freeze too. Krank knew that, new man or not, Devon still had a taste for cocaine – in fact, they'd had some lines last night. A bunch of cops from Hollywood Division marching all over his house hadn't been in Devon's plans for this morning.

Just then the doorbell rang. The chimes echoed through the house. They faded.

'Why did you do that? Why did you do that, Lauren?' Devon sounded exactly like the whiny child he'd been when Krank had first met him. Why did women do anything? thought Krank. *Because they're crazy.*

The doorbell rang again. No one moved, not even Lauren. Krank feared for what would happen if either Lauren or Devon opened the door to the two cops they could all now see on the small video intercom system mounted on the wall. Lauren must have left the gate open because they were already on the property. One was waiting for someone to answer the door while the other was already checking the side gate that led into the garden and pool area.

'Lauren, we're leaving, okay?' said Krank. 'Let me speak to them.'

24

Lock had slept fully clothed, his gun next to him, in one of the upstairs guest bedrooms. He'd fallen asleep as soon as he'd lain down, and woken, four hours later, without the need for an alarm. His ability to sleep and wake on cue was as important to someone in his line of work as shooting a gun or giving a bad guy the good news in a hand-to-hand situation.

He rubbed his eyes, then got up, pulled his washbag from the overnight case he always carried in the car and headed into the bathroom, taking his gun with him. He had a hot shower, thinking over the events of the previous day. *A day?* It already felt longer.

Lock rinsed off. He turned the shower handle and killed the water. As the pressure fell away from a blast to a drip, he heard someone beyond the bathroom door, walking around in the guest bedroom. He slid back the shower door and stepped out, realizing as he did so that he couldn't see a towel.

He went to the bathroom door and cracked it open. Tarian stood there, a large white bath sheet in one hand. The shaken, uncertain Mrs Griffiths of the day before was gone.

She was wearing a lilac silk dressing-gown that finished just above her knees, revealing a killer pair of legs. Her hair was up in a towel, accentuating the high cheekbones and plush red lips. Lock had always figured that the true mark of a woman's beauty was seeing her without make-up. Tarian Griffiths was beautiful. There was no question.

She was holding the towel just out of his grasp. Something approaching a smile hovered on her lips. Normally game-playing like this from a client would have irritated Lock. Normally. He made a mental note that, once this gig was wrapped up, he really needed to find himself a girlfriend and start getting laid on a semi-regular basis.

'Why don't you throw it to me?' he said finally.

Tarian smiled. Her eyes ran from the floor all the way up the edge of the door to Lock's face. 'Did you get some sleep?' she asked, making no effort to either throw the towel or step closer.

Lock nodded. The top of her robe had slipped open a little to reveal her cleavage. 'Yes,' he said. 'Thank you. You?'

A little of the self-assured Brentwood cougar seemed to leave her and he saw the sadness in her eyes that had been present the day before. 'First time in weeks. I think it was knowing that you and Tyrone were here.'

'That's good,' said Lock. He stretched his hand out a little further. 'May I have that towel, Mrs Griffiths?'

'Mrs Griffiths?' she said. The way she said it seemed to suggest that the title amused her. 'Not Tarian?'

'The towel?' said Lock.

She still didn't move. From the corridor the sound of small feet came to him. Not so much a pitter-patter as a steady thump as the two younger kids made their presence in the house known. Tarian stepped toward him, and held out the towel. As he reached for it, she momentarily snatched it away, her eyes never leaving his.

'Teddy and I are separating,' she said, finally handing him the towel. 'He would have moved out already only for this drama with Marcus. We thought that the kids were already upset enough. We've been sleeping in different beds for the last few months.'

Lock already knew that from his walk through the house. There was a camp bed set up in one of the vast walk-in closets in the master bedroom. Judging by the clothes, it was Teddy's. He gripped the towel in his hand as the words kept tumbling out from between Tarian's plump red lips.

'It wouldn't be cheating,' she said.

Was she looking for affirmation that she was still attractive? If it was that simple she would have little problem finding someone younger than Lock for a casual hook-up. This area was full of handsome young actors waiting tables or providing personal training to women like Tarian. Not all of them were gay.

He doubted it was as simple as that. More likely her making a pass at him was tangled up in the nature of what he was doing. He was a literal protector. This was the equivalent of a male patient falling in love with an attractive young nurse. And yet? He was attracted to her. It was a raw, visceral attraction. The kind that had him standing behind the door with one hell of an erection. If they'd been alone in the house, he would have thrown her down on the bed and taken her right there and then. Ripped that goddamn robe right off her.

The children were screaming outside the door. It snapped Lock back to the present. He looked at Tarian as she stood there, vulnerable and expectant. He just about managed to remind himself that what she was proposing was one hell of a bad idea. 'I'm here to keep everyone safe,' he said. 'That's all. I have a firm policy about not getting involved with either clients or principals or anyone directly connected to them.'

Downstairs the doorbell chimed. Tarian turned away. She was still smiling. She must have sensed he hadn't entirely meant what he'd just said.

'Hey, Marcus is here! Marcus is here!' shouted the boy.

His sister took up the chorus. 'Marcus is here, Mommy!'

Lock closed the door on Tarian Griffiths and hastily dried off. With the towel still wrapped around his waist, he walked back into the bedroom and changed into the fresh clothes he kept in the case that lived in his car. He stepped out into the corridor, his SIG on his hip. This was one homecoming he didn't want to miss.

25

From the photographs Lock had been shown, Marcus Griffiths wasn't much to look at. In the flesh, he achieved the rare trick of being even less impressive. He stood about five feet seven, but the shadow of a post-adolescent stoop shaved off another inch. His hair managed to be both curly and lank. He stared down at the floor of the hallway, occasionally deigning to mutter a reply to the volley of questions coming at him from every direction. All Lock could think was that if, at that age, he had given off half the attitude Marcus did, his father would have slapped the shit out of him. Lock's home had been warm, loving, but also a place of simple virtues such as saying 'please' and 'thank you', being respectful to your elders and generally behaving like a human being. Hormones had not been seen as a free pass for rudeness.

Ty was standing off to one side as Lock came down the stairs, while everyone apart from Teddy, who was framed in the kitchen doorway, smirking, fussed around the prodigal son. Marcus shot Lock a glance that settled somewhere between contempt and disdain. Lock could hardly pat the kid down but he did do a quick visual scan for a weapon. None that he could see. He walked into the kitchen. Teddy retreated with him. The housekeeper was busy making a mountain of food for breakfast.

'Mind if I grab some coffee?' Lock asked.

'Rosa will get that for you,' said Teddy. 'Get me one too, Rosa,' he added, doing that white-people thing of raising his voice, as if that would magically make the English language more discernible to a native Spanish speaker from south of the border.

The housekeeper poured two mugs and set out half-and-half and sugar on the kitchen island for them. She never said anything. She didn't make eye contact. Lock didn't blame her. In a nuthouse like this, keeping your head down was usually the best policy, especially when your pay check depended on it.

'*Muchas gracias*,' said Lock, taking the coffee with a smile that Rosa returned with a raise of her eyebrows that spoke volumes. They were both hired help, after all. He took a sip. The coffee tasted great. Freshly made. The expensive stuff, Blue Mountain from Jamaica.

Teddy hefted his mug to his mouth, and regarded Lock with bloodhound eyes. 'Oh, boy, do I need this. And some painkillers. Probably a blood transfusion too.'

With a glance at the door, where Tarian was still fussing over Marcus, Lock asked, 'He say anything about where he's been?'

'With friends,' said Teddy.

'Anything about the shooting?'

'He's not mentioned it, and I think Tarian is scared to. Case he freaks out. I asked him when he was last at his place and he said three days ago. I was going to say more but she cut me off. You must have seen that look she has, like she's going to cut my goddamn balls off.'

Lock ignored the last part. Whining was never to be encouraged, particularly not when it came from a grown man who had likely contributed his part to the breakdown of his marriage. In Lock's experience, despite what men would have their fellows believe, women didn't start out as nags: they got that way because of the men they were married to. If they had started out like that, more fool the men who married them.

'You want me and Tyrone to handle it?'

'Boy, would you? That'd be great. He doesn't listen to me. It's like talking to a wall. I'm just the guy who pays all the bills around here.'

'Leave it to us,' said Lock, draining the rest of his coffee.

26

Lock signaled for Ty to follow him. They walked back out into the hallway. Tarian and the two kids were still fluttering around Marcus. The little boy was trying to show his stepbrother some toy car while the little girl was asking him a million questions. Tarian looked like she was someplace between relieved and apprehensive.

Marcus stood in the middle of all the activity. When he saw Lock and Ty, Lock thought for a moment that he might bolt for the door. He looked scared. It didn't take a genius to see it. He was staring at Lock with an air of defiance but his folded-in body language spoke of fear.

Tarian broke the ice for them: 'Marcus, this is Ryan, and Tyrone.'

Lock winced a little at the first names. She was making them sound like camp counsellors. He stepped forward, hand out. 'Ryan Lock. Good to meet you, Marcus.'

Marcus offered a sweaty hand. Ty followed Lock's lead. 'Hey, brother, Ty Johnson.'

'What's going on?' Marcus said to Tarian. 'Who are these guys? I already told you, I'm not seeing another shrink. I'm fine.'

Lock and Ty traded a look. Ty took the lead, moving next to Marcus and clapping a hand on his back, imposing himself on the boy. 'It's nothing to worry about. But we need to talk to you for a few minutes. Bring you up to speed. That's all.'

Lock had physical presence but not the way Ty had it. There weren't many people who would turn down a polite request from the six-foot-four, former Marine.

Marcus managed a weak 'Mom?' but she was already shooing away the kids. 'They just want to talk, Marcus.'

Lock fell in on the other side of Marcus and they walked him into the living room. Ty closed the door behind them. Lock gestured for Marcus to sit down.

'What is this? Are you cops?' said Marcus.

Lock stayed standing. 'Private security. Your mother was concerned about you. She wanted us to make sure you were okay. That's all. Nothing you have to worry about.'

'Well, I'm fine,' said Marcus, getting up only to find Ty's hand pushing him back down.

'We ain't done getting acquainted yet, son,' he growled.

Marcus sighed and took a swipe at the curly hair that had fallen forward over his face. 'I said I'm fine.'

'When were you last at your apartment, Marcus?' Lock asked.

Marcus shrugged. 'Like three days ago. I've been staying with friends. Why?'

Lock studied his face. 'We visited your apartment yesterday with your mom. Someone shot out one of the glass balcony doors. Then they took a shot at us.'

Marcus seemed surprised. It was hard to tell if he was acting or genuine. Lock always looked for the speed of reaction. Someone who reacted too fast to news like that usually knew it was coming. Either Marcus didn't know or he'd prepared.

'A shot? Like a gunshot?'

That came off to Lock like someone trying a little too hard to play the innocent. 'Yeah,' said Lock. 'Bang. Bang. You know anything about that?'

Marcus got up and walked to the window. This time Ty let him go. 'Maybe. I mean, I can't be sure, but . . .'

'You can't be sure about what?' said Ty.

Marcus turned round. He looked upset. He wasn't faking that. 'How much has my mom told you?'

Neither Lock nor Ty replied. They both just stared at him.

'She tell you about the girl at USC?' Marcus asked.

'She didn't, but we made it our business to find out,' Lock said.

Marcus didn't reply. Lock could tell that his answer hadn't gone down well, judging from the fleeting expression of rage that flitted across the young man's face.

'She has friends. Well, a boyfriend,' said Marcus. 'Maybe it was him that took the shot. Or one of his buddies. They're like big-time jocks, think they're tough guys.'

'With guns?' said Ty.

'Maybe,' stuttered Marcus. 'I don't know.'

'You been bothering her again?' said Lock.

'No! No way. It was stupid. The whole thing. I didn't even do anything to her. Just some notes and stuff. She was a bitch anyway.'

Lock looked at Ty. They'd both registered some real emotion there. The girl was a sore point.

'Did her boyfriend or any of his friends threaten you, Marcus?' said Lock.

Marcus shrugged. 'Maybe like stay away from her. Stuff like that. I didn't think they'd use a gun.'

'And did you stay away from her?' said Ty.

'Like I had a choice. Not that I'd want to go anywhere near her anyway. Like I said, she's a cun—'

Lock held up a hand, cutting him off. 'Ladies don't like that word. I don't much like it either.' He turned to his partner. 'You like the C-word, Ty?'

Ty solemnly shook his head. 'Nope. Disrespectful. Don't think your momma would like it either.'

'Okay. Well, I haven't breached my court order. And as for guns or people firing them, I don't know anything about that. Now, can I go? I mean, if you're not cops you can't keep me here, right?'

'You can go,' said Lock. 'Thanks for your help. We'll look into what you told us.'

'Good,' said Marcus, stalking out of the room. 'I hope you do.'

He opened the door and slammed it behind him. They heard him thudding up the stairs.

'What do you think?' Lock asked Ty.

'I think he's one lying little motherfucker,' said Ty.

'Yup,' said Lock.

27

Marcus pushed open the door to his old bedroom. He opened the cupboards, and began to rifle through them. Someone knocked at the half-open door. It was his mom.

'Are you okay? I've been so worried.'

He rolled his eyes. 'Apart from being interrogated like I'm some kind of a criminal, I'm fine. When you were poking around my apartment, did you happen to see my laptop? I can't find it.'

'I wasn't poking around. I was looking for you. Making sure you were okay.'

He turned on her. He wished his shot had been better and that he'd blown her stupid head off. Krank was right. They were all the same. *Stupid bitches*. 'Have you seen it? Yes or no?'

'Yes. We brought it back. Mr Lock was worried it might get stolen, what with the door being broken and everything.'

'So where is it?' Marcus shouted. He wanted to punch her. Her and those two goons she had downstairs. Maybe he'd come back and kill them all. Teddy too. Put that poor bastard out of his misery.

'It's right there,' said Tarian, pointing a manicured finger at his desk.

In his panic he hadn't noticed it. He scooped it up and threw it into a rucksack, along with some fresh clothes.

'Where are you going?'

'I'm leaving,' said Marcus. 'You can't stop me.'

She grabbed at his arm as he pushed past her. He shook her off.

'I'm worried about you. We need to talk. Stay for a little while at least,' Tarian begged.

He ignored her, shoving her out of the way and heading for the stairs. The rucksack slung over his shoulder, he took them two at a time. At the bottom he dug out his cell phone and texted Krank to come meet him and take him back to the kill house.

The two security guys watched him head for the front door. Teddy called after him but he ignored him too. He opened the door and went out into the fresh air. He felt a sense of relief. He had what he'd come for. No one knew anything about what he and the guys had planned. It was all good.

The next time his mom saw him he would be on the news. The national news. International. Worldwide.

28

Lock and Ty stood next to each other in one of the big bay windows that fronted onto the garden. They watched the heavy black iron gates at the bottom of the driveway swing open and Marcus dart through them without a backward glance. Lock had watched most of what had gone on from the upstairs hallway.

'Pretty keen to get hold of that laptop of his,' he said to Ty.

Ty dug into his pocket and pulled out a plug-in hard drive. He held it up for Lock's approval. 'Just as well I already cloned it, huh?'

'You looked at it?' Lock said.

'He's got some security that I can't get past. Gonna drop it off with someone who'll crack it. Chinese dude by the name of Li. Might take him a while, though.'

'Hold the fort for me here?' said Lock, as he glanced at his watch. 'I'm heading out.'

'Sure, but where you going?'

'Few people I need to talk to down at USC,' said Lock.

As he reached the door, Ty called him back. 'Yo! Ryan?'

Lock turned.

'She likes you,' said Ty.

Lock knew exactly who he was talking about. 'She's married.'

'For now,' said Ty. 'Good-looking woman. All I'm saying.' He made a show of taking in the sweep of the room. 'Got money too. You'd make a cute couple.'

'Do me a favor, would you?' said Lock.

'What's that?'

'Just watch the house. Anything I should know about, call me.'

29

Kristina Valeris had reached a point where she had given up wishing for rescue. Now she could only wish for death. But death did not feel close. She had always assumed that someone in her position would be so traumatized by the shock of abduction and imprisonment that they would feel numb. Instead she felt raw, like her skin had been peeled away to leave her nerve endings naked and exposed.

They had her in some kind of shed at the back of the property. She had a belt around her waist. The belt was locked and connected to a length of chain that was attached to the back wall. It allowed her to move about six feet from the dirty single bed that had been pushed up against one wall. There was a bucket for her to urinate and defecate into, along with some wipes and hand gel. There was bottled water. There were some crackers and peanut butter for her to eat between meals. Once a day she was blindfolded and unshackled and taken, at gunpoint, to a shower.

Sometimes one of them came in to sit with her. They always wore masks, though she had seen most of them through one of the grimy windows, walking around outside in the garden. She had seen the guy she thought of as the taxi driver just once since she'd been taken. The one she had picked out as the leader was Asian, short but muscular, like he spent a lot of time at the gym. She'd heard them call him Krank.

Krank seemed to control the others. She heard them speaking about him when he wasn't there. They seemed to be intimidated by him but it was more of a hero-worship thing than something that came from fear. It was like he was a guru. They talked endlessly about something he'd said and what it might mean. Or they would compete among each other about how close they were to him.

It creeped her out almost as much as the nightly visits when she closed her eyes and took herself away until they were done. At first she hadn't understood how they could treat another human being like they treated her. Slowly, as she listened to them talk, she understood.

They talked incessantly about women and girls but never by those names. Women were bitches, hos, freaks, hamsters, sluts. Each one they mentioned had a number that related, as far as Kristina could tell, to how attractive they were. There was no recognition of women as people. They weren't even objects. It was hard to hate an object as much as they did.

There was something else. Or, rather, someone else. They had turned up the morning after Kristina was abducted. At first she'd thought they had come to rescue her. She quickly realized that she was wrong. They had come to gloat.

That person made Krank, the driver and the other one look like well-adjusted members of society. Kristina was left alone with them for an hour. It was the most painful, horrifying hour of her life. She had tried to let her mind escape and float free, but they wouldn't allow that. They kept calling her back. They would lean down and whisper in her ear: 'Be here, Kristina. Experience the moment. Live in the present.'

It was the voice that had shocked her back, that wouldn't allow an escape. If she lived, Kristina knew that she would hear it in her nightmares. She had never seen the person the voice belonged to. She was always blindfolded before they arrived.

The voice. Not just what it said, but the sound of it. Just thinking of it made her shake uncontrollably.

It was a woman's.

30

Stacy Becker, the object of the misguided affection that had made Marcus subject to a court order, lived in Cardinal Gardens, a USC student-apartment complex, on the north side of Jefferson Boulevard. As with a lot of the country's illustrious seats of higher education, the USC campus was not based in the nicest of neighborhoods. Lock parked his Audi on McClintock Avenue and walked the short distance to Cardinal Gardens.

The complex was made up of nine town-house-style buildings that faced onto a central courtyard. It looked pleasant but functional, a shorthand that could have applied to a lot of the city. Everything was pleasant and going along just great – until it wasn't, and then it could get very unpleasant indeed.

Lock took a seat in the middle of the courtyard. He had already called ahead to let Stacy know he was dropping by. She was going jogging but said she'd meet him at one of the benches that were dotted among the trees. Lock had a lot on his mind, not least the fleeting return of Marcus and what was on the laptop he had been so keen to recover.

He couldn't lie to himself either. Lock was thinking about Tarian. It was stupid to deny that he found her attractive. She had made it very clear that it was mutual. *Perhaps when this was all resolved, if it could be resolved, and when she was clear of Teddy . . . Perhaps what? They'd be in a relationship?*

That was the problem with getting older. You already knew when things had no chance of working out with someone before you could even give them a chance. With age came complications. Kids. If not yours then the other person's. People had careers and family that tied them to a location. It was a world away from the college kids he was surrounded by. No commitments. No baggage. Free to flit in and out of each other's lives as they wished.

It made Lock wonder about Marcus and the anger he seemed to carry. He was one of those people who had it all yet believed that the world was out to get them. The kid was hardly a male model but he wasn't unattractive. He was white, which already gave him a jump (as Ty never reminded of reminding Lock), he came from money and privilege. And yet Marcus had a festering resentment.

'Hey!'

Lock looked up to see Stacy standing with a tanned athletic guy in his early twenties. They were both in shorts and T-shirts. Looking at what he assumed had to be Stacy's boyfriend, it was evident that Marcus might have had a lot going for him but Stacy was still out of his league.

Stacy introduced her boyfriend, Brad. He shook hands with Lock while giving him his don't-mess-with-my-girlfriend-bro face.

'What did you want to see me about?' Stacy asked, earnest.

'Just a few more questions about what went on with Marcus. I promise not to take up too much of your time. I also wanted to let you know to stay alert. If you see Marcus you should call campus security and the LAPD straight away. They should both be aware of the situation because it's already gone to court so they'll respond quickly. Get somewhere safe, stay there, and wait for them to arrive.'

'You're kind of freaking me out, Mr Lock,' said Stacy.

Brad slid his arm around her waist. The gesture seemed more territorial than protective. 'Maybe you should come stay with me this week.' He stared at Lock. 'I live off-campus.'

Lock gave Brad his moment. Clearly living off campus was the mark of a man. 'I think it's probably better if you're on campus, Stacy. I'm going to speak to USC security later and make sure they all know who to look out for,' he said. 'I don't think anything will happen, or even close, but it's always better to be prepared.'

'Okay, thanks,' said Stacy.

Lock had led with the warning for two reasons. One, he wanted Stacy to take it seriously. But he also wanted to establish some trust, to make sure that she knew he was working for Marcus's family but that that didn't mean he wasn't on her side. Which was true. He didn't want to see her hurt and he didn't want to see a troubled young man do something stupid that would hurt not only him but everyone around him. It took only a moment of idiocy to ruin a bunch of lives.

'I wanted to ask you about people that Marcus might have been hanging out with when he was here. Guys. Like a group of them.'

Brad was the first to react. He threw back his head and laughed. 'Those losers.'

'So you both knew them?'

'Not really,' said Stacy.

'But you did, Brad?' Lock pressed.

'One of them, kinda. He was called Loser, or some dumb nickname like that. They both lived over on Severance.'

'Was he a freshman too?' Lock asked.

Brad shrugged. 'Senior, I think. Older definitely.'

'You know his real name?'

'Drew something,' said Brad. 'Sorry, that's all I got.'

Something occurred to Lock. 'What about Marcus? He must have had a name, right?'

Stacy rolled her eyes. 'Oh, yeah, it was real imaginative. They called him MG – y' know, his initials.'

Lock spent another fifteen minutes talking to them before he sensed he was exhausting their patience and starting to go round in circles. He mentioned, in an oblique way, the shots fired at Marcus's apartment and was met with a blank stare by both Stacy and Brad. That left him with a couple of nicknames. He could only hope that the copy of the hard drive from Marcus's laptop computer would yield something more.

From what Brad had said, which chimed with what Teddy had told them, Marcus had fallen in with a crowd of self-styled pick-up artists. On the surface it didn't seem to Lock like the most troubling thing in the world, especially for a kid like Marcus, who needed to bolster his confidence and social skills. Marcus would go out with his friends to pick up girls – just like every other bunch of young men since the dawn of time. But that wasn't the worrying part. That came when girls weren't interested. It seemed that Marcus wasn't the only one who couldn't take no for an answer.

But how did that fit with what else that had happened? The gunfire. Marcus's moods and habit of going AWOL. His threats to Stacy. Did it add up to anything?

Perhaps the best thing would be for Tarian to give her son some space. To let him find his own way. It was a tough thing for a parent to do, perhaps the toughest, but it might also be the right thing. Marcus had seemed pretty together when Lock had met him. Surly, sure, but that hardly made the boy unique.

And what would end up happening if he stuck around Tarian? By the time he started the drive back to Brentwood he had made up his mind. He and Ty would finish up their security review. They could look some more into the hard drive, and what Marcus Griffiths might be hiding, but if that yielded nothing, they were done. Marcus wasn't missing. He didn't appear to be in danger – at least, not from an external source. The LAPD and USC security could cover Stacy and her boyfriend. There was no job to speak of for Lock and Ty, and there were plenty of people out there who actually needed help. It was over.

Lock was in his car heading back to Brentwood when he thought of something. He couldn't work out anything from the nicknames. Krank. Loser. They might as well have been named John Doe I and II. Instead of staying on the 10 freeway, he took the next exit and headed down Sepulveda, back to the Marina.

    At the apartment complex, he parked outside the main office but didn't go inside. They might have the information he needed but there was no way they'd give it to him. He headed for the booth that controlled access into the complex. A middle-aged Hispanic guard was on duty. Lock introduced himself, told him who he was. He got a break when the guard, who was called Ramón, mentioned that he'd served in the Middle East. Lock had been with Britain's Royal Military Police specialist close-protection unit, but shared service gave him a platform on which to build.

Twenty minutes later Lock got back into his car and left the complex. He was a hundred dollars lighter but he had a promise from Ramón that he would provide Lock with a list of visitors to Marcus's apartment. No one would have got past Ramón or his colleagues with something as flimsy as a nickname like Krank.

31

Marcus pulled the laptop from his rucksack and dumped it casually on the kitchen table. Loser and two of the other guys were busy cooking while Krank pored over a map that was laid out on the dining-table. Krank glanced at him.

'Anyone try and access it?' Krank asked.

'Yeah, last night,' said Marcus. 'Probably one of those security guys my mom has working for her.'

Krank gave Marcus his death stare. 'Tell me you're kidding.'

'Relax,' said Marcus. 'They didn't get past the first log-in, and even if they had, they wouldn't have known what they were looking at.'

'We're taking no chances,' said Krank. Fingers spread out at the two upper corners of the map, he went back to his studies. 'You ready for tonight, MG?'

Marcus had hoped that Krank had changed his mind and decided to let her go. After all, she had never actually done anything to Marcus. Not like that stuck-up little bitch Stacy or his mom. He should have known better. Once Krank had decided on a course of action that was it. There was no knocking him off course.

'You want me to do it?' Marcus said, looking at Loser.

One of them was busy chopping garlic. He lifted the knife from the cutting board and made a slashing motion in the air. 'It's easy, dude. Just slice her carotid. She'll be done in, like, five, ten minutes.'

'Yeah, I want you to do it,' said Krank. 'You're the only one who hasn't popped his cherry. How can we take you along on this,' he stabbed a finger at the map, 'if you're still a virgin? Blood in, remember.'

'I thought that maybe taking that shot at—'

He was cut off before he could finish. Krank was getting pissed. He stood up and glared at Marcus. 'What's "maybe"? What does "maybe" count for? No. Tonight you do her. She goes. We shouldn't have kept her here this long in any case. Too risky.'

Marcus was cornered. He swallowed hard. He really didn't want to do this. He wasn't sure he could, even if he'd wanted to. As ever Krank sensed his unease. Krank always picked up on weakness.

'Don't worry,' he said. 'You'll have some help.'

32

There was a Toyota Prius parked at the front of the Griffiths family home as Lock arrived back. Any other unknown vehicle might have raised his heart rate by a few beats per minute, but Lock had yet to encounter a Prius driver capable of providing a credible threat to someone he was charged with protecting. He got out of the Audi and walked to the front door. Ty opened it as Lock approached and he went inside.

'Visitor?' Lock asked.

'The father,' said Ty. 'Showed up about a half-hour ago.'

Lock could see him sitting in the living room with Tarian. Her first husband, Peter Blake, was perched next to her on the couch. A tall, thin man with greying hair and frameless glasses, he was, according to *Forbes* magazine, worth somewhere north of half a billion dollars. He took off his glasses and sat rubbing his eyes. At least Lock now saw where Marcus Griffiths had got his social awkwardness. Everything about Peter Blake, from his body language to a slight stutter as he spoke to Tarian, indicated a man who was far from comfortable in his own skin, never mind the world.

'Where's Teddy?' Lock asked Ty.

'Sulking in his den with a big ole glass of whisky. You find anything out?'

'Not really,' said Lock. 'Spoke to the girl at USC. Told her to be careful. Guard at the apartment complex is going to see if he can get us some actual names for Marcus's buddies.' Lock nodded at Peter. 'What's his deal?'

Ty shrugged. 'You jealous?' he said.

Before Lock could respond, Tarian called, 'Mr Lock, would you join us?'

Lock made his way over.

'This is Peter, Marcus's father,' said Tarian.

Peter got up to shake Lock's hand. He had the grip of a recent stroke victim.

Pleasantries out of the way, Tarian gestured for Lock to sit down. 'I've already told Peter that you're helping us try to figure out what might be going on with Marcus.'

Lock felt that was a stretch but he let it go. He wasn't a shrink, and he had no desire to be seen as one. He was interested in psychology in as much as it would allow him to assess whether Marcus was a danger to himself or others. That was where his interest began and ended.

'When did you last see him, Mr Blake?' Lock asked, taking a seat across from them.

'See him? A couple of months ago. But I speak to him regularly.' Peter glanced over at his ex-wife. From the way he looked at her, it didn't take a genius to figure that he might have gotten wind of her impending of break with Teddy. 'I've offered him a job with one of my companies. An apartment close to me in Palo Alto. Whatever he needs.'

Lock wondered if Peter had ever taken his son out to a ball game, or coached his soccer team, or done any of the regular stuff. Everything his parents offered Marcus seemed to revolve around material things. Not that they were unique in that regard. That seemed to be most of modern parenting. *Take this, and shut the hell up.*

'He wasn't interested?' said Lock.

'Sadly, no. That's why I came down. There have been a few things he's said to me over the past months that concern me. Outbursts.'

'Can you be a little more specific?' said Lock.

Peter took a deep breath. 'He's spoken about hurting people. At first I thought he was blowing off steam. You know, teenage hormones, being angry at the world, that kind of thing.'

Lock stayed quiet, allowing Peter to go on. The problem was that Marcus was hardly a teenager. He was a young man who would be held accountable for his actions. Lock wasn't sure how much of a get-out clause hormones would provide, if Marcus did something really stupid.

'You never told me this,' said Tarian. 'What did he say?'

Peter looked troubled. 'Some of it was about you and Teddy. And the children.'

Tarian grabbed for his hand. 'What did he say?'

'He said that he hoped that one day he'd come home and find you all dead. That he didn't feel part of the family. That no one cared about him. That you favored the children you've had with Teddy more than him. He was venting, Tarian. I'm sure he didn't mean it. But it did worry me.'

The color had drained from her face. It couldn't be news to her but to hear it from her ex-husband had to be shocking.

'Kids say a lot of things in the heat of the moment,' said Lock, trying to make her feel a little better.

'This wasn't in the heat of the moment. He was perfectly calm. That was what worried me,' Peter said. Tarian still held his hand. 'I've spoken to a family counselor and I think we need to stage some kind of an intervention. Perhaps if we all sit down with him and talk this through we can let him know that we're here for him. Mr Lock, if you could find a way of getting Marcus back here?'

Lock had the sudden desire to walk out and take Ty with him. This was domestic stuff and, as a rule, he stayed well away from such matters for very good reason. 'Mr Blake, I'm not sure what Mrs Griffiths told you about me, but I'm not a babysitter. Nor do I help people stage interventions. Now, my business partner and I are happy to gather further information and do a risk assessment on your son. We're also happy to review security for Mr and Mrs Griffiths. But that's it.'

Tarian stood up suddenly. 'An intervention? With all of us? That might work. Let me go speak to Teddy.'

Lock watched her leave the room. It was as if she hadn't heard him.

'You know,' Lock said, 'you might want to speak to someone with expertise in this area. If Marcus is demonstrating violent tendencies, pushing him into a corner might have the opposite effect to the one you want.'

Peter seemed to bristle. 'I think I know my own son, Mr Lock. Now, given that you're no doubt being paid very handsomely, I'm sure you'll have no problem accommodating us.'

In the hallway Lock was sure he heard Ty mutter something less than complimentary about the tech tycoon. Neither he nor Ty had much time for entitled assholes.

For a man who had spent time in the military, Lock wasn't always the best when it came to being ordered around, as more than one officer had discovered. It had held back his career in the Military Police. It had cost him money in the civilian world.

Peter Blake was already wilting under Lock's stare. 'Excuse me?' said Lock.

'I don't mean to sound like I'm telling you what to do,' he stuttered.

'Uh-huh,' said Lock. Maybe this was another clue to why Marcus had turned out as he was. He was surrounded by parents who thought that money was a substitute for persuasion or good manners. People did what you wanted them to do. Then, of course, you got into the real world and discovered that life didn't work like that. At least, not all the time.

Stacy had told Lock that Marcus's first attempts to woo her had revolved around a date she hadn't realized was a date. That had been followed by a series of expensive gifts that had creeped her out rather than softening her. 'It was as if he thought he could buy me,' she had told Lock.

'If you need an extra fee for tracking down my son and making sure he's here and that he stays—' Peter said.

'He stays?' Lock asked. 'You planning an intervention or a kidnapping, Mr Blake?'

'A friend I spoke to told me that sometimes people can be initially resistant to having a dialogue and confronting their issues.'

Confronting their issues, thought Lock. Right now he was fantasizing about pulling his SIG and helping Peter Blake confront some of his. What the hell had happened to America that no one could speak plain English anymore? Instead they descended into psychobabble, with emphasis on the babble. '*If* your son wants to sit down with you, that's up to him. Now, if you'll excuse me . . .' Lock walked out of the room leaving Peter stumbling over a half-assed apology.

In the hallway, he told Ty, 'Five minutes we're out of here.'

'You got it,' said Ty.

Lock headed for the den. It was located near the back of the house and looked out over the pool, spa and barbecue area. Not that Teddy could see the view as he'd had heavy-duty blinds installed, along with the home-theatre system and another wet bar, with enough whisky to maintain the population of a small Irish island during a bad winter.

He hadn't even pushed open the door when he heard the shouting. It was a real old-school knock-down, drag-'em-out, no-blow-too-low domestic. He knocked at the door and waited.

'Well, maybe if you could actually get it up once in a while instead of drinking yourself to death, I might not have had to file for divorce.'

'Oh, fuck you, Tarian. You were sleeping around long before any of this.'

'You're so full of shit.'

'What about that Pilates instructor then? The one with the lisp.'

'He was from Barcelona. They all speak like that, you redneck asshole, and he was gay for your information.'

Lock knocked again, this time louder. The shouting match seemed to die down. Finally, Teddy opened the door. Tarian was pacing the den behind him. She was crying. Lock did his best to remind himself that their marriage, or divorce, was none of his business.

'I think we've done what we can here,' he said to Teddy.

'But we need you,' said Teddy, as Tarian stalked over to them. 'You can't leave. Not without giving us some notice. I mean, what if someone comes to the house.'

Lock looked at them both. At least he'd stopped them fighting. 'Ty will be back tomorrow to suggest some updates to your security. If I find out anything more about your son, I'll let you know. But there's nothing more for me to do.'

'What about the intervention?' said Tarian. She seemed to be genuinely upset by Lock's leaving. He wondered if it was personal.

'Oh, sweet Jesus,' said Teddy. 'An intervention. What we gonna do? All sit round the barbecue pit singing "Kumbaya" until the little psychopath finds the Lord?'

Tarian drew back her hand to slap Teddy's face. From pure reflex, Lock reached out and grabbed her wrist. He didn't have time to think about. It was an action that was ingrained in him. Teddy took a step back, leaving Lock eye to eye with Tarian.

'Can I let go now?' he asked her.

Her eyes were still moist from tears. There was something behind them too. Not rage. Despair, maybe. Or defeat. She was trying to do her best but her best wasn't good enough. Lock felt for her. He couldn't help himself. She and Teddy must have seen something in each other at one point. They'd not only gotten married but had stayed together long enough to have two kids. Lock wondered where it had gone wrong. It was different for women, and especially a woman who was finishing her second marriage. It wasn't fair that it was different, but it was.

'I lost my temper,' she said. 'Sorry.'

Lock let her go but it took a moment for her to move her arm away from him. She never broke eye contact. He really did need to get out of there.

'You and me both,' said Lock.

He turned and walked back to the hallway where Ty was waiting for him with their overnight bags, packed and ready to go. The last thing he heard as he left was Tarian Griffiths calling after him.

33

At five minutes past ten, while they were debating whether to go out or stay in, and Marcus was praying no one would mention the girl they hadn't yet killed, Gretchen's car pulled up outside. She walked straight in, without a word to anyone, and grabbed a beer from the refrigerator. She popped the cap off and took a long sip. 'Got your text. Figured I'd swing by. So, Devon's back to being a little bitch, huh?'

Krank was sitting at the table, his iPad in hand, scrolling over a map of northern Malibu. From time to time he would swipe at the screen, cross-referencing the contours of the map with a database. He glanced up at Gretchen as she pushed herself onto the kitchen counter. 'Lauren's the problem. But don't worry, I'll deal with her.'

Gretchen tilted back the beer bottle and took a slug. She was short, barely five feet two inches, with spiky blonde hair, striking blue eyes and so many tattoos and piercings that even she had lost count. She was wearing pink Chuck Taylor high tops, skin-tight jeans, a crop top that showed off a muscular torso, and an over-sized black leather biker jacket. Apart from the air of menace that she carried with her, she could have stepped straight out of a Japanese anime cartoon.

'You'll deal with her?' Gretchen said, her sharp chin jutting out as her head tilted back. 'What you gonna do, Krank? Kill her?'

Loser pushed back his chair from the long wooden kitchen table, and stalked out. Gretchen smirked. 'Pussy,' she called after him. 'You boys are all such pussies.'

'I'm not even going to dignify that with a response,' said Krank, swiping back to his map.

'You just did, asshole,' Gretchen shot back. 'Hey, how are you, MG? Awfully quiet over there.'

Marcus shrugged. Even though he was much more confident with women than he had been before, Gretchen set him on edge. Not that he was the only one. She could unsettle most people if she set her mind to it.

No one knew for certain how Krank had hooked up with Gretchen. It was lost somewhere back in the mists of time. They had spun so many different versions of how they had come to be friends that neither Marcus nor Loser knew for sure. One version was that they had got into a fight in a club while they were both trying to pick up the same girl. Krank had once told the rest of the guys that he had picked

Gretchen up in a mall while day-gaming, most often on the street, in malls or at college campuses. Gretchen had just about wet herself laughing when she'd heard that one. She told them that there was no way, game or no game, Krank was her type. Not that there wasn't a connection between them. There was. They both acknowledged it. They were like twins who had been separated at birth. They would finish each other's sentences; they knew what the other would do in a situation before they had done it. They seemed able to read each other's mind. At first, to someone who didn't know them, it was entertaining, if a little spooky. After a while it was more than spooky. It was frightening.

Krank and Gretchen were like two Great White Sharks that had decided to hunt together. And hunt they did. First for women as sexual conquests and, when that became unfulfilling, for more than that. Worse, they seemed to feed off each other. Gretchen would do something outrageous, and Krank would feel compelled to go one step further.

Again the details had been lost but Loser had told Marcus it was Gretchen who had killed first and that was what had given Krank the taste for it. Loser also said that all the cute stories about how they'd met were a lie. The real story was duller. They had met online, on a message-board that Krank moderated, which was dedicated to the men's rights movement. It seemed counter-intuitive but perhaps the most radical voices in the movement, and the most outspoken, were women opposed to feminism.

Loser's story, that Krank and Gretchen had met online, had made more sense to Marcus. He had found a freedom online that he felt was denied him in the real world. He could build relationships with strangers that went deeper than anything his offline life offered. Anonymity, far from distancing him from others, had made him more relaxed, freer to be the person he wanted to become.

But however Krank and Gretchen had met and joined forces, Marcus knew that Gretchen held a special place in their group. She was the alpha female to Krank's alpha male. At times she was more alpha than he was. As was the way of these things in their world, Gretchen had become the leader of their leader. She carried herself that way. Tonight was no exception.

Gretchen slammed her hand down on the kitchen counter. 'You still got that bitch out back?' she asked.

'You wanna go visit?' Krank said, laying down his iPad on the table.

'Depends,' said Gretchen. She leered at them. 'How's she taste? Fish goes off, y' know.'

Krank reached into his pocket and dug out a set of keys. He threw them over to MG. 'You go with Gretchen,' he said. 'Maybe she can teach you a few things about manning up.'

Marcus had been dreading something like this. It was bad enough being alone with Gretchen. She scared him in a way that not even Krank did. Krank could do messed-up stuff, but he could give you a reason. There was a belief system that seemed to underpin his actions. He was driven by the desire to stand up for men, to help return the world to a time before feminism screwed everything up in America.

Gretchen was different. From what he could tell she did things for the sake of them. Or because she enjoyed them. He knew that she liked to inflict pain. Not just the physical kind either. She would watch the news when she came over sometimes. If someone was being interviewed about a terrible tragedy she yelled for everyone to be quiet and turned up the volume. She would peer at the screen with this huge grin on her face. The more upset the person was, the more Gretchen seemed to enjoy it. It creeped him out.

And now here he was, pushing open the door and stepping into the shack with her.

The girl startled at the noise. She had been sitting next to the back wall when he had opened the door. Marcus's stomach turned over as he thought back to what she had looked like only a few short days ago. She had been vibrant, beautiful, and now she looked less than human. It was the way her eyes darted about, like an animal's did when it was trapped and frightened. Her every movement was cramped and furtive. As Gretchen moved toward her, the girl flinched.

Marcus held back. Gretchen hunkered down next to the girl. 'It's okay, sweetie,' she said, stroking the girl's hair. 'I'm here. Now, what have these horrible boys been doing to you, huh?'

A few moments later, Marcus closed his eyes as the girl screamed. It was a low, guttural scream, the kind of sound an animal might make as it was being pushed toward its death in a slaughterhouse with barriers on either side to make sure there would be no escape. The screaming subsided, replaced by low moans. All the while Gretchen spoke softly to the girl, her words at odds with the pain she was inflicting.

'Don't worry,' she said. 'It will all be over soon.'

After a few minutes, Krank burst in. He was carrying a bundle of rags. He stormed over to Gretchen. 'The whole neighborhood can hear her. You want to have the cops show up?'

'They'll think someone's watching a movie,' said Gretchen. 'Hey, that's an idea. We should have filmed this.' She dug into her pocket for her phone.

Krank grabbed her wrist. 'You're not filming anything here.'

Gretchen shook him off and jammed her phone back into her pocket.

The girl flinched as Krank grabbed a handful of her hair. He pulled her head back. Marcus saw her eyes roll back in her head for the briefest of moments as she slipped out of the present. He hoped, for her sake, that she might stay like that. A few seconds later she came to and the screaming started up again.

Gretchen helped Krank hold her as he shoved one of the rags into the girl's mouth. She must have nipped him because he yelped a little and drew back his hand, shaking it violently. He looked at the damage, clenched his fist, drew back his arm and punched her full in the face.

'That was hot,' said Gretchen. 'Do it again.'

'Shut the hell up,' Krank shot back, as he found purchase, and got the rag into the girl's mouth.

He stepped back and admired his handiwork. With the fingers of his left hand he worried at the edge of the right where she'd bitten him. Marcus could hear the girl's breath whistling through her nose.

Gretchen had a knife in her hand. It was small, the kind of knife a chef would use to debone a piece of chicken. She held it up to the girl's left eye. 'Don't have to watch if you don't want to, sweetie.'

Marcus swallowed hard. This wasn't what he had signed up for. He might have fantasized about having his revenge on all the girls who had rejected and humiliated him but not like this. He looked across at Krank.

'Want Gretchen to stop, MG?' Krank said, anticipating his thoughts. Krank could always do that. Sometimes Marcus believed that Krank knew what they were thinking before the thought had even formed.

Marcus nodded as Gretchen looked back over her shoulder at him.

'You guys are no fun,' said Gretchen, as she slashed the air in front of the girl's face and she flinched. Her body was shaking now, like someone who had been plunged into a freezing cold bath. Marcus could smell urine.

Krank walked over to him, and pulled a short, snub-nosed revolver from the waistband of his pants. He held it out toward him. 'Up to you, MG. Either Gretchen keeps going or you do the right thing here.'

Marcus swallowed again. It hurt. He could feel himself close to tears. He couldn't afford to cry in front of either Krank or Gretchen, he knew that. They already saw him as weak. If he broke down now he might be next to face Gretchen's wrath. He doubted her sadism was limited to young women. That was merely her preference.

He knew what Krank was asking him to do. He took the gun from him. He thumbed back the hammer and walked over to the girl. Gretchen stood off to one side.

'This I have to see,' said Gretchen.

Marcus shoved past her. Krank stood next to him. 'Go ahead, MG. And remember, you're a soldier. This isn't personal. We have to show these bitches who's boss. Take back our country. That's all.'

The gun raised, Marcus stepped off to the side. He moved back and aimed at the side of the girl's head. He could see her straining to twist round and look at him. His hand was trembling as he found the trigger. It took more pressure than he had imagined as he squeezed. At the last minute, he closed his eyes.

The gun went off. It was loud. There was a buzzing in his ears. Above it he could hear Gretchen laughing. He opened his eyes and saw her doubled over with laughter. She was looking straight at him.

'You missed!' she said, between gusts of mirth.

Marcus looked at the girl. Her chin was resting on her chest, her eyes closed, but she was unharmed.

Gretchen's cackles continued. 'How the hell does someone miss from a foot? Oh, man, MG, you're such a little pussy.'

Marcus felt the rage surge. He raised the gun back up and fired, his eyes open. This time the bullet found the girl's head, tearing off her jaw. He adjusted his aim, and fired again. He fired twice more into her, and she slumped. The final shot must have caught her neck because blood arced from her, spraying his face. He stepped back and swiped at it with the back of his hand. He could taste it on his lips, salty, metallic.

He felt Krank grasp his shoulder and squeeze.

'There you go, MG. I knew you'd get over the line. Proud of you, man.'

Marcus turned to look at Krank first, then Gretchen. Gretchen's laughter had faded. The look on her face had changed. She seemed to be weighing him differently. There was a little fear mixed in there too. At least, Marcus hoped there was.

The horror subsided. He felt a rush rise up in him. It was as if he was somehow taller. He looked down at his T-shirt, stained with blood, and the gun in his hand. He felt good. He was ready for whatever came next. He had finally killed, and now he understood a little better why the others said it was better than sex.

34

Within only forty minutes' warning, Lock had to haul ass from his condo in the Palisades to downtown so he could meet the security guard from the apartment complex in a coffee shop. He didn't blame the guy for not wanting to meet up anywhere near the Marina. For all LA's sprawl, its neighborhoods were small towns. What the guard was doing was cause for dismissal and, as low-paid security work went, you could do a lot worse than signing people in and out of a pricey apartment complex at Marina Del Rey.

Lock grabbed some water and took a seat inside at a corner table that gave him a good view of the entrance. The sidewalk was busy as office workers flitted back and forth. Across the street a construction crew were at work.

He saw Ramón, the security guard, walking toward the door of the coffee shop. He was dressed in grey pants and a white shirt with a tie, a belt containing the spill of a gut that came from sitting in a guard booth for most of the day. His head was on a swivel. He pushed through the door and made for Lock's table.

Lock got up and motioned for him to sit down. 'You want anything? Coffee? Water?' he asked the man.

It seemed a complicated question for the guy, though his lack of clear decision-making might have come down to nerves. 'No. Yeah, wait a minute. I'll take a water.'

'Do me a favor?' said Lock. The guard glanced up from a folded piece of paper he had pulled from his inside jacket pocket, and gave him an expectant look. 'Chill out. This ain't WikiLeaks, 'kay? No one's following you, and apart from me, no one gives a shit about any of this.'

It seemed to work. The guard managed an uncertain smile. 'Can I get a muffin?'

'Sure thing,' said Lock, heading to the counter where he picked up a water and a couple of muffins. He paid and sat back down across from the guard.

The guard smoothed the paper out on the table in front of Lock. 'I figured it was easier just to write the names down. I didn't know if you wanted all the dates and stuff but I can get those.'

Lock picked up the paper and began to scan what was a very brief list. In the six months Marcus Griffiths had lived there he'd had seven visitors. Four were men. Three were women. One of the men named was Teddy Griffiths. One of the women was Tarian. That took it down to five people that Lock wasn't aware of.

Teddy Griffiths had said that the leader of the group of kids Marcus had gotten mixed up with was Asian. There was only one obviously Asian-American name on the piece of paper. Charles Kim. Lock would start with him and work his way to the others. The problem he had was that, when it came to surnames, Kim was about as common as Smith or Jones. Charles wasn't much better. He could guess an approximate age but that still left a lot of young men in their twenties in the greater Los Angeles area.

The guard had already demolished one muffin leaving only a scattering of crumbs on the table top. He pointed at the second. 'You going to eat that? Hate to see waste.'

'Go right ahead,' said Lock, fishing an envelope from his back pocket and sliding it with the muffin toward the guard. 'Thanks for your help with this.'

The guard shrugged, seemingly more excited by the prospect of a second muffin than the additional three hundred dollars in fresh bills tucked into the envelope. He pawed some more muffin into his mouth with the tips of his fingers. 'My wife's got me on this diet. Like a paleo thing. You heard of that shit? It's like nuts. I mean, literally, she sends me into work with these big bags of nuts and shit. I tried to tell her, like, "Baby, there's a reason we left that kinda thing behind," but she won't listen.'

'This guy here,' Lock said, cutting short the chit-chat about diet crazes with a finger tap at the list. 'Charles Kim. You remember him any?'

'Yeah, real nice kid. Very funny. Always took the time to ask me how I was. Most people don't make the effort, know what I'm saying?'

'Can you describe him? How old do you think he was? How tall? Any tattoos? Anything I can use to track him down?'

The second muffin was gone. The guard licked the end of his right index finger and started dabbing at the crumbs before popping the finger into his mouth. At least Lock knew that he could keep him talking with another muffin. Hell, he could probably have skipped the cash entirely and gone for a basket of pastries instead.

'He was twenties, maybe like twenty-five, twenty-six. Didn't see any ink on him, Always dressed preppy. Not crazy big but like he worked out.'

'How tall?' pressed Lock.

Another dab of crumbs disappeared from the table top. 'Can't help you with that. He was always in his car.'

'You remember what he drove?'

'Sure. BMW 5-series. Dark blue or black. I remember thinking it was a nice car for a kid that age. I kinda thought that maybe he was dealing or something.'

'Because of his ride?' Lock asked.

'Well,' said the guard, 'that and the fact that one time I saw he had a handgun. It must have slipped out from the under the seat when he stopped to talk to me. I acted like I hadn't seen it. Car guns aren't that uncommon in this town.'

'What kind of gun?'

'I don't know. Like a Glock. Something like that.'

Lock spent another twenty minutes running through the rest of the names. The details on the other visitors that the guard could remember were sketchier. Charles Kim was the one who had stood out, which fitted with what Teddy Griffiths had told him. It was always dangerous to assume too much, but Charles Kim sounded like the real name of Krank.

The other male visitors were white and in their twenties. One was dressed rather flamboyantly ('Kinda like a pimp. Looked dumb as hell to me, a white boy trying to pass like Superfly') but that was it for defining characteristics.

Of the two women who had visited, all the guard could recall was that they were both early twenties and white. They had only visited Marcus once, maybe twice at most, and that had been some time ago, closer to when he had first moved in. He thought that one had been 'kinda alternative-looking' but when Lock pressed him he wasn't sure.

Lock thanked him with a couple more emergency muffins, and watched the guy leave while he held back. Five minutes later, Lock walked back to his car, which was parked near the Federal building. He dug out his own laptop, drove out of the parking structure and pulled over to the side of the street as soon as he had a decent enough internet connection.

Opening a secure, anonymized browser he began to search for Charles Kim. When broad search engine results yielded too many hits to be of any use, he logged on to a pre-paid account at one of the web's many people-finder and background-check sites.

An initial search for Los Angeles threw back around twenty results. About two-thirds had ages attached to them.

Lock discounted anyone in their forties or over. That left him with four men named Charles Kim under the age of forty, who were living, or who had lived recently, in the greater Los Angeles area.

He bore down into the results. Ten minutes later he had a shortlist of just two names. The first Charles Miller Kim was a twenty-seven-year-old with an address in La Puente. Lock made a note of the address. He had a cell number and could have called ahead, but that would have meant letting the guy know he was looking for him. In turn that could make him harder to speak to face to face.

He worked the other names on the list. They were less common and he quickly located the other visitors to Marcus Griffiths's apartment without any great difficulty.

Lock closed his laptop and headed back to the Audi. He got in and set his GPS for the address he had in La Puente. There was one more thing about the two Charles Kims he had to speak to. It could prove significant or not, but it was one of the first things he had looked for. Neither of them had a criminal record. Nor did any of the other visitors – with one exception.

One of the female visitors, twenty-five-year-old Gretchen Yorda, not only had a criminal record, she'd done time. Once he'd found Krank, Lock figured she'd be next on his list of people to speak to.

35

La Puente was a nice enough neighborhood in east Los Angeles that was made up of mostly middle-class Hispanic families. It was a long way from the wealth of the west side, but Lock guessed it was tagged as respectable, whatever the hell that meant, these days. He rolled into a neat cul-de-sac of five single-story ranch homes, and parked.

He got out and quickly located the house he was looking for. There was a red Chevy pick-up truck parked in the driveway but no sign of a BMW. It looked more like a Toyota kind of place than a BMW but maybe Charles Kim was out cruising.

Lock walked to the front door, rang the bell and waited. He saw someone peel back a curtain in the living room, then retreat. Lock stepped to the side of the door. A few seconds later it opened to reveal a young Asian mother in her twenties with a toddler on one hip and a slightly older child clinging to her leg.

'Sorry to disturb you, ma'am,' said Lock. 'I'm looking for Mr Charles Kim.'

She was clearly taken aback. He had a feeling that, if he lived there, he was not the Charles Kim he was looking for.

'That's my husband,' she said. 'He's at work.'

'This may sound like a strange question, but does he drive a dark-colored BMW sedan?' Lock pulled out a piece of paper. 'I'm trying to track down a Charles Kim with a BMW and I have a couple of possible people. It's nothing to worry about if it is him.'

The toddler on her hip began to fret. 'No, you have the wrong house. I'm sorry.'

Before Lock could ask her anything else, she had closed the door on him. He didn't blame her. She'd been more polite than he would have if someone he didn't know had turned up at his home asking questions.

Glancing around, he saw an older man busy in his front yard, trimming back a rose bush. Lock headed over to him and asked him the same question. The man put down his shears and, in heavily accented English, told Lock, with a wry smile, that no one there drove a BMW.

Unless this Charles Kim had a secret life, he wasn't the person Lock was looking for. Lock headed back to his car, got in and headed west, back to the apartment address he had in Santa Monica for the other Charles Kim, the one he was guessing did have a BMW and a nickname.

36

Tarian Griffiths was upstairs when she heard Rosa shouting up to her, sounding panicked. She rushed from the master bedroom and down the stairs. She could hear Teddy talking to her. He was doing the thing that drove Tarian crazy – speaking loudly in English when he knew that Rosa only spoke Spanish, apart from a few phrases.

Tarian bustled through the kitchen and into the laundry room. Rosa was holding a grey T-shirt over the sink, her fingers pinching the sleeves. It looked like one of Marcus's. Even from the doorway Tarian could see what looked like a bloodstain in the center.

Teddy was trying to persuade Rosa to give him the shirt. 'It's the design,' Teddy said. 'It's not blood. It just looks like it. Or maybe it's ketchup.'

'Teddy, let me handle this, would you?' said Tarian.

'With pleasure,' he said. He pushed past her, stopping long enough to whisper, 'She found it hidden in the back of his closet when she was collecting laundry. She thinks we should call the cops.'

'*Uno momento*,' Tarian said, to the flustered housekeeper. She followed Teddy back out into the kitchen.

'What's going on, Teddy? He hid a bloodstained T-shirt in his closet?'

Teddy wouldn't make eye contact. He looked everywhere but at her. 'We don't know it's blood. It looks like blood, but who knows?'

'Wait right there,' Tarian told him.

She walked back into the laundry room, and reached out to take the T-shirt. 'May I, please?'

Reluctantly, Rosa handed it to her. Tarian held the edges and looked at the stain. It was a reddish-brown that had soaked into the fabric. It did look like blood. Maybe it wasn't. Or maybe it was, but there was a rational explanation. But, then, why would Marcus have hidden it at the back of the closet rather than placing it in the laundry basket?

She held up her hand toward Rosa in a let-me-deal-with-this gesture. She was sure that Rosa wouldn't call the police off her own bat. But should they?

Teddy was still in the kitchen. She was amazed that even though it was midday this latest discovery hadn't made him hit the Scotch. She grasped the T-shirt in her hand, her eyes pulled toward the stain. 'It looks like blood to me,' she said.

He took a deep breath and exhaled slowly. 'Yeah. I know. I just didn't want to let Rosa get any more excited.' The words fell away. It was a moment before he spoke again. 'Maybe we should call the cops. Let them deal with it.'

Tarian had a hard time imagining the phone call. Not just because the idea of calling the cops on her son went against her every instinct as a mother, but because she was scared of where it might lead. It had been hard enough to contact Lock, and she had only done that because she had figured that if she were paying him she would have some degree of control.

'And say what? That I'm scared of my own son and the people he's hanging around with? That we found blood on his clothes and we think he might have hurt someone?'

Teddy walked to one of the cupboards, opened it and reached for a crystal tumbler. Tarian stepped in front of him, took the tumbler and put it back in the cupboard. 'Whisky's not going to help us.'

'Might not help *you*,' said Teddy, sounding as sullen as a kid caught with his hand in the cookie jar.

'I just think,' said Tarian, 'that we don't want to get the police involved unless we actually know what's going on with him. We were planning on speaking to him anyway. We can ask him what this is about.' She held up the T-shirt.

Teddy gave her a sour look. 'Might be a better idea if I took it out into the yard and burned it before Rosa decides she should speak to the cops anyway. I mean what if it belongs to that girl at USC? What if he's . . . ?' He trailed off.

'We would have heard if something had happened to her. The police would have been here. They already have his name.'

'So if it's not that, then what?' Teddy asked.

'We'll speak to him,' Tarian said. 'Just like we planned. It's only fair that we give him a chance to explain before we go jumping to wild conclusions.'

She looked back down at the bloodstained T-shirt. Whether she could admit it out loud or not, she knew there was no rational explanation for what Rosa had found. She knew it in the same way she had known that her son had become a stranger to her, not just someone she didn't know any more but someone she feared. She needed to give herself a final chance to get through to him. If she couldn't, then calling the cops might not be the worst idea. At least that way he'd be safe, and so would they.

37

The Pacific Ocean shimmered in the near distance as Lock parked the Audi on 5th Street in Santa Monica. The apartment block was five minutes' walk, tucked away on California Avenue just past 3rd Street. It was a handsome red-brick building with an ornate black metal entryway. Lock hit the button for the apartment and waited for someone to answer. No one did. He stepped back from the entrance as he saw a young woman with short blonde hair walk through the lobby toward the door. She was dressed in yoga pants and a crop top. A French bulldog puppy trotted behind her on the end of what looked like a diamond-encrusted lead.

As she pushed through the door, Lock stepped forward and held it open for her. 'Cute dog. How old is he?'

'It's a she.'

Lock knelt down to pat it. 'Sorry, she. I had a dog just like this,' he lied. 'Wife got it in the divorce. Broke my heart.'

'That's too bad.'

'Hey, you wouldn't know Charles Kim, would you? I'm sure he lives in this building. Only I lost his number, and he doesn't seem to be in.'

Her expression changed as soon as he said the name from one of polite interest to one that suggested he'd just farted. 'You're a friend of his?'

With the sense that this was going to be a short conversation, Lock asked, 'Drives a BMW?'

'I really have to go.' She started to move past him.

He took a half-step in front of her, letting his jacket ride up enough at the waist that she could see his SIG Sauer 226 sitting neatly in its holster. 'I'm not a friend of his, no. I get the impression you aren't either. But I do need to find him.'

'Are you a cop?' she said.

He sensed the uncertainty in her voice. She was on the verge of making a scene. 'I'm trying to trace him for someone. I can't say too much more than that.'

'So you're not a cop?'

He had to hand it to her: once she got on a track she stuck with it. Then again, so did he. He held his position. 'Does a Charles Kim who drives a dark-colored BMW live here? Yes or no?' Lock stayed focused on her face. 'He sometimes goes by the nickname Krank.'

She pursed her lips. 'I haven't seen him here for weeks but, yeah, he's here sometimes.'

Lock had the primary information he needed. He stepped to one side allowing her a route past him. 'I'm not a cop, but if there's anything else you can tell me that would help me find him I'd really appreciate it.' He put out his hand. 'Ryan.'

The puppy barked, keen to walk. She reached out and shook Lock's hand. 'Kimberley.'

She started down the steps and Lock fell in beside her.

'The guy you're looking for, Krank, or whatever he likes to call himself, is a total asshole. And you can tell him I said that.'

Now all Lock had to do was listen. They walked down California Avenue toward the ocean and Kimberley spilled her guts to him about Charles Kim.

She had run into Charles, a.k.a. Krank, shortly after she'd moved into the building. She lived in apartment 4C. Her shower was blocked and had overflowed into the apartment beneath. That was his apartment, 3C. Rather than losing his temper, he had been cool about it. Although she didn't say so in as many words, he had got her into bed but, when she'd mentioned the relationship word, had cooled off. That might have been okay but she told Lock he had then made a point of bringing home a string of young women. Because her bedroom was directly above his, she could hear everything.

After that he'd smirk at her every time their paths crossed. Again, as far as Lock was concerned, it didn't seem that abnormal. Then he moved from being a regular asshole to making veiled threats that suggested she might want to find somewhere else to live. Things quickly escalated and late one evening in the building's parking lot he had told her that if she didn't move something bad might happen to her.

She'd called the Santa Monica PD. They'd done their best, but it had been a case of her word against his. She had thought about moving but then he'd begun to drop off the radar, spending less and less time at his apartment. In fact, she hadn't seen him in over a week.

'You have any idea where he's living at the moment?' Lock asked, as they passed a group of people doing yoga on a grassy area.

'Don't know. Don't care. I think he may have said something about moving back to San Diego.'

'He mention where in San Diego?' Lock pressed.

She shrugged. 'I didn't ask. I'm sorry. I've kind of tried to forget about him. It's bad enough that he still has the apartment below me. Wherever he is, I just hope he stays there.'

Lock didn't blame her. He thought over what she'd told him. Certain pieces were starting to fall into place. He was getting an idea of who Charles Kim, or Krank, was. He was charming. He had the ability to disarm others. He could get young women into bed. He obviously had money. He drove a nice car, and an apartment in this part of Santa Monica wasn't cheap. So, with all of that, what did he want with someone like Marcus Griffiths?

He had been ready to thank her for her time and walk back to the car. Instead, he turned around. 'Can I ask you one last favor?'

38

Lock stepped into Krank's apartment and closed the door behind him. He walked down a stub of narrow hallway passing a bathroom. He pushed open the door with his right foot. It was empty, the shower curtain pulled back along the rail to reveal a deep bathtub. A sink. A toilet. Both clean and dry.

He moved back into the corridor. He noted that there were no pictures on the walls. The absence made the place feel transient somehow, like the occupant was merely passing through rather than making a home for himself. He kept going, emerging into an open-plan kitchen and living room. Bookshelves lined two walls. That he hadn't expected. Off to one side was a desk with an Apple computer. A small filing cabinet was tucked beneath the desk.

Apart from a couch, the main feature of the room was a weights bench. Lock had already noticed a pull-up bar clipped above the frame of the door that led into the apartment's solitary bedroom. Krank liked to work out. That was good to know.

There were two windows each on the west and south sides of the apartment. One looked down into a small open courtyard; the other faced out onto California Avenue. All four windows had been cracked about six inches to allow in a fresh ocean breeze.

Leaving the computer for later, Lock walked into the kitchen area. The surfaces were clean. The dishes had been put away. He pulled open the dishwasher. The top rack was empty.

There was something in the bottom rack. It wasn't dirty dishes. Reaching into his pocket, he pulled out a pair of gloves. If it was what he thought it was, he didn't want his prints anywhere near it. Gently, he lifted out the heavy cardboard box of ammunition and placed it on the counter.

Magtech. Solid copper .223 caliber. Hollow point. Designed to circumvent legislation that prohibited armor-piercing bullets. Capable of making a very nasty entrance wound and a devastating exit wound. Plenty able to punch through most body armor. There were twenty in the box.

He laid it on the kitchen counter and looked at it, confused. Nothing about the apartment suggested that Krank had left in a hurry. The exact opposite. Everything had been left clean and tidy. There wasn't even a stray dirty sock on the floor. Yet there was a box of armor-piercing bullets hidden in the lower rack of the dishwasher.

He left the ammo where it was for now and walked toward the bedroom door. It was ajar. He pushed it open. Unlike the rest of the apartment, which was wooden flooring, the bedroom was carpeted. He stood in the doorway and surveyed the bed. Perfectly made. A California king-size. The bed for a single man who had a lot of company. From what the ex-girlfriend had told him, Krank wasn't averse to having more than one guest for a sleepover. The room looked hotel-occupant ready. Everything had been squared away. Just like the rest of the place. No family pictures. Nothing personal. Apart, of course, from the books.

Those turned out to be the most revealing part of the entire apartment. Helpfully, they were arranged neatly by subject matter, then by author.

The bookcase consisted of six shelves. The top two shelves were devoted to history, economics and politics. From a quick scan of the titles, it was clear that Krank's economics and politics interests skewed toward the libertarian end of the spectrum. The history was mostly accounts of America from the 1960s onwards.

The third shelf was principally fiction. Ayn Rand featured heavily, with two copies of her defining book, *The Fountainhead*. The fourth shelf held more obscure titles.

With some of them, the subject matter was obvious: *Women Who Make the World Worse*, *Weak Link: The Feminization of the American Military*, *The Politically Incorrect Guide to Women, Sex and Feminism*, *Feminist Fantasies*, *Spreading Misandry: The Teaching of Contempt for Men in Popular Culture*, and *Taken into Custody: The War Against Fathers, Marriage and the Family*. Other titles were more obscure, but a quick leaf through the pages confirmed the same subject matter.

The fifth shelf focused on self-defense, weapons, guerrilla warfare. Everything from owners' manuals for a range of handguns to *The Anarchist Cookbook* and volumes on Krav Maga and close-quarters combat.

Lock hunkered down to take a look at the bottom shelf. He could immediately see why these titles had been placed where they would be difficult for a casual visitor to browse. They focused on American mass shootings from before Columbine all the way up to the Sandy Hook Massacre and beyond. He pulled a couple of titles out and flicked through them. Someone had underlined sections and scribbled notes in the margins.

Standing up, Lock felt a sudden chill. You could rarely infer too much from a person's choice of reading.

People read for escape. Little old ladies who wouldn't hurt a fly could be big fans of gruesome horror without it signifying anything. This seemed different, though. Put all the titles together, throw in what he already knew about Krank, along with the case of shells hidden in the dishwasher, and he was more concerned about Marcus and his family than he had been before.

He had remembered something else too. A detail the girl upstairs had told him.

He walked into the bathroom, switched on the light and looked up at the ceiling. He put down the toilet lid, put his foot on it, and tested his weight as he stood on it. He reached his hand up to the ceiling. There was no sign of any water damage. No sign of any leak. And no sign of any repair. The plaster was slightly faded and matched that of the walls on either side.

He got down, and walked out of the apartment, pulling the door closed behind him. The corridor was empty. He walked to the end, pushed through into the stairwell, and took a flight of stairs to the next floor.

Pushing open the door, he walked down to apartment 4C, and knocked. The girl he'd met outside lived there. She had told him she was going to run errands and had let him into the building. She hadn't mentioned a room mate.

He knocked again. He could hear someone walking to the door. 'Okay, okay, I'm coming.'

The door opened to reveal an elderly man in jeans and a baggy T-shirt. He stared at Lock. 'What is this? Who let you in?'

'I take it you don't share this place with a young woman called Kimberley?' Lock held his right hand at chest height. 'About so high. Spiky blonde hair. Has a French bulldog.'

The look on the man's face gave Lock his answer. A minute later he was back in Krank's apartment, picking up the box of cartridges from the dishwasher. A minute after that he was standing in the bright sunshine on California Avenue. 'Kimberley' and her dog were nowhere to be seen.

39

Gretchen stood on the corner of California and 3rd Street. Though she was still holding the puppy's lead, the animal was gone. She tapped Krank's number on the screen of her cell phone and waited. He picked up immediately. An elderly couple walked past her. She stood side on so that she had a view of the apartment building that she had just let Ryan Lock into.

'What's up?' said Krank. 'You get everything?'

'You got someone looking for you. Think it's the same guy that MG's parents hired. His name's Lock.'

When Krank next spoke, he sounded panicked. Gretchen enjoyed it. He wasn't the ice-cold character he liked to project. He was alpha for sure, but he could still behave like a total pussy. 'He didn't catch you in the apartment, did he?' Krank asked.

'I was on my way out. But we had quite the talk about you.'

'You did what?' Now Krank sounded apoplectic. 'Why did you do that?'

'Chill,' she told him. 'I told him I lived upstairs and gave him a false name.'

'You shouldn't have done that. What if he figures out you're lying?'

Gretchen rolled her eyes. Krank was such a worrier. He talked a good game, but sometimes she wondered if he was actually capable of putting his plans into action. 'And how's he going to do that? Relax. It's fine. I got everything you asked me to pick up. I'll be back at the house in an hour.'

40

Tarian Griffiths laid the phone on the kitchen counter. Teddy, already nursing the first Scotch of the day, stood next to her ex-husband, Peter. Both men were expectant as they waited for news of how her call to Marcus had gone. Like everything else in her life with both men, it had fallen to her to actually do something about the mess they were in. Just once, she thought, she would have liked to be with a man who took charge of the situation rather than wringing his hands or pounding down whisky like they were about to stop distilling the stuff.

She managed something approaching a smile. 'He's coming over tonight.'

Both Teddy and Peter looked relieved. Tarian wasn't certain that she was. She still wasn't even sure this was the right thing to do. Part of her thought they should have gone with their initial gut instinct and called the police. After all, if Marcus had hurt someone . . .

She had spent an hour or so searching the internet for any report of a USC co-ed being murdered or attacked. Apart from a couple of stories that were a few years old, there was nothing recent. With the restraining order in place, she didn't dare contact the girl directly to make sure she was okay. Although the court hadn't prohibited her from such she didn't want to raise suspicions.

Teddy had been the one to talk her round. What if Marcus hadn't done anything? What if there was a perfectly innocent explanation for the blood on his shirt? Maybe he'd gotten into a bar fight. If they called the cops and they asked him about, she would have lost her son for good. He'd never trust any of his family again. Wasn't it better that they confronted him themselves? If they didn't believe his answers, Teddy had argued, then they could call the cops.

The seed of doubt Teddy had planted was all she had needed. Tarian had called Peter and they had agreed they would talk to Marcus together. But in order to talk to him they needed to persuade him to come home, and the way he had stormed out last time, Tarian knew that wasn't going to be easy. They needed some kind of bait.

Marcus had a trust fund that had been part of her divorce settlement with Peter. They were co-signatories. Most of the money wouldn't come to Marcus until he was thirty. It was one more thing that had driven a wedge between Tarian and her son. Marcus wanted the money now.

She had dropped a hint to Marcus during her phone call that they might have reconsidered. She hadn't said anything upfront, just that she, Teddy and Peter wanted to discuss some financial matters with him, but first they needed to know he was stable enough to make good choices.

It had worked. After some discussion at the other end of the line, presumably with his 'friends', Marcus had told her he would be there at seven o'clock sharp.

'How did he sound?' Teddy asked.

'Yes, was he okay?' said Peter.

Tarian wasn't sure how to answer. He sounded the way he had for the past year or more. Distant. Disconnected. The only time he didn't sound like that was when he was screaming at them and blaming them, her in particular, for ruining his life.

'He sounded like . . . I dunno, like Marcus.' She looked at Teddy. 'I don't think the children should be here tonight. You know how he can get.'

Thankfully Teddy didn't argue. 'I'll see if Sylvia can take them.'

Sylvia was Teddy's cousin. She lived in West Hollywood. She was a little on the flaky side but the kids loved her and it would be only one night. 'We should call Dr

Stentz.' He was a psychiatrist Marcus had seen before. 'See if he can come over.'

Peter held up his hand. 'Already did it. He'd be happy to help us.'

'Speaking of which,' Tarian said, 'what about asking Ryan and his partner if they could be here?'

'Ryan?' said Teddy, staring at her over the top of his crystal tumbler as he drained the last of his Scotch.

She rolled her eyes. 'Mr Lock, then. That better?'

Teddy tilted the glass and crunched loudly on an ice cube. He glanced at Peter. 'She has the hots for him.'

To his credit, Peter cut him off. 'I don't think that is helpful.'

'Should we ask him to come over, or not?' said Tarian.

'I can handle Marcus if he gets overexcited,' Teddy said.

Teddy 'handling' her son was what worried Tarian. Teddy wasn't the most diplomatic of men at the best of times. Mix in the best part of a bottle of whisky and it was a recipe for disaster if he and Marcus started to go at it. 'That's what concerns me, Teddy,' she said.

'What's that supposed to mean?' Teddy shot back, his hackles rising.

Tarian bit her lower lip hard to stop herself responding. She didn't need a row with Teddy. Not on top of everything else.

'If I could say something,' Peter said quietly. 'If Marcus has hurt someone and these security consultants become aware of it, won't they go the police?'

Teddy could barely keep the sneer out of his voice. 'They both signed a non-disclosure agreement. I made sure of it.'

Peter wasn't knocked off track. 'I'm fairly sure knowledge of criminal activity trumps any NDA. And even if it doesn't, if they do go to the police or the DA then suing them for breach of contract hardly matters.'

Despite his mild, almost meek manner, Tarian had forgotten what a voice of reason Peter could be. She'd never felt the excitement with him that she had with other men, but in a crisis he kept a cool head, unlike Teddy. 'You're right. We can't get them involved.'

'So what about the shrink?' said Teddy. 'Don't we have the same problem with him?'

'Patient-doctor confidentiality is a little more robust,' said Peter. 'He can claim an ethical exemption. In any case, if Marcus has hurt someone, we'll have no choice but to go to the authorities, will we?'

Tarian looked from Peter to Teddy and back again. The weight of the question hung in the air between them. Could she turn in her own son? 'There's probably a simple explanation for all of this. Isn't there?'

Neither man answered.

41

Gretchen heaved the last of the backpacks onto the kitchen table. As Marcus and the others busied themselves stacking the contents of the other two packs on the floor, ready for deployment, Krank opened the drawstring of the last. He began to take out boxes of ammunition. He stacked them neatly in blocks on the table. When he was done, he stood back, puzzled. 'You're missing a box,' he said.

'That's not possible. I took everything that was in the apartment.'

'You must have panicked when you saw that guy snooping around,' said Krank.

Gretchen glared at him. 'I'd already moved everything out before I even ran into him.'

Krank scraped an index finger down the block of boxes in front of him, counting off as he went. 'There were nine boxes of these. I can only count eight.'

Gretchen rolled her neck, reaching up and probing at a knot in her upper back with her right hand. 'Maybe one box fell out. I'll go check the trunk.'

She skipped past him and out of sight. Gretchen never sweated this kind of stuff. That was why they needed her. No matter the situation, she could always be relied upon to stay calm.

Outside, she hit the clicker. The trunk popped open. She peered in. Nothing. Apart from a first-aid kit, and a spare handgun she kept in its carry case, the trunk was empty. She slammed the trunk shut and opened the rear passenger door. She checked the back seat and under the front seats. She closed the rear door and opened the front passenger door. The glove box was empty. Maybe Krank's count was off.

Then she remembered. *Shit*. She had been clearing the dishwasher, and thinking what an idiotic hiding place it was when the puppy had started barking. As she'd gone to see if there was someone outside the apartment she had kicked over a bowl of water she'd put down for him. She'd closed the dishwasher door and cleaned up the mess. The puppy was still barking and circling by the door. She had grabbed the final backpack, left to put it in the car, and when she came back she'd forgotten about the last box of shells.

One her way out, after running a final check, which hadn't included the dishwasher, she had run into that private security creep hired to babysit Marcus. The ammunition had gone clean out of her mind. Then, of course, she had let Lock into the building.

Gretchen speed-walked back inside the house. Krank was in the kitchen, busy drilling Marcus about how to handle dinner with his parents. Krank wasn't going to like what she was about to tell him. 'I fucked up,' she said. 'That last box is still in the apartment.'

Krank swiveled slowly to face her. Marcus and the others fell silent, and stared at their shoes.

'You did what?' said Krank.

Gretchen stood her ground, legs evenly apart, chest out, chin tilted up. 'You heard me. I didn't pick it up.'

Krank's eyes narrowed. 'You let that guy into the building. Which means he would have been in the apartment. And if he was in the apartment he would have found them.'

Gretchen shrugged. 'So what if he did? Lots of people have stuff at home that they shouldn't have. Guns. Blow. You had a box of ammo. Maybe you're planning for the zombie apocalypse.'

'Armor piercing,' said Krank. 'Illegal.'

Gretchen couldn't help herself. She burst out laughing.

'This shit isn't funny,' said Krank.

Her hand swept out, taking in all the gear stacked in the kitchen. Body armor, Bushmasters, handguns, incendiary grenades that Krank had conjured up from God knew where. 'With what we have planned you're worried about being *arrested*?'

Krank took a step toward her. Gretchen lowered her hand. It fell to the knife clipped onto her belt. Her fingertips stroked the handle.

'If I'm arrested this is all over. Or if they find this place. What about that? It'll all be over before we've gotten started,' said Krank.

Gretchen stood her ground. 'No one's going to find anyone. No one knows about this place. Or any of this. So why don't you stop acting like you have your period and chill out?'

The others were waiting to see how Krank would react. Would he freak out or stay calm? If it had been Marcus or Loser who'd admitted to a slip like this he would have been screaming by now. He wasn't, though. His hands were bunched into fists and he was angry but he hadn't gone crazy. He seemed to be thinking. After a few long moments of silence, he turned to Marcus.

'See if your folks say anything about it. If they don't bring it up, ask them about this Lock guy. Don't say anything about knowing where he's been. Let them do the talking. Soon as you know what's going on, or what they know, you call us. Understand?'

Marcus swallowed so hard that everyone in the kitchen could hear it. 'I understand.'

42

The armor-piercing bullet rolled across Ty's open palm. .45-caliber. Copper-jacketed. Handgun ammo. Copper was soft. It allowed the charge to push through easier upon impact. When the government had banned Teflon-coated bullets, they hadn't realized that the hard coating had nothing to do with the bullet's ability to punch through armor. Teflon was used to protect the barrel and cut down on ricochet. After the ban, manufacturers had simply started using copper. Show me a law, thought Ty, and I'll show you a way to work round it – or, in this case, simply make a bad situation worse.

A private individual couldn't purchase ammunition like this for a handgun. But armor-piercing rounds for rifles were easy to come by. Not that they were always needed. If you had the correct rifle for the job, it didn't matter too much. In reality, there was no such thing as bulletproof. Only degrees of bullet-resistant. But, for obvious reasons, handgun ammunition of this type was more tightly controlled.

Handgun ammo that could punch through a standard non-plated vest, though? That was a lot tougher to come by. But not impossible. Not if you found the right person at the right gun show. Ty guessed that was what Charles Kim had done. It would have been a two-minute transaction in the parking lot.

'What do you think?' Lock asked him.

Ty pinched the bullet between two fingers and held it up to the light streaming through the front windshield of Lock's car. 'This right here is cop-killer shit. You want to get a civilian wet, you don't need anything close to this. Long as you can shoot straight and you have the right hardware, you're already good to go.'

Lock didn't say anything. He'd obviously had the same thought.

'What else you find at Homeboy's crib?'

Lock took out his cell, tapped at the screen and handed it to Ty. 'Take a look.'

Ty took the phone and began to work through the pictures that Lock had taken inside the apartment. The wide shots of the hallway and rooms didn't give much away, apart from the fact that the guy was a neat freak and kept his place clean. Ten pictures in, Ty got some close-ups of the bookshelves in the living room. He had to squint to make out the titles on the spines.

'Your eyesight going south, Tyrone?' said Lock.

'Don't worry about my eyesight. How about you maybe learn how to zoom the next time, motherfucker?' said Ty.

Lock did a bad job of biting back a grin. Ty kept swiping until he got to the pictures of the bottom shelf. He looked up again from the screen. 'Columbine. Sandy Hook. Virginia Tech. All the chart toppers.'

'Keep going,' said Lock.

Ty did. Not that he understood why Lock had developed such a sudden fascination with bathroom ceilings. He turned the cell around and held it up. 'What am I supposed to be looking at?'

'Absence of the normal. Presence of the abnormal,' said Lock.

It was one of his partner's little mantras. But Ty still didn't know what Lock had seen when he took the picture that he was missing.

'Or, in this case,' said Lock. 'presence of the normal.'

Ty could feel himself getting irritated. 'We going to stand here and talk in riddles all day, or are you going to tell me what I'm missing?'

'What did I say about the story the girl I ran into spun me about how she met Krank?' said Lock.

Ty remembered. 'The flooded shower?'

'Exactly. Except the ceiling in his bathroom wasn't damaged or patched.'

'So maybe they took out the whole ceiling in there. Made over the whole thing.'

'That's what I wondered,' said Lock. 'So I went upstairs to check and guess what? Whoever I ran into doesn't live in that apartment. So I got curious. I asked round some of the other people in that building. No one recognized the name Kimberley. There's no one that lives in that building who matches the girl with the French bulldog. In fact, they don't allow dogs that are any larger than handbag-sized.'

'But she knew enough to make up some bullshit story about living there to throw you off the trail.'

'And,' said Lock, 'she sure knows our boy.'

'Girlfriend?' Ty asked.

'That's what I'm thinking,' said Lock. 'But why say anything to me? Why not just keep walking when I ran into her?'

Ty didn't have to give it much thought. 'Why do people do dumb shit every day? Especially when they have something to hide.'

'A lot of the time I think it's because part of them wants to get caught. So their subconscious gives them permission to screw up.'

Ty smiled. 'Maybe, but you might be going too deep. People do dumb shit because they think they're smarter than they actually are. You ever hear of this thing called the Dunning-Kruger effect?'

Lock shook his head.

'I read this article about it. These two professors at Cornell worked it out. A dumb asshole doesn't know he's a dumb asshole because he's dumb. Instead, they think they're slick. And smart folks listen to dumb people telling them they ain't as smart as they think they are,' Ty said.

'I don't know. She asked me a lot of questions too. Like who I was, and why I was interested in this guy.'

'You didn't tell her anything, though, right?'

'Not much more than I was comfortable sharing.'

'So what's the problem, then? We've established that we're not dealing with some kind of brains trust here.'

Lock stuck out his hand. Ty dropped the bullet into it. Lock put it back in the box with the others and jammed it back into the glove box of his Audi. 'Well, let's hope you're right, because a dumb asshole with a bunch of these, and who-knows-what other hardware, can still cause a world of pain.'

43

Tarian reached over and plucked the crystal tumbler from Teddy's hand. She dumped the light yellow remnants of whisky and half-melted ice cubes into the sink. As Teddy started to protest, she interrupted, 'Just slow down. Please. For me? Drink all you like tomorrow but tonight I need you.'

Teddy's face softened. He leaned over to kiss the top of her head. Usually she would have pulled away. This time she closed her eyes and imagined someone else was drawing her in close to them.

Someone rapped their knuckles on the frame of the kitchen door. She pulled away, hoping it wasn't Marcus arriving early. She knew that her son hated seeing any intimacy between her and Teddy. He always had.

She turned to see Dr Stentz standing in the doorway, Teddy having buzzed him in and left the front door open for him. Stentz was dressed in a sport coat and slacks. He had curly dark hair flecked with grey and always seemed to be happy about something. Teddy had told her Stentz always smiled because he got to charge three hundred dollars an hour to listen to people spout bullshit – who wouldn't be happy with that kind of money for doing so little?

'Dr Stentz,' said Tarian. 'We didn't see you there. Can I get you something? A glass of wine? Some juice? Water?'

'Water would be fine. And Marcus?'

Like a lot of shrinks Tarian had met, Stentz had a habit of speaking in shorthand, as if the fewer words he spoke, the more profound he'd seem. Tarian checked the clock above the range. 'He should be here in about a half-hour. Peter's in the dining room. I thought we could all discuss how we wanted to handle this before Marcus got here. I'm sure you have some ideas.'

'I'll go speak to Peter,' said Stentz.

Tarian opened one of the kitchen cabinets, and took out a glass. Her cell phone buzzed its way across the marble counter. She walked over and picked it up. The display read: 'Ryan Lock.' Even with everything that was going on, she couldn't escape the slight flutter in her stomach at seeing the name. Maybe, she thought, she'd find some way of seeing him again once this was all over. Although Peter and Teddy had been right about not involving Lock, part of her wanted him here. Not for the sake of Marcus, but for her own selfish reasons.

She hit the answer button, and tried to sound calm. 'Mr Lock, what can I do for you?'

She gestured at Teddy to pick up the glass. 'Can you get Dr Stentz that water, Teddy?'

She moved toward the window near the sink that looked out onto the backyard cabana area and beyond to the swimming-pool. At the other end of the line, Lock said, 'You have a doctor there? Is everyone okay?'

'Oh, that, he's a family friend who's come over for dinner. We're all fine here. Thank you.'

'Glad to hear it,' said Lock. 'And how about Marcus? Have you heard from him lately?'

Now she wished she hadn't sent Teddy off. She wasn't sure how to answer. She wasn't a good liar, never had been.

'Yes,' she said. 'In fact we should be seeing him soon. To talk things over. There are some financial matters we have to discuss.'

Lock didn't say anything. She thought the call had dropped. She'd heard traffic in the background.

'Mr Lock?' she said.

'I'm here. Listen, Mrs Griffiths, when you see Marcus, can you try and find out where his friend Krank is living at the moment? Get an address for me, if you can, and as soon as you have it, call me.'

The hairs on the back of her neck were standing up. There was something about the way Lock had spoken that scared her. She thought back to the bloodied T-shirt that Marcus had hidden. 'Why? Is there anything I should know? Is his friend in some kind of trouble?'

'I don't know, Mrs Griffiths. But listen, what I said earlier about not being able to help you, forget that. If you or your husband need either myself or Ty to help you with anything, or if Marcus shows up with his friends, just call us. No fee required.'

The butterflies had turned to lead weights in her stomach. Now she knew that something was wrong. But how could she ask Lock what it was without giving away her own fears and having him ask her questions she couldn't answer until she'd spoken to Marcus? Perhaps it wasn't too late to ask him if he could come over. She could run it by Teddy. If she could persuade him, Peter wouldn't stand in the way.

'Thanks, Ryan. I appreciate. Listen, we have some people here right now. Could I call you back in a little while?'

'Sure. And remember that offer. If you need us, you only have to ask. Don't forget to see if Marcus knows where we can find his friend.'

'I will. And, Ryan?' Tarian said. She waited for him to say something. He didn't. Flustered by the silence, she kept going: 'I really appreciate this. I only wish we'd met under different circumstances.'

'Me too,' he said.

44

Lock pulled into the rear parking lot of the strip mall on Lincoln Boulevard in Marina Del Rey. It was after five in the afternoon and the business they were visiting was officially closed. The owner had told them he'd wait for them until half past the hour.

Lock reversed the Audi into a space directly beyond the next-door yoga studio, and switched off the engine. For the past twenty minutes, Ty had kept sneaking glances at him from behind his Oakley sunglasses, a perpetual smirk etched on his lips.

'You have something you want to say, Tyrone?'

Raising a finger, Ty pulled the Oakleys down his nose and peered over the top. 'Why don't you just admit that this isn't just business anymore? You got the hots for her.'

'She's married,' said Lock, hoping to cut the conversation short.

'If I was a gambling man I'd say not for too much longer,' said Ty.

'Well, then, if things change maybe I'll do something about it.'

'So you do like her?' said Ty, opening his door.

Lock followed suit, the two men moving to the back of the premises. 'Okay, yeah, I do. I find her attractive. Happy now?'

Ty grinned as he knocked at the door. 'I'm happy if you're happy, brother.'

A man's voice called out, 'Who is it?'

'Li, it's Mr Johnson and Mr Lock,' Ty answered.

'Where'd you find this guy?' Lock asked Ty.

'Comes highly recommended,' said Ty. 'When you absolutely, positively, have to get past computer security then apparently this is the dude. He's kind of like a grey hat.'

'Grey hat?'

'Yeah,' said Ty. 'You got your white-hat hackers who stay within the law. Your black hats who break the law. And then there are guys like Li who skirt the line.'

Ty knocked again. 'Li? It's Ty Johnson. You in there?'

They heard someone walking toward the door. 'Okay, hang on, guys. I'll have to open up.' There was the sound of locks beings thrown and a bolt being drawn back. The door opened to reveal a tall, weedy Asian kid in his early twenties. He was wearing jeans, sneakers and a white T-shirt with a couple of dubious stains on the front.

Ty had already filled in some of the details that would have explained the kid's paranoia. His name was Li Zhang. His parents were Chinese dissidents who had both fled China following the government crackdown that took place after the Tiananmen Square protests had been brutally crushed. Li's father had been a leading research scientist working on the nuclear program. His mom had been the daughter of a high-ranking Communist Party official, who had used his connections to get them both out of the country. After they had left, he had been arrested and executed for his trouble. They had lived under pretty much constant threat of reprisals, even in the relative safety of Southern California. It had left their only son, Li, with a healthy fear of authority and a rebellious streak. That, combined with a love of hacking computer systems, had made him some enemies of his own. However, Ty had said, if anyone could get access to the contents of Marcus's hard drive it was Li.

The two men followed Li into a storeroom where work benches were covered with various pieces of computer hardware. A twenty-four-inch screen glowed green in one corner. Next to it was a keyboard and a mouse. Li clicked on the mouse and hopped up onto a stool as Lock and Ty stood either side of him.

The screensaver cleared to show a desktop arrangement. 'This is the hard drive right here,' said Li. 'It had some fairly serious encryption but it's all yours now. I made an unencrypted clone drive that you can take away but there's some stuff you might want to see now.' Li glanced back at them. 'It kind of creeped me out. I was hoping it's, like, from a movie or something, but I watched it again and I'm not so sure.' He twisted round to Ty. 'That's when I called you.'

Lock traded a look with his partner. 'Li, can you show us what you're talking about?'

'Sure,' said Li. He moused across the screen and opened a folder, then clicked on a sub-folder and did the same. 'He buried it pretty deep,' he said, clicking a few more times until he hovered over a file name that was mostly numbers and ended with '.mov'.

He double-clicked the file and a media player opened. 'I'll turn the volume up a little, but I don't want it too loud in case anyone hears.' He nodded toward the opposite wall that divided his unit in the strip mall from the one next door. 'Those yoga ladies, I had a client use one of their parking spots last month and they smashed his windshield.'

Li clicked the mouse and the video footage filled the computer's screen. The first thing they saw was a young woman standing alone on a deserted street. The footage had a green tinge to it, indicating that it had been shot at night. The video camera, almost certainly a tiny GoPro or something similar, was mounted, facing out on the dashboard of a car. Lock could hear the whisper of the engine and someone shift in their seat.

She was young and blonde, dressed in a short skirt and a crop top. She tottered on high heels to the edge of the sidewalk and back again. Every few seconds she would check her cell phone. From the deliberate way she took every step, Lock guessed that she was either high or drunk.

Arms folded, Ty glanced across at him. 'Hooker?'

That had been Lock's first thought but it was an assumption, and it was way too early to assume anything. 'Or she's waiting for a ride.'

The person inside the car spoke. It was a male voice. 'You see her?'

There was no reply, only a pause before the same person said, 'That's the one.'

It suggested that the young woman had been selected somehow. The nature of the selection wasn't yet clear. Did the person in the car know her? Lock wondered. For that matter, who was the person on the cell phone? Li had recovered the footage from Marcus's computer but it didn't sound like Marcus. The voice was too deep for a start.

On screen the girl kept up her pacing and phone-checking. Seconds turned over. Lock could feel himself tightening with his own nervous energy. From what Li had already said, this didn't end well for the girl. She was prey. The person in the car, and the other end of the line. They were the hunters.

The male inside the car spoke again. 'Okay. Over to you. But don't be too obvious. Give it, like, a minute. Forty-five seconds minimum.'

The scene didn't change. The seconds rolled by. The minute seemed eternal before headlights flared at the end of the street.

The car that turned into the street rolled toward the camera. It stopped next to the girl. There was an exchange between the driver and the young woman who was waiting. She opened the rear passenger door and got in. The car pulled away from the curb. Lock was about to check his notes to see what Marcus drove. He didn't have to. As the car rolled past the camera, he could see Marcus Griffiths at the wheel.

'We're going to need some copies of this,' Lock said to Li.

'Sure. I can do that,' said Li. He was nervous. He kept shifting his weight from one foot to the other and back again.

'Li?' said Lock.

The young hacker looked at him.

'Relax, okay? We're white hats,' said Lock.

Li didn't look all that convinced. Lock didn't blame him. If your parents had fled a country where the people you had most to worry about were the authorities, it was hardly surprising that you ended up being a little confused about who the good guys were. Lock was confused sometimes.

The car with the camera turned round and took off. At the end of the street it hung a left. 'You see any street signs?' Lock said to Ty.

Ty shook his head.

'I saw one for Olive,' said Li. 'It's downtown. I can go back and show you. The sign only shows up for like half a second.'

Up ahead, Lock could see the tail lights of Marcus's car as it kept moving. The engine of the camera car slid up a gear as it tried to stay in touch. The Honda that Marcus was driving began to drift out of its lane. Marcus over-corrected and the rear of the Honda began to fishtail before he got it back under control.

Seconds later, the brake lights flashed red. The car skidded to a halt. The rear passenger door popped open and the girl bailed out, landing hard on the sidewalk. She got to her feet. Lock noticed that she was barefoot, having presumably shaken off her high heels in the back of the car. She took off running as the camera car pulled up directly behind the Honda.

There was the sound of someone swearing under their breath as they exited the camera car. He was an Asian male of average height and build. Lock guessed this was Krank. He jogged toward the Honda as Marcus got out. Words were exchanged. Marcus was animated. He was rubbing at his eyes and pointing in the direction that the girl had taken off in.

A few moments later a white van pulled up. There was a quick consult and everyone got back into their vehicles and took off.

The next few minutes were of Krank's car prowling the area. On the audio Lock could hear Krank, assuming that was who it was, cursing Marcus under his breath. It was becoming clear that this abduction had been a task handed down, though Lock wasn't sure of the motivation behind it.

The camera rounded a corner. The girl was walking away from a nightclub entrance. She was barefoot and limping slightly.

Inside the camera car, Krank made a phone call. 'She's heading your way. Soon as she turns the corner, do it. Fast and rough as it takes. RV back at the usual place.'

Lock clasped his hands together in a quiet thank-you. Krank had fucked up. He was about to lead them straight back to wherever his RV point was.

Just then there was a muffled sound next to the camera and the image cut out. A few seconds later it was back. This time, though, it was a close-up of the girl from earlier. She was screaming in terror as a shadow fell over her.

Lock turned to Li. 'Where's the rest of the footage? Where's the drive back?'

Li shrugged. 'That was everything. He must have switched off the dash cam. Anyway, that's enough for the police to arrest them. It's all right there.' He jabbed a finger at the screen.

Ty reached in and clicked the mouse to pause the video. 'Yeah,' he said. 'That's enough. But we have to find them first.'

Lock moved for the door. 'Well, we may not know where Krank is, but I know where Marcus should be right about now.'

'What about the rest of this video?' asked Ty.

Lock pushed through the door and out into the corridor, heading back to the car. He called over his shoulder, 'We already know how it ends.'

45

The fingers of his left hand drumming out a frantic beat on his knee, Marcus Griffiths stared at the house from the back seat of Krank's BMW. Up front, Gretchen rode shotgun. Krank killed the music that was playing and turned round. 'You all set?' he said to Marcus.

Marcus didn't look all set. Far from it. He looked like he was about to throw up. He would rather have stayed back at the house, playing a video game and drinking beer. Not even the ten milligrams of Xanax that Krank had palmed him earlier had done much to calm his nerves.

'Hey!' snapped Gretchen. 'We need to know if you're ready to do this.'

Her face had clouded with anger. She scared him way more than anyone in the house did. He doubted that any of this would have happened if not for her. Krank had liked to preach about men's rights but Gretchen had taken it to a whole other level. Marcus had never met anyone who hated a group of people as much as Gretchen seemed to hate women, although she almost always referred to them as 'feminazis' or with the C-word.

'I'm ready,' said Marcus.

'Got the cell?' Krank asked.

Marcus patted his pocket. 'Got it.'

The phone was new. A week before, Krank had taken their cell phones from everyone who spent time at the house. They had each been given a replacement. On Marcus's an app had been installed that meant that if he called any member of his family his old number would show on their caller display. His 'new' number was known only to Krank and the others. When Marcus had asked, Krank had called it a security measure. Cell phones could be used to trace people – not just where they were, but where they had been. Krank was worried about someone using their cell phone to find the house. The app threw out their old number but that number was connected to a physical cell phone that had been placed elsewhere by Gretchen.

'We need to know what they know. And we need information on this security guy they hired,' Krank told him.

Marcus stared along the street. A couple jogged past. The guy was in his late forties, and the woman he was with looked half his age. Marcus felt a pang of jealousy. He choked it down and tried to focus on what Krank had said, but the Xanax had made his thoughts fuzzy. 'I got it.'

Marcus opened the car door and began to get out. Gretchen reached between the gap in the seats and grabbed the back of his shirt collar. He could have shaken her off but that would only have made her worse. 'Any problems, you let us know. Understood?' she said.

They were worse than his own family, thought Marcus. Just as likely to nag him. Just as unable to trust him to do anything. He would be glad when this was all over. Krank had shown him the place they were headed to down in Uruguay. It looked incredible, like a paradise come to life.

'I understand. Call you if there's a problem.'

Gretchen let go. Marcus got out. He closed the car door and walked toward the gates. He pressed the button and waited. A video camera caught him in its gaze. The gates began to open. He walked through.

Krank watched Marcus as the gates closed behind him. He glanced at Gretchen. She had pulled a set of earphones from her pocket and had jammed them into her cell phone.

The cell phones they had given out as replacements had a feature the others hadn't been told about. They had pre-installed surveillance software that relayed every text, every email, every audio, chat or video conversation to a central server. They could also be remotely activated as live surveillance devices so that Krank and Gretchen could listen in on whatever was happening.

Krank pulled up the remote server app on his phone and selected 'MG'. He plugged in his earphones. He could hear the crunch of gravel followed by the sound of Marcus ringing the doorbell.

'You think he'll be able to do this?' he asked Gretchen. 'He seems kind of antsy.'

Gretchen chewed thoughtfully on her bottom lip. Her hand slipped to the handle of the knife that dangled from her belt. 'He'd better.'

46

Marcus stopped in the doorway of the living room. His mother hovered behind him. It seemed that him that she'd been standing behind him his whole life. Perhaps she thought she was 'being there' for him, but the way he saw it, she was smothering him. He had never been allowed to become his own person, to have his own thoughts or come to his own conclusions. At least, not until he had gone online and met Krank and the others.

The three men – his father, his stepfather and his therapist – sat uncomfortably in a triangular arrangement. Apart from Stentz, who was no doubt being paid for his attendance, Marcus doubted any of them actually wanted to be there. They would have been browbeaten into it by his mother, nagged and worn down by her *faux*-concern until they finally agreed.

Marcus glanced toward Stentz, who gave him that creepy fake smile of his. 'Marcus, good to see you. Please, have a seat.'

Whatever nerves Marcus had experienced on the ride there had gone. He almost regretted accepting Krank's offer of the Xanax to settle his nerves. He walked over to the fireplace. 'Thanks, but I'll stand.'

'You may want to take that seat. We'll be here for a while,' said Teddy, trying to make it sound like some kind of a threat.

For all his Texas-tough-guy act, thought Marcus, he was just like the others. Blue pill through and through. Too scared to stand up to Marcus's mom. Rather than live life on his own terms, like Marcus had chosen to do, he drank too much and screwed around on the side.

'Let him stand if he wants,' said Peter.

Marcus saw the dirty look that Teddy threw him. Out of all four of them, the only person that Marcus had any time for was his father. He was blue pill too, but he seemed at peace with it.

'Can I get a drink?' Marcus asked.

'I'll get you some water,' his mom said.

'A real drink,' said Marcus. 'Teddy, you look like you could use one. What's it been? At least an hour since your last Scotch?'

Teddy got to his feet. He took a couple of steps toward Marcus. Marcus stared at him. He might be scared of

Gretchen and Krank, but not Teddy. Not after everything he'd seen. If only Teddy knew . . .

'Teddy,' said his mom. 'Sit down, please.'

Teddy did as he was told. Of course he did, thought Marcus. Totally conditioned to do what he was told and completely whipped.

Tarian walked across and perched next to Teddy. 'Marcus, we're all here because we're worried about you.'

'So you didn't get me here for dinner and to talk about my inheritance?' Marcus said. Even though he'd known it was coming, he could feel rage building in him at the deception. He choked it down. He had to remember that he was there for a reason too. He needed to find out what they knew, but to do that he'd have to be patient.

Stentz made a big show of placing his hands in his lap, palms up. 'So how have you been, Marcus?'

Marcus glared at him. Stentz's fake concern made him want to retch. Krank said that therapists and shrinks were a symptom of the problem, not the solution. Men were designed to conquer and dominate the world, not to sit on a couch and cry about how unfair life was. Life *was* unfair. The world owed you nothing. Being told that had been a liberation for Marcus, one among many.

'I've been enjoying life. How about you?'

The phrase 'enjoying life' seemed to cause a ripple in the room. Teddy muttered something Marcus didn't catch and Stentz pursed his lips so hard that they all but disappeared. From his sessions with Stentz, Marcus knew that a lip purse or a closing of the eyes was the therapist's equivalent of one of Teddy's drunken tirades.

It was his father's turn next. 'That's what we'd like to talk to you about, Marcus. 'How you've been enjoying your life.' He paused. 'Listen, we realize that you perhaps haven't had the easiest time of it, and that you're a young man, and that young men like to cut loose once in a while.'

Marcus folded his arms. 'Why don't you just ask me what you want to ask me? And while I'm here, perhaps you can explain why you have some guy sticking his nose into my life.'

No one spoke. It took a few moments of silence before Marcus realized that all three men were waiting for Tarian to respond. To him it was yet more evidence of what they'd all become and what Marcus had vowed to avoid. Krank was right: the sickness in society, the collapse of what passed for civilization, came down to men surrendering power and decision-making to a gender that was driven by hormones and the reproductive cycle.

Tarian cleared her throat. 'Why don't we all move through into the dining room, and we can start over? I'll get you that glass of water, Marcus.'

One by one, Stentz, Teddy and Marcus's dad got to their feet. They began to walk out into the hallway and beyond that into the dining room. Marcus stood and watched them. Tarian said, 'Marcus?'

Marcus stared at his mom. He loved her. He couldn't deny that. But Krank was right. She and others like her, they were the problem.

47

An elderly man in running shorts and a T-shirt shuffled toward the car at a snail's pace. Krank grabbed a bottle of water from the center console and took a swig. Gretchen had one of the earbuds pressed into her right ear as she listened intently to the audio from inside.

'What are they saying?' Krank asked.

'Just lots of touchy-feely bullshit about how much they all love him. It's like some half-assed intervention,' said Gretchen.

'What about MG?'

'He's being too confrontational. He needs to ease it back a little or he'll never get anything out of them.'

Krank sighed. It was a bad time for Marcus to finally find his balls and start standing up to his family. 'Maybe I should text him,' he said.

'Maybe we should ditch him entirely. He's always been a drag,' offered Gretchen.

This had been a recurring theme with Gretchen. Krank didn't blame her. As much time as Krank had spent with Marcus, he was fundamentally a beta male. He would never be alpha. Not in a million years. He was a follower, not a leader. But what Gretchen sometimes struggled with was that they needed followers. A cell full of leaders could never work. It would be pulled apart.

'No argument from me,' said Krank. 'But it's too late to lose him now. He knows everything.'

Gretchen's eyes narrowed as the early-evening jogger shuffled past. 'It's never too late.'

48

A shoal of red tail lights curved north along the 10 freeway from the Lincoln on-ramp in Santa Monica. Lock nudged the front of the Audi into the left-hand lane to escape the turn lane that would take them down onto the freeway. An SUV tried to cut off his escape. Ty lowered his window and leaned out, scowling at the SUV driver, who hit their brake, allowing the Audi the lane change.

Traffic ahead of them on Lincoln Boulevard wasn't much better. Nose to tail as far as Lock could see. The drive from the Marina to where they were now in Santa Monica had already taken twice the amount of time it should have. Traveling on the streets to the Griffiths home on Rockingham Avenue in Brentwood would typically be a ten-to-fifteen-minute journey. This was looking more like an hour regardless of the route.

'Try them again,' Lock told Ty.

Ty jabbed a finger at the screen of his cell and put it on speaker. It rang out and went to voicemail. They had already left several messages to contact them immediately. All they could do was keep trying and hope that the traffic cleared.

'LAPD?' Ty asked. 'They could get there faster than we could.'

Lock shook his head. 'I want to let the family have a heads-up. Better if Marcus walks in with an attorney to give himself up.'

'So what do you think that shit we watched was about?' Ty asked.

Lock had been asking himself the exact same question. It looked like a gang initiation. Los Angeles street gangs often required a prospective member to commit a homicide before they were granted entry. Sometimes the target was someone they wanted rid of anyway. Many times it was almost entirely random, although race could play a part.

This type of initiation served a number of purposes. It proved that the individual was capable of committing violent crime. It also ensured that the gang had something on that person.

'I don't know,' said Lock. 'They don't exactly look like gang-bangers.'

'Rich white kids can do that shit too,' Ty reminded him.

'Yeah, but why?' said Lock. 'What's in it for them? They don't need money. From what Teddy said, that Krank kid and his crew could get girls. It doesn't make sense.'

Ty shrugged as they edged forward a few feet, the traffic showing no sign of clearing. 'Does it have to make sense? Maybe they're just, y' know, getting off on it. I'll tell you one thing for nothing, brother. Watching that video . . . that ain't the first time.'

Lock had had the same thought. No one all of a sudden decides out of nowhere to abduct a young woman. Crimes like that had a pattern to them. It reminded Lock of a serial rapist he and Ty had gone after in Mexico. But he had been a loner. Or, at least, that was how he'd started. This felt very different. This seemed like a bunch of people feeding off each other, seeing how far one could push the others to go. But to what end?

Maybe Ty was right. Perhaps Lock was seeking a motive where there was none. Or none of the usual ones – money, sexual gratification.

And what about all those books about mass shootings? Lock wondered. This type of crime – a lone abduction, even one committed by a group – seemed a long way from something like that. But was it?

One of the few people who might be able to answer that question, and a whole lot more besides, was Marcus Griffiths. 'Try their house again,' Lock said, as all around them they were hemmed in by people rushing back home to normal lives.

49

They all sat at the long polished mahogany dining table. The Xanax must have made Marcus thirsty because he drained the glass of water his mother had brought him almost immediately. At first no one appeared eager to say anything. It was Teddy who broke the silence.

'Marcus, you and I haven't always gotten along. I take my share of responsibility for that.'

As he spoke, Teddy kept sneaking glances at Marcus's mom. Marcus guessed that this speech was really for her, a way of Teddy showing that he was 'in touch with his feelings' and all that other bullshit. Stentz had that far-away shit-eating grin on his face.

Marcus was growing bored. He looked around the table at the four adults. He wondered how they got through the day while resisting the urge to put a gun in their mouth. They were so full of lies and hypocrisy. If his father had really cared about Marcus, then perhaps he'd have tried to serve as some kind of role model. Instead he seemed to be a walking, talking doormat. Teddy covered his weakness with whisky and cheap bravado. As for Stentz, he was what Krank liked to call 'a shiver in search of a spine to run up'.

Twenty-five minutes had passed and Marcus was still no clearer about what any of them actually wanted from him. It was time for him to do them all a favor and help them get to the point. He spread his hands across the table. 'Would one of you tell me why you wanted me here? Because I'm no clearer than I was when I arrived. And while we're at it, why do you have some kind of private detective checking up on my friends?'

That final question got a reaction. There were lots of hurried looks between them. His dad cleared his throat. 'It's your friends we're concerned about. At least, that's part of it.'

Marcus ran a finger round the rim of the water glass. 'You didn't like that I had no friends and now when I do . . . ?'

'It's the type of friends you have,' said Teddy.

Marcus could feel rage building. He had to fight the urge to get up, walk over to Teddy and stick the glass in his bloated, whisky-flushed face. Teddy wasn't fit to lick Krank's boots.

'What type are they, Teddy?' Marcus said. When he had married his mom, Teddy had tried to get Marcus to call him 'Dad'. He hated when Marcus called him Teddy.

'If we can all stay calm,' said Stentz.

Marcus rounded on him. 'I was asking him, not you.'

'Marcus!' said his mom. 'Don't speak to Dr Stentz like that.'

'Doctor?' said Marcus. 'He's a shrink. He thinks that all the bad things in the world are down to lack of breastfeeding.' He turned his attention back to Teddy. 'Come on, Teddy. What don't you like about my friends?'

'You want me to be honest, Marcus? Is that it? Can we talk man to man now?'

'Sure,' said Marcus. 'A bit of truth would make a nice change in this family. You want to go chug down some Scotch first?'

Teddy's jaw tightened. The barb had hit home. 'You want the truth, son?'

'That's what I just said, wasn't it?'

'Teddy!' said Tarian. 'This is not helpful.'

Teddy waved away her objection. 'No, Tarian, the kid has a point. There's been too much pussy-footing around him. Maybe if you'd stopped treating him like such a special snowflake he wouldn't be like this.'

Marcus couldn't help but smile. This was way better than the passive-aggressive jibes and usual sarcasm he had to tolerate from his family. 'So what am I like? I'd love to know.'

'Perhaps that's a discussion for another time,' said Stentz.

Marcus waved him away. 'I'd say this is exactly the time. What do you think, Teddy?'

Teddy,' Tarian warned. 'Please.'

Marcus didn't take his eyes from his stepfather. 'Mom, maybe if you'd let one of the men in your life actually have an opinion once in a while rather than cutting off their balls and keeping them in a box, we wouldn't be here right now. Come on, Teddy, get it off your chest.'

Teddy's hands were trembling. Either he needed that Scotch, thought Marcus, or he was about to lose it. Perhaps both.

'Okay, Marcus, you want to know what I think? I'll tell you. I think that you, just like all the other kids your age, have spent your whole life being told how special and unique you are and now you're actually convinced that you are. Well, let me tell you, you're not. You're just a self-absorbed, selfish little asshole.'

Marcus leaned back in his chair. For the first time since he had walked through the door he was actually enjoying whatever the hell this was. An intervention? Family therapy? A reunion? 'Well, you'd know all about being self-absorbed, Teddy,' he said, lacing his fingers behind his head.

'Oh, I'm not finished yet. That's only part of your problem,' Teddy continued. 'It doesn't make you unique, it makes you typical. Being a spoilt brat would make you pretty much average, these days. But that's not enough for you. It's not enough that you've never had to work a day in your life. Or that you have no idea that all the crap you have doesn't just magically appear. No, even then, you want more.'

'That's pretty rich coming from a guy who inherited his fortune,' said Marcus. He noticed the trace of a smirk creeping across his father's face. At least his real dad had actually made his own fortune – for all the good it had done him.

'Hey, I had to go work for my family's company from the time I was eighteen. But you think what you like about me. That's fine.' Teddy's face was red. Marcus had hit a nerve.

'So, what else you got?' Marcus asked. 'I'm spoilt. Is that it?'

'Like I said,' Teddy went on, 'that would just make you average for your generation. But that's not why we're here.'

'Finally,' said Marcus. He glanced around the table. 'So you're not here because you're worried about me?'

Both Stentz and his dad began to interrupt but Teddy cut them off. 'No, Marcus,' he said. 'We're not worried about you. We're worried about what you've been doing, you sick little fuck.' Teddy put his hands, palms down, on the table, and levered himself to his feet. 'That girl you were stalking at USC not enough for you, huh? Leaving creepy messages for her and following her around campus not enough to get you off?'

Marcus could feel his enjoyment drain away. What was Teddy talking about? What did they know? What had Teddy meant when he said that stalking hadn't been enough for him?

He had to focus, he told himself. What was he here for? Krank needed that information about the private security guy. 'That why you hired that private security asshole Lock and his buddy? To check up on me? So what's he been telling you?'

Teddy just glared at him. Marcus looked at his mom. 'Someone want to tell me? Or am I just supposed to sit here and be accused of all kinds of stuff without any evidence?'

Mention of the word 'evidence' seemed to clear the air from the room. Both his dad and Stentz stared at the table top. His mom brushed a tear away with the back of her hand.

'Oh, we have evidence, Marcus. But we didn't need anyone snooping around to find out. You left it all right here,' said Teddy. 'Go get it, Tarian. Show him what you found in his closet.'

The room seemed to spin around Marcus. He knew what Teddy was talking about as soon as he'd said it. The T-shirt. He'd been in his room and his mom had knocked. He'd thrown it in the back of the closet so she didn't see it. She'd walked in, they'd argued, and he'd forgotten all about. He hadn't gone back for it. The blood belonged to the girl. He'd had to move her body outside so that they could bury it. There had been blood. Not a huge amount, but enough to soak into his T-shirt. Krank had told him to burn it, but he'd held on to it. It was a trophy. A reminder of what he could do. Of the red-pill man he had become. Old Marcus would never have been able to touch a dead body, never mind bury one.

'Not too cocky now, are you?' Teddy said.

His heart beating out of his chest, Marcus tried to find some words. He had none. Teddy was right. What confidence he'd had was gone. He had screwed up. Even if the others wouldn't call the cops, Teddy sure as hell would. He'd throw Marcus to the wolves without a moment's hesitation. Krank, Gretchen and Loser would be arrested too. Their lives would be over. They be spared the death penalty because it was California, but they'd get life without parole. And for what? Marcus asked himself. Krank had wanted to make a stand, go out in a blaze of glory that would set down a marker for those who came after. Instead they'd be hung out to dry for some dumb initiation ceremony. He had to think of something, and quickly.

'There was a car wreck,' he said finally. His dad and Stentz looked up from the table.

Teddy's mouth twisted into a sneer. 'Bullshit there was.'

'It's true,' said Marcus, addressing his mom. 'I'd been drinking. That's why I didn't want to tell anyone.'

He could tell from the look on her face that his mom wanted to believe him. Maybe he'd be able to dig himself out of this, after all. 'It's your blood?' she asked.

'Look at him,' sneered Teddy. 'There's not a mark on the kid. Show us this injury then, Marcus.'

'It wasn't my blood,' Marcus said. He could feel his confidence returning. One of Krank's early lessons had involved what he called 'setting the other person's frame'. It was something that came from neuro-linguistic programming but what it boiled down to was having confidence in what you were telling someone. People created their own reality. If your reality was stronger than theirs you could bring them into line.

Krank had demonstrated it over and over again in front of Marcus. He didn't just use it to get girls, it was integral to how he lived his life. His frame was stronger than everyone's – apart, maybe, from Gretchen's. Now all Marcus had to do was create a frame, a story, that was stronger than everyone else's. A big part of that was allowing people to hear what they wanted. Teddy might have wanted to see him shoved into the back of a cop car, but the other three, for their own selfish reasons, didn't. He would use that.

'So whose blood was it?' said Teddy.

'Let him speak,' said his mom. 'Marcus?'

'It was my fault, okay? I'd been drinking and I got into my car. I didn't even see them until it was too late. I rear-ended the other car. I got out. There was a girl in the front. She was bleeding pretty bad and I could smell gas. I was scared in case the whole thing went up so I got her out and moved her to the side of the road. Then I dialed nine-one-one and split. I should have stayed, but I was scared.'

As Marcus spoke, the story took on a reality in his own mind. He could see the sudden flash of red as he looked at the car in front of him. He could feel the shudder of the impact. The gasoline smell, mixed with the metallic tang of blood, was real.

Teddy was looking at the others in disbelief. 'Oh, come on. You don't actually believe this crap, do you?' The others didn't say anything. 'Okay, so where's this damage to your car? Show me that and I might start to buy into this.'

'It would explain the blood,' said Stentz. 'I can understand someone panicking under the circumstances. Not that I endorse your behavior, Marcus.'

Marcus ignored Stentz and focused on Teddy. 'I took it to a shop. They repaired it and I paid the guy another five hundred bucks not to say anything if anyone came round asking about it. But, hey, don't believe me. I already know what you think of me, Teddy.'

The room was turning against Teddy and he knew it as well as Marcus did. 'That's right. I don't believe you, son.'

A cell phone trilled in another room. It had been ringing on and off for the past ten minutes. Everyone had ignored it per Stentz's rules. 'That's mine,' said Tarian. 'I'll just check, okay? It might be the kids wanting to say goodnight.' She stopped in the doorway. 'Teddy, don't say anything, please, for my sake.'

50

'I got her,' said Ty, handing his cell phone to Lock. Ahead of them was the same wall of metal, vehicles bumper to bumper. If anything, the traffic seemed to have gotten worse in the past few minutes. It had taken them five minutes to move a half-block.

Lock took the cell. 'Tarian, it's Ryan.'

'Ryan, sorry I didn't answer before. Marcus is here and it's been a little tense.'

Lock hit the mute button. 'He's there,' he told Ty. He cancelled the mute, and said, 'Is anyone else with him?'

'No, he's alone,' said Tarian. 'Why?'

'Okay, that's good. I need you to listen carefully. But don't react to what I'm about to tell you. Just act like this is a perfectly normal conversation and that everything's fine,' Lock told her.

She hesitated. To his relief she had seemed fine when she'd answered. Now he could almost hear her deflate. It left him feeling bad that he had to be the bearer of bad news. His reaction made him uncomfortable. She was a client. This was business. And yet . . . 'Okay. I can do that,' said Tarian.

A gap opened up in the lane next to them. Lock ducked into it so he was on the outside. A few cars ahead, a Ford Bronco pulled a U-turn in front of some light oncoming traffic. Its move prompted another driver further back to pull the same stunt. Presumably they were heading back to the freeway to see if that had cleared.

Lock took a deep breath. 'Who else is there with you?'

'Teddy, Peter, and Marcus's therapist, Dr Stentz. We thought that if we all sat down with him and told him how worried we were about his recent behavior . . .'

Jesus, thought Lock, only in California. He wasn't going to tell Tarian this now but Marcus was already way beyond being helped by a touchy-feely love-in, though maybe the shrink would make for a decent defense witness when it came to the sentencing.

'What about the kids?' Lock asked.

'Staying with Teddy's cousin, Sylvia,' said Tarian.

'Okay, that's good,' said Lock. 'Ty and I are on our way. Now, I want you to keep Marcus there. Make sure he doesn't leave. Take his car keys from him if you have to.'

There was a long silence at the other end of the line.

'Tarian? You still there?'

'His car isn't here,' said Tarian.

Lock already knew what she was thinking. In LA, and especially in a neighborhood like Brentwood, public transport was for the help. A kid like Marcus had probably never been on a bus in his life.

'Did someone drop him off?' Lock asked.

'Not that I saw,' said Tarian.

'Are you sure?' Lock asked. 'You haven't seen anyone?'

'He probably isn't comfortable driving right now. That'll be it. He must have taken a cab.'

'Why doesn't he want to drive?' Lock asked. 'What do you mean he's not comfortable driving?'

She lowered her voice. 'He just told us he was in an accident a week or so ago. He'd been drinking and he rear-ended this woman. I'd found something in his closet. One of his T-shirts. It had blood all over it. When we confronted him he told us about the accident.'

I bet he did, thought Lock. But now wasn't the time to challenge Marcus's story. He and Ty could do that when they got there – if they ever did.

Tarian went on: 'He'll have to speak to the police, of course, come clean, but with a good attorney . . .'

'Okay, Tarian, just give me a yes or no answer. Did you see a cab drop Marcus off?'

'Well, no, but how else would he . . .' She trailed off. 'These friends of his. What did they do exactly?'

Lock leaned out of the window of the Audi. There had to be a wreck up ahead because the only people moving were those who were turning round and driving back in the other direction. 'That doesn't matter right now. In fact, forget I said it. Like I said, we're on our way. Here's what I want you to do. Take it easy on Marcus. Don't confront him. Don't challenge him. And whatever you do don't open your front door unless you see us outside.'

'Ryan, what is it? What's going on?'

'Just follow my instructions for now. Marcus is going to need an attorney. The best you can afford, which I'd imagine is someone who's pretty good. But that's for tomorrow. Right now just have everyone stay cool and wait until we get there.'

51

Krank's fingers drummed furiously against the steering wheel. Gretchen lowered her window, sparked her Zippo and lit a cigarette. She offered one to Krank, who waved the pack away. 'You know I don't smoke,' he said, irritable.

'Maybe you should start,' said Gretchen. She blew a series of perfect smoke rings out of the open window. 'What are we gonna do?'

Krank didn't know. On one level he was proud of Marcus. Most people would have folded. Instead Marcus had improvised a story on the spot. They'd all bought it, apart from that asshole of a stepfather, but that worried him. Teddy wasn't about to let this go. He'd want to see the car. They couldn't rule out him contacting the cops. And if the cops got hold of Marcus it would all be over before it had even begun.

'I don't know,' said Krank. 'But this isn't good.'

Gretchen took another drag and deliberately blew the smoke into Krank's face. She was trying to provoke him. She was one of the few people who could. 'Isn't good?' she said. 'Duh.'

'So what do you think we should do?' he asked her, waving a hand at the clouds of smoke.

'You already know what we have to do. Marcus knows where the house is. He has to go.'

Krank knew she was right. Marcus was his boy. He'd taken him a long way. He'd personally slipped him that red pill and watched him spread his wings. But he would never be the kind of true alpha male they needed. It was like putting down an old, sick dog rather than having it suffer. It was better for everyone.

He dug out his cell and dropped Marcus a text.

52

Marcus felt the vibration from the cell as the text arrived. He excused himself to go to the bathroom. Teddy glared at him as he got up. His dad, Peter, reached out a hand as he passed. 'Don't worry, Marcus, we'll be here for you, whatever happens.'

The poor sap, thought Marcus. No wonder his mom had taken him for half his fortune. He was completely gullible. As for Stentz, here was a man whose whole career was based on understanding human behavior and yet he'd buy any old bullshit that was thrown at him.

In the hallway, Marcus ran into his mom. She looked flustered. 'You're not leaving, are you?'

'Relax, I'm just using the bathroom.'

He started to walk past her but she called after him. 'Marcus?'

He stopped.

'There's someone else I want you to talk to before you leave,' she said.

'Another shrink?' he asked.

'No. Mr Lock's on his way over.'

Marcus froze. He didn't like Lock. Not one bit. He had a cop vibe about him, only worse.

'Not sure I can stay that long,' he told her. 'I have stuff to do.'

'Such as?' she pressed.

'Just stuff.' He was hoping that she'd drop the questioning but she seemed determined.

'Marcus, did you get a cab here?' she asked.

'No,' he said. 'Someone dropped me off.'

'Your friend Krank?'

'Just a friend,' he said.

She stared at him. The look she had on her face made him feel uncomfortable. It was like she was seeing him for the first time. 'You asked about Mr Lock.'

'Yeah. So?'

'I don't think he'll believe your story about the car. It is a story, correct? Something you made up so that you wouldn't get into trouble.'

First Teddy and now her, he thought. She had never been on his side, and he'd been crazy to think this time would be any different. 'Why should I care what some private security goon you hired because you want to sleep with him thinks? Or have you slept with him already?'

She slapped him hard. He didn't see it coming. It was so fast. One minute they were stood facing each other, the next her hand had whipped out and struck him across the face. She seemed as shocked as he was.

He wished he hadn't missed her when he'd taken the shot back at his apartment. His eyes narrowed. He wished her dead. He could feel his hands ball into fists. And yet somewhere deeper he knew that the slap had come because she was scared. Scared of him and who he'd become.

'Marcus, I'm sorry. I didn't mean to . . .'

Teddy called through to her: 'Honey? Are you okay?'

The doorbell rang. He started at the noise. So did his mother. The doorbell didn't ring out of the blue. The gates had to be opened to allow someone in before they got to the door.

It had to be Lock. He would have all the codes. Marcus could feel his heart sink into his boots.

'I'll get it,' shouted Teddy.

Marcus heard the front door opening. Then he heard Teddy say: 'Who the hell are you?'

There was the sound of three gunshots, one after the other. Pop. Pop. Pop. His mother screamed and ran past him. He grabbed at her arm to stop her, but she was already gone.

53

Marcus took off after his mom. He heard her scream again. She shouted, 'Teddy!' Two more gunshots followed. These ones louder. There was more shouting. It sounded like his father, or maybe Stentz, yelling at someone to get out.

Marcus found himself walking toward the sound of the gunfire. His heart was racing a hundred miles an hour, but his mind felt like it was wrapped in cotton wool. Everything around him suddenly seemed alien. The walls seemed to buckle and the floor to slide from underneath him.

Sounds were muffled and distant, as if he was swimming under water. He found himself in the front hallway. The front door was wide open. Teddy was lying on the floor, blood pooled around his head. His eyes and mouth were open. Blood poured from his nostrils into his mouth and down his chin, pooling on the floor by his neck. He wasn't moving.

Krank and Gretchen were standing over him. They both had black Glock handguns. Marcus recognized them as part of the armory Krank had assembled.

Tarian stood in the hallway. Marcus watched as Gretchen turned toward her and leveled the gun at her chest.

A minute ago he'd been ready to kill her himself because she had slapped him. That anger was gone, replaced by fear and a terrible, all-consuming guilt.

Everything that had gone before seemed unreal to Marcus somehow, like a movie he'd watched but not really been part of. This was different, though. This was completely real.

If he didn't do something he was about to watch his mother being shot right in front of him. He couldn't let it happen. He might have been a shitty son but he wouldn't be responsible for this.

He took three steps forward so that he was standing between his mom and Gretchen. Krank stepped over Teddy's dead body and trained his gun on Stentz and Marcus's father. Peter had his cell phone in his hand. He must have hit the speaker because Marcus could hear a call being connected to a police dispatcher.

'Yes, my name's Peter Blake. I'm at . . .'

Before he could get the address out, Krank fired. The shot hit Peter's right hand, shattering it, and blowing off two of his fingers. The phone fell to the floor with a clatter. The back flew off. The screen shattered. Peter looked down in disbelief at what was left of his hand. By the time he looked back up, Krank had fired again. This time the force of the shot took him off his feet and sent him spinning backwards.

Marcus reached behind to his mother and shoved her back. 'Get out of here. Now.'

Krank fired once more. This shot sent Peter to his knees. His body twisted one way and then the other, like a fish caught on a line. Marcus half turned. His mom was staring in horror at the scene unfolding. Down the corridor was the bathroom. It had a lock on it. The internal doors in the house were fairly heavy. It would at least buy her some time.

Marcus shoved her again. Harder this time. 'The bathroom. Lock the door behind you.'

She still wouldn't move. 'Go!' Marcus yelled at her. It seemed to snap her out of it. Her eyes focused on his face. Something passed between them that was honest in a way that it hadn't been before. She started to run.

As Marcus turned back, Gretchen fired in his direction. At first he thought she was taking aim at the fleeing figure of Tarian as she sprinted toward the sanctuary of the bathroom. Then he realized that she was staring at him.

Behind Gretchen, Krank had walked over toward Marcus's father. He raised his good hand, the one that hadn't been blown away. His breathing was coming in fits and starts as he gasped for air. His fingers opened and closed. 'Please,' he said, before Krank shot him full in the face.

Stentz took this as his cue to run back into the living room. Krank glanced over his shoulder at Gretchen. 'Take care of him,' he said, waving his gun toward Marcus. 'Then we'll split.'

Marcus had seen that look from Krank before. It was as if he went into machine mode. There was no sign of humanity, no flicker of compassion, he was robotic.

Glancing behind, Marcus could see that his mom had almost reached the bathroom. He turned back to face Gretchen. 'You'd better get out of here now. That security guy is on his way,' he said.

She looked over to where Krank had been, nervous. 'Krank, hurry up!'

Marcus's relief was short-lived as Gretchen turned back toward him, raised the Glock and took aim. As she began to squeeze the trigger, he ducked down. The shot flew over his head. The next one wouldn't. He knew that as surely as he knew anything. He had to do something. There was no sound of sirens, and he couldn't assume that the cops, or anyone else, would get there in time to save them. Still in a crouch, he rushed toward Gretchen.

In the distance, he could hear Stentz pleading for his life. Marcus straightened up and kept running toward Gretchen. He could see a flicker of uncertainty cross her face as she took fresh aim. He kept moving, presenting a bigger target with every step but hoping that his momentum would carry him forward even if he was hit.

He saw Gretchen close one eye, and take a final breath as she centered the metal sights at his chest and pulled the trigger. Marcus dove for the floor.

54

As the vehicle in front inched forward, Lock finally lost patience. He spun the wheel hard and, spotting a gap, moved the Audi out into oncoming traffic. Next to him Ty was incredulous: 'Dude, we're almost there and now you want to head back to the freeway?'

'Not exactly,' said Lock. Rather than turn he kept moving forward at a steady clip. The needle of the speedometer edged toward thirty as cars blared their horns and swerved out of his way.

Ty's hand pushed out to the dashboard as he braced himself for a possible collision. His other hand lowered his sunglasses so he could peer at Lock over the top of the frames. 'You are aware that you're on the wrong side of the road?'

'I'm aware,' said Lock, as he ducked into the middle lane to avoid a head-on collision with a station wagon. He veered back into the opposite outside lane as traffic ahead of him cleared. He could see people on their cell phones as he passed. A trucker flipped him off as he wrestled his rig out of the way, air horn wailing as it passed. Other drivers screamed at him, leaning out of their windows as they sped past.

'What are you gonna say if we get pulled over?' Ty asked, in a tone that leaned more toward curiosity than genuine anxiety.

Lock's eyes flicked to the rearview mirror 'They're probably stuck back there in the same traffic we were.'

Ty lifted a hand and pointed at a black and white police car heading straight for them, lights blazing and siren wailing. 'That one ain't,' he said.

Lock held his nerve as Ty went back to his brace position. He poked down harder on the gas, bringing the car's speed up to forty. The patrol car kept coming. Lock accelerated, flashing his lights as he bore down on the patrol car, which was still moving.

At the last second, it swerved out of his way. The Audi scraped through. Ty, eyes closed, was muttering to himself.

'They moved,' said Lock, slowing down and drifting across two lanes before taking the corner onto North Rockingham Avenue. Behind him, the LAPD vehicle was still struggling to turn around. They'd likely catch up with him at the Griffiths residence, which was fine with Lock. It would save a phone call.

55

Under ten minutes later, Lock pulled up at the gates of the Griffiths home. There was no sound from inside but that was hardly surprising. The house itself was set back several hundred yards from the street. The neighbors on either side were even more distant. That was why people paid a premium to live in this part of town. In Los Angeles, a city that faced outwards like no other, privacy was a valued commodity.

Lock lowered his window, then leaned out and hit the call button on the keypad. It would buzz inside the house. While he waited for an answer, he checked on Ty. 'You okay?'

'Need some fresh underwear but, yeah, apart from that, I'm good,' said Ty. 'Next time, let me drive.'

There were few things that Lock enjoyed more than freaking out his partner. 'That patrol was always going to move. Now, if I'd gone at the same time they did? That would have been messy.'

No one had answered. Lock buzzed again. He grabbed his cell and called the number he had for the house. It rang out before diverting to voice mail. Screw it, he thought. Tarian knew he and Ty were dropping by. This was no time for the proper observance of social niceties. He leaned out and keyed in the four-digit number that opened the gates.

They swung open. He drove through.

Lock's Audi moved up the long, curved driveway past a stand of neatly trimmed trees that further shielded the house from view. He hit the brakes as he saw the open front door, and the body – at least one that he could see – lying inside. Ty was already tapping 911 into his cell. Lock positioned the Audi so that it was side on to the house.

He got out of the car, his SIG Sauer 226, with a fully loaded magazine in the clip, drawn, as Ty calmly began giving details to the person at the other end of the line. They needed the LAPD, but they didn't want a unit pulling up on the scene without knowing that they were the good guys, and the good guys were armed.

As he exited his vehicle, Lock gave Ty his immediate plan. Go in through the front door and sweep downstairs first. If that was clear he'd move upstairs.

He walked slowly toward the front door. There were four vehicles parked out front. He recognized one as belonging to Tarian and the other to Teddy. Two of the vehicles, one a Lexus, the other a Prius, he didn't recognize. He didn't see the Honda that belonged to Marcus.

Even at a distance of twenty yards, and with a lot of blood pooled around his head, Lock recognized Teddy Griffiths. Skirting left to take himself out of a direct line of fire from the front door, he moved to the living-room window. He peeked inside waiting for a sign of movement. He edged back to the front door, staying close to the house, his back to the wall.

He got to the hinge side of the door, and took another look inside. There was another body in the entrance foyer. It looked like Peter Blake's but Lock couldn't be sure because the man was lying face down. Both he and Teddy showed no signs of life. Teddy was certainly dead. Lock had seen more than enough dead bodies to make that assessment. Glancing behind him, he saw Ty exit the car and low-run toward the back of the house, gun drawn. He had already made a point of noting what Ty was wearing, not that he needed much additional help in being able to instantly ID the giant African American.

Stepping carefully over Teddy's body and the blood pooled around it, Lock moved inside the house. Backing up so that the wall was behind him and he had a clear one-eighty view of the entrance hall, he stopped to listen. He was met by relative silence. No house is ever completely silent. A refrigerator hums. A breeze moves through an open window. Lock tried to tune into the background noise of the house as best he could.

He allowed a few more seconds to pass and moved across to the other body. He hunkered down next to it. As he'd thought it was Peter Blake's. He'd been shot in the head and chest. The exit wounds were substantial. Whoever had shot both him and Teddy hadn't been messing. They were either packing a powerful handgun or a rifle, some serious ammunition, and very likely both. Both bodies were an unholy mess. For a second, his mind flashed back to Krank's apartment and the book collection on mass shootings.

From outside came the wail of sirens drawing closer. Lock kept moving. Time allowing, he wanted to finish his search and be outside to meet the cops when they rolled up. That way there would be less chance of a nervy cop shooting either him or Ty. This division of the LAPD – officially known as West LA, and unofficially referred to as West Latte – was not noted for these types of incidents, which raised the response level to something approaching nuclear. A pile of freshly killed rich white people put cops significantly more on edge than a pile of their poorer brown counterparts from the eastern part of the city.

Next, Lock moved to the other side of the entrance hall that led toward the kitchen. Next to the curved double staircase there was yet another body.

He hunkered down next to Marcus Griffiths. Or, at least, that was his best guess of who it was. The face had been all but obliterated by a shot fired from close range but Lock was fairly sure he recognized the curly mop of brown hair. There was no sign of a weapon nearby so Lock guessed Marcus could be ruled out as a shooter. Not that it would be much consolation.

That left only one family member unaccounted for. Tarian had told him that the kids were with Teddy's cousin. Lock called out: 'Tarian? It's Ryan Lock!' Are you there?'

No one answered. The silence told its own story. Lock started toward the kitchen, bracing himself for yet more horror.

A sound from behind him. A door being opened. He spun round, gun up, his finger on the trigger, testing the pressure and leveling his breathing so he could get off a clean shot. The bathroom door opened a crack. Lock took aim.

56

Lock took his finger from the trigger and lowered his SIG as Tarian stepped out from behind the door. Her eyes were black and blotchy from where her mascara had run. At first she didn't seem to register Lock's presence. She looked straight past him and began to scream. She fell to her knees and began to crawl toward the dead body behind him. 'No! No! Marcus!'

Lock went to her. He reached down with his free hand and pulled her back to her feet as he scanned the area around them for a shooter. 'Tarian, listen to me. I need to get you out of here.'

'My son!' She was doing her best to break free.

Ty emerged from the kitchen, stepping into the hallway, his gun drawn. 'What we got?' he asked Lock.

'Three dead that I've found. There could be more. I'm going to get her outside. What about the kitchen and the laundry room?'

'Both clear,' said Ty.

There was a door at the back. He could take Tarian out that way without her seeing the rest of the slaughter. He tried to pull her gently toward the kitchen door as Ty fell in behind to provide cover. He could hear an LAPD patrol car rolling its way up to the front of the house. Lock grasped Tarian's arm at the elbow as he escorted her out of the hallway. She was in shock. He looked back to see a hole the size of a fist that had been blown in the bathroom door.

Tarian Griffiths had survived. They had a living, breathing witness. But the killer, or killers, was nowhere to be seen. If this was Krank's bid for the history books, Lock figured that, no matter how devastating it would be for Tarian, it would still only figure as a footnote.

57

Lock took a sip of coffee and stared across the table at the two LAPD homicide detectives. His rush-hour traffic avoidance stunt had not exactly enamored him to the city's finest. However, as was the way with the US justice system, he'd called an attorney, who had swiftly traded the offer of the information both Lock and Ty had about the killers in return for an agreement that any traffic infraction would be ignored. The way Lock saw it, it was a pretty sweet deal. He hadn't exactly delivered Charles Kim and the other perps to them on a silver platter but as near as made no difference.

The interview itself had been good-natured. Again, in Lock's experience, cops were always affable when you were making their life easy. That was human nature.

He had taken them through everything, from his initial contact with Tarian to their visit to the apartment in the Marina and his and Ty's subsequent digging. The only time the two cops seemed to get hung up was when it came to his motive.

One of them had said to him, 'You don't strike me as the *pro bono* type. If you don't mind my saying so.'

'I'm not,' Lock had told him.

'So why with this job?'

Lock knew the answer. He didn't want to admit it to himself, or at least he wasn't going to admit it to two cops, but he knew. If he'd been asked for help by Teddy Griffiths or Peter Blake he wouldn't have gone as far as he had. He would have bailed sooner. He wouldn't have followed up, or asked Ty to get the contents of the hard drive forensically examined.

The answer he gave the lead detective was a shrug. 'Didn't do much good in the end, did it?'

The detective had smiled. 'That's not much of an answer.'

At that point Lock had been talking to them for almost four hours solid, with only one brief break to use the restroom and get fresh coffee. He was close to out of answers. He sure as hell wasn't about to admit that he had feelings for Tarian Griffiths that went beyond a concern for her wellbeing. He thought of saying something glib, like 'It's nice to be nice,' but chose not to. Instead they had to settle for another shrug.

The interview was winding down now. They'd shifted back to the small-talk that they'd begun with. Did he have another job lined up? Could he try to avoid driving head on into one of their patrol cars because next time they might not move over? His answers were, no, he didn't have a next gig and, yes, he would do his best to be a more responsible driver.

They thanked him for his time, and walked him out into the corridor. That was it. The LAPD were actively seeking two individuals in connection with the murders of the four people found dead at the Brentwood house. They also had Krank and the others linked to a series of ongoing missing-person cases and one other active homicide where a young woman's body had been found dumped in a canyon north of Malibu. They were confident they would find them, charge them, put them in jail, bring them to trial and send them to prison for the rest of their lives. As far as law enforcement was concerned, it had been a good end to a bad day.

Lock walked out into the cool night air where Ty, who'd been interviewed by a different set of cops, was waiting for him.

'Wanna eat?' Ty asked him.

'Not really,' said Lock.

Ty slapped his shoulder. 'Too bad. I know a place not too far from here.'

58

The restaurant that Ty had selected was in fact a strip club with a buffet of such dubious hygiene credentials that it was a miracle the whole place hadn't yet been condemned by the Department of Public Health. It was three blocks north of the Beverly Center and, in true Los Angeles fashion, came with a high-concept twist. The strippers, or 'featured dancers', as the billboard termed them, were also celebrity lookalikes. As far as Lock could see, the real entertainment came from trying to discern which celebrities they were supposed to look like. He wanted to find a regular place but Ty was insistent that, in times of high trauma, such establishments were best designed to take their mind off the day's horrors.

As they took a seat at the bar, a dancer allegedly impersonating Beyoncé, but who was also sporting a worrying six o'clock shadow, was on the featured stage, giving it her all. Ty ordered them both a beer and they did what two men alone together in a strip club have a tendency to do when not yet drunk: they lapsed into an embarrassed silence.

Their beers arrived. Ty tried to engage the bartender in small-talk. The man took his money, brought the change, gave them a couple of comped tickets for the buffet and went back to drying glasses.

The two men sipped their beer for a few more moments. Lock had always wondered what Purgatory – the way station between damnation and salvation – would look like. He figured Ty had found it.

Ty seemed to agree. He drained his beer, gave a final scowl in the direction of 'Beyoncé' and stood up. 'Sorry, man, this was a bad idea.'

Relieved, Lock left what remained of his beer, prayed he hadn't caught a communicable disease from the bar stool and followed Ty out into the parking lot at the rear of the club. 'There's an actual restaurant with actual food a few blocks down. Italian. They might still be open,' he said.

'Sounds good,' said Ty, getting into the passenger seat of Lock's car.

Lock swung out of the parking lot and onto La Cienega Boulevard. It was getting late. The streets were beginning to clear. In millions of homes rolling news coverage still crackled with the killings in Brentwood. Much was being made of the fact it was the same street where O. J. Simpson had lived at the time of another of LA's more notorious murders. But Lock knew as well as anyone that public attention would move on. It always did. There would be another outrage. A fresh mass shooting. It had reached the point where they had become monthly if not weekly events. He would have loved to believe that there was a ready-made solution. Experience had taught him differently.

Without warning, he pulled over to the side of the road. A taxi cab swerved round him.

'You okay?' Ty asked him.

Lock shook his head. 'This isn't over,' he said quietly. 'That thing today. That was a warm-up.'

'How you figure that?' Ty asked.

He wasn't sure how he could answer in a way that would make sense. It was a hunch, but how had he reached it? He wasn't sure, but he just knew that someone like Krank wasn't about to go quietly.

'The books that kid had about mass shootings,' he said. 'What did all those events have in common?'

'Lot of dead bodies,' Ty offered.

'But today was different,' said Lock.

Ty looked at him. 'Looked pretty typical to me.'

'But it wasn't,' said Lock. 'Columbine. Sandy Hook. Isla Vista. They all ended with a suicide or death by cop. None of those shooters escaped, or even made any real attempt to escape. It was like they'd done what they'd come to do, made their point, and that was it for them. But today they made sure they were gone by the time anyone could get there.'

'We only missed 'em by a few moments,' said Ty.

'Yeah,' said Lock. 'That's what bothers me.'

Ty shrugged. 'Not our problem anymore.'

'You said it yourself – we missed them. That kind of makes it our problem.'

'Ryan, you got the whole of LAPD and everyone else in law enforcement going after them. They ain't gonna get away. Not for long. Now, can we eat?'

59

Gretchen and Loser hefted the last wooden crate into the back of the rental truck. Krank took one last look at the BMW. He took out the key fob from his pocket and dropped it on the ground next to the driver's door.

The truck had been rented a week before, using a false ID and credit card. It wasn't due to be returned for another week. They would drive it to the new location. It would be unloaded, then Loser had been tasked with driving it up the coast into Ventura County and dumping it. Once that was done it was quad bikes all the way. Those had already been purchased and stashed at what Krank lavishly referred to as the Ranch.

The Ranch was a parcel of land with a shack and a stream right next to their target, carefully chosen for its very specific geographical features. Krank didn't own the Ranch. They would be squatting. But it would be temporary. Even more temporary since the events in Brentwood. He figured that they had maybe three days max.

That left only one question. Would Nature favor them? For the past few weeks the weather had been hot and dry. Now they all needed were the winds. Then they could begin. Columbine. Sandy Hook. Isla Vista. They would all be eclipsed – forever and completely.

Krank climbed into the back of the truck with Gretchen. It was too risky for them to ride up front in the cab with Loser. Theirs were the headline faces on the news.

He took one last look at Loser before he closed the door. 'Drive slow, okay? If you get pulled over just follow what we agreed.'

Loser nodded. He closed the door. Darkness engulfed them. A few moments later the engine chuntered to life and they were moving.

60

Tarian opened the door and Lock walked past her into the hotel suite. It was one of eight at Shutters on the Beach in Santa Monica. Each one faced out onto the Pacific Ocean. Lock had made sure it wasn't a hotel that Tarian had stayed at previously before he'd deemed it acceptable. Marcus would have spoken about his mother to Krank, and Lock didn't want to take any chances that Krank might have connected a location Marcus had mentioned to where she'd be staying until he was captured. A sociopath like Krank would know as well as anyone that people were creatures of habit, especially when they were scared.

Tarian was in a bathrobe. Lock followed her through into the living area. 'Thanks for coming, and arranging everything,' she said.

'How you holding up?' he asked her.

'It still seems completely unreal,' she said, her voice cracking. 'All of it. I keep thinking I'll wake up at home and none of it will have happened. The kids are still with Sylvia. She hasn't told them yet. I wanted to do it. But I need a little time first.'

Lock understood what she was saying. Death was one thing, but a violent death, one that was wholly unavoidable, was different somehow. It came with a special bitterness that old age or lingering illness didn't have. It was harder to move on from. If you weren't careful, it could corrode you from the inside out.

She stopped talking and stared at him. 'You've seen a lot of bad things, haven't you?' she said.

'It doesn't get any easier,' said Lock. 'You'd think it would, but it doesn't.'

'So why do you keep doing this kind of work?' she asked him.

It was hardly a unique question. Women seemed to ask it a lot. Women he became involved with, at any rate.

'It's a drug,' he said. 'The adrenalin is a drug. And I'm good at it. Most of the time anyway.'

'You couldn't be blamed for what happened today. You weren't even supposed to be there,' Tarian said.

He didn't detect any bitterness in her tone, though he wouldn't have blamed her if she had. 'You're right. I'm not to blame, but that doesn't stop me second-guessing.'

She crossed to the bar area, opened a small fridge and pulled out a bottle of white wine, then took a corkscrew out of a drawer and handed it to Lock with the wine. 'Could you?'

Lock set to work while Tarian got two glasses. He filled a single glass.

'You don't want one?' she said.

'I need to have a clear head. In case anyone shows up here.'

She took a sip of wine. 'Pretty good. The doctor gave me some pills to help me sleep. I think I'll have this, then take one and go to bed. Or I can skip the pill and you can join me?'

She walked over and stood in front of him. 'Don't let me make a fool of myself here, Ryan. I need this.'

He leaned in, pinching her chin between his thumb and finger and kissed her softly on the lips. She kissed him back, harder.

Lock didn't say anything. They stayed there for a few more seconds, her lips on his, her tongue sliding into his mouth. He pulled back.

"I can stay with you tonight. You need someone to hold you? Or you want a shoulder to cry on? I got that covered. But anything else will have to wait."

61

A group of college girls, dressed Malibu-casual in shorts and T-shirts, crowded the corridor as they waited for the teaching assistant to open their classroom. Gretchen, her freshly cropped hair dyed bright blue and sporting oversized black-framed glasses with clear lenses, pushed past them, toting a heavy backpack. No one gave her so much as a second glance. The more unique or out there your 'look', the more anonymous you became on a preppy college campus.

The college was women-only, one of a dwindling few in California. The total enrollment was under five thousand students, fewer than some LA county high schools. But what Barnes College lacked in numbers it more than made up for in tuition. A four-year undergraduate degree program would cost a cool one hundred and fifty thousand dollars in fees alone. Female-only also made for a lower alumni endowment, which meant financial aid was sparse. As a result it tended to draw students from higher-income groups and offered places to those who might not have had offers from other colleges.

As Gretchen had described it to Krank, it was for 'dumb, rich, self-entitled white bitches and granola lesbians'.

Certainly all the students she had seen so far that morning pretty much fitted her description. They didn't have to work a job. They stayed in campus dorms. They all had brand new cars paid for by Daddy. At the same time, as far as Gretchen was concerned, they held themselves up as some kind of downtrodden minority. They were women born on third base who thought they'd hit a triple but resented not being at home plate. They represented everything she had come to despise. Killing them would be a service to the nation.

At the end of the corridor, she ducked into a restroom. She walked straight into a stall and closed the door. She opened the backpack, took out the contents, primed them, set the timer and waited for the one occupied stall to clear. When the bathroom was empty she climbed out, leaving the stall door locked from the inside.

Outside in the main college square she sat and waited. Groups of girls flitted past. A tweedy professor hustled from his car with a stack of papers. No one looked at her twice.

She waited for the series of pops from inside the building she had just exited. She pulled out her cell phone and hit the number for campus security. Someone picked up straight away.

'Hi, listen, I just came out of Broughton Hall and I think I heard gunshots. It sounds like someone's shooting at people,' she said.

Before the person at the other end of the line could ask for her name or any additional details, she killed the call, stood up, and walked quickly toward the main dorm buildings. Within seconds blue-uniformed security officers were peeling out of buildings. She counted twelve. They immediately began directing anyone walking on campus back to their dorm. They were panicked.

She followed the directions the students had been given. The main entrance to the dorm was open. A heavy-set woman in security uniform was busy shooing co-eds inside. 'Everyone to their rooms and wait for the all-clear.'

A young blonde student asked about her friend who was in a lecture. She was told that everyone in a class would have to stay there until the all-clear was given.

Gretchen smiled to herself as she listened to the conversation escalate. The blonde student argued that she wanted to go check on her friend, and wasn't it a free country? The female security officer responded that freedom of movement was suspended until they had clearance. It went on for a few more rounds before the blonde girl finally relented. Gretchen ducked out of a fire door and headed back to her bike.

The all-clear would come as soon as they found the pack of firecrackers rigged to a timer. It would be put down to a prank. Security would be heightened for a day or two. No one would make any connections between this and Brentwood. If the Brentwood killers had been on campus, they would have done more than play a prank. That would be the thinking anyway.

As she straddled the bike, she called Krank. It took a couple of tries before he picked up – signal was spotty up in the canyon where the Ranch was.

'How did it go?' he asked.

'Too easy,' she said. 'Like shooting fish in a barrel.'

'I was thinking more along the lines of a barbecue, but whatever. You heading back?'

'Yeah. See you in twenty,' said Gretchen.

62

Tarian was still sleeping when Lock woke. He didn't envy her the morning. He knew from experience that, after bereavement, mornings were the worst. The slow, creeping sense of dread as your new reality formed itself in your mind. Today would be the day she had to tell her two surviving children about what had happened. It would not be easy. It was better that she slept.

He leaned over and kissed the top of her head. She barely stirred. He got up and headed into the bathroom. He showered, dried off and got dressed. He dug out a complimentary bag of toiletries, brushed his teeth and rinsed with mouthwash, then went into the living area and stepped out onto a balcony that looked over a deep shelf of beach and beyond that the ocean. It was going to be hot. A breeze had picked up as the Santa Ana winds whipped down through the canyons.

His phone brought him the latest local news. No arrests had been made in the Brentwood killings. The search was ongoing and the LAPD were 'actively pursuing several promising leads', which could mean almost anything. He read on. A house in the Hollywood Hills, believed to be linked to one of the killers, was being searched. A number of bodies had been found. Lock's mind flashed back to the haunting green-black video excavated from Marcus's hard drive by Li Zhang. He wondered if the girl was among them and whether her parents had yet had the knock at their door that brought closure and fresh torment in equal measure.

Scrolling down, other local news was light. A chimpanzee had escaped from the LA zoo. A bad crash on the 405 with three fatalities. An alarm at a women's college in Malibu that had turned out to be a prank. The rest was sports news and weather. He'd already worked out the day's weather – hot, dry and windy.

He walked back inside and through to the bedroom. Tarian was still fast asleep. He debated waking her. He grabbed a piece of paper from the desk and wrote a note, asking her to call him. He left it where she would be sure to see it. The last thing he wanted was for her to think he was ducking out on her, but right now the absolute best thing for her was rest. She would need whatever last reserves of energy she had remaining over the next few days.

He could have stuck around, waited for her to wake, and spent the morning with her. If Krank and the others had been found, he would have. But they were still out there, and right now he felt that he was more in Charles Kim's head than anyone else.

63

Two LAPD Hollywood Division patrol cars were parked nose to nose at the entrance to the Hollywood Hills property. Lock pulled up in his Audi and got out, Ty with him. He'd spent the night poring over the data from the hard drive that Li had cracked, a copy of which was also with the LAPD. Lock had made sure that, straight from the jump, he and Ty had given their full co-operation.

Ty sipped from a cup of coffee as they walked toward the two patrol cars. 'How'd your evening go?'

'It was fine,' said Lock.

'Tarian holding up?' said Ty.

Lock ignored him as one of the patrol officers, a barrel-chested Hispanic sergeant, walked over to them. Lock introduced himself and Ty, name-dropping the two detectives who had said they'd keep him as informed as they could, and quickly explained the circumstances. The sergeant was polite but wasn't going to give away much more than was in the public domain.

'So far we got three vics. All female. All buried out back next to some kind of firing range. House has been occupied until recently, either before the shooting in

Brentwood or shortly thereafter. That's about as much as I know,' he told them.

'The house belong to Charles Kim?' Lock asked.

'Not directly. Some kind of family trust deal. But he was living there with his crew,' said the sergeant.

'He leave anything interesting behind?' said Lock. 'Only I found some fairly heavy-duty ammunition at his apartment.'

The sergeant shook his head. 'Some milk in the fridge, clothes, but nothing like that. You have any other ideas where he might be holed up?'

'None,' said Lock.

Lock and Ty walked back to their car. Lock called Tarian's cell. She was awake but sounded groggy. She thanked him for staying with her and for the note. She was fine. If she needed him, she'd call.

They headed back down into Hollywood. It was only mid-morning but the crazies and tourists were already out on the streets. Lock kept driving. The trail was cold. Los Angeles had twelve million people and there was no guarantee that Krank and the others were even there. In a few days the story would start to fade. The longer it took for them to be found, the less likely it would happen. People did just disappear. Krank and his crew had money, resources, and they'd already proven that they were good at vanishing into thin air.

At the same time, they weren't career criminals. They weren't robbing banks or kidnapping for ransom. They were cult-like. They clearly had an axe to grind with society or, more specifically, with women. They were operating like a terrorist cell. That made them even harder to locate.

Career criminals had associates, patterns, places they tended to hang. The three people currently on the loose, if it was three and not more, had each other. Lock could feel his frustration grow as he drove, and Ty kept flipping through the contents of the hard drive on his tablet computer. They were missing something. Lock knew they were.

'Anything good?' he asked Ty.

'Just lots of crazy shit. Blog posts. Message-board stuff. None of it makes any sense. AFC, alphas, the natural order, they got their own language.'

'AFC?' Lock said.

'Stands for "average frustrated chump". Like a dude who's a regular Joe.'

'You wanna drive?' Lock said. 'Let me take a look.'

'You think you speak crazy better than I do?' said Ty. He smiled. 'Wait. You don't need to answer that one.'

'Very funny,' said Lock. He pulled the car over. The two men got out and switched seats. Ty pulled back out into the traffic. Lock began swiping at the screen as he scrolled through the fevered thoughts of one small corner of the internet.

'Where we headed?' said Ty, as they came to a freeway on ramp.

Lock didn't look up. 'Santa Monica. I want to check on Tarian.'

For once Ty bit back whatever wisecrack was on the tip of his tongue. He spun the wheel of the Audi, powered up the ramp and merged onto the freeway heading west.

64

Having checked in with the front desk, Lock called Tarian from the lobby. Before he left he had told her not to answer her hotel-room door unless she was expecting someone. Hotel security, whom Lock had found to be more than capable, had instructed housekeeping to let their guest know ahead of time if they needed access. The front desk were also being extra vigilant in not allowing anyone who wasn't a guest or a verified visitor near the suite. The suites came with a hefty price tag and were typically used by celebrities or high-net-worth individuals so security around them tended to be fairly high level.

Not that Lock anticipated Krank turning up to finish the job. Tarian had already identified both him and Gretchen. Forensics would likely confirm their guilt. The more Lock had thought about what had happened at the house, the more convinced he'd become that the killers had left Tarian alive deliberately. Going by the wounds evident on the other victims, they'd had the firepower to get access to the bathroom. So why hadn't they? There was one obvious answer. They didn't care whether they left behind a witness or not. In fact, a witness who could identify the killers to the authorities might have been a positive. So far it was a hunch.

Lock proceeded to the bank of elevators that would take him to the suite. As he waited he thought about the material he'd read that had been recovered from Marcus's computer. Lock wasn't a big internet guy. Like a firearm, it was a tool. Something he used when he needed to. From the sheer volume and the records of when material had been accessed, Marcus had spent a huge part of his time reading blogs, writing his own, or commenting on various message-boards that revolved around what they called the 'manosphere'. After a while it appeared that Marcus had discovered an extreme edge where it wasn't sufficient for young men to pick up and sleep with as many women as possible – not that Lock fully understood even that mentality.

As a young man and then an adult, Lock had never lacked female attention. He had never sought it out. He had never had to. He was, he guessed, what Marcus would have called a natural alpha, possessing certain qualities without being aware of them. Thinking about it, he guessed that much of his attractiveness lay in his self-containment. He had never needed a woman to be content until he had met

Carrie. Losing her had devastated him. Work had allowed him to cope. Since her death he had found some women attractive but he had never been able to open himself up with them like he had with her. Part of it was the fear of another loss. He wondered if that was what had attracted him to Tarian. She was beautiful. She found him attractive and didn't hide it. But she was married. Or had been. And now? If he'd gotten a call from her a few months down the line telling him she'd left Teddy, that would have been one thing. But this scenario, her family killed in front of her, hardly made for the start of a fairytale happy-ever-after.

The elevator doors opened. Lock stepped out. He spotted the man lurking in the hotel corridor. He was wearing a jacket that was better suited to Maine in winter than LA's year-round sunshine. He had a ball cap pulled down low over his eyes. He was about five nine and had some weight to him. He was standing with a clipboard making a show of inspecting a fire alarm. The fire point was about twenty yards from Tarian's suite.

The man hadn't heard the elevator doors opening, or he was ignoring Lock's presence. Lock drew his SIG Sauer 226 in one fluid motion. There was already a round in the chamber. He was good to go.

He aimed for the man's back. 'Keep your hands where I can see them,' he said to the man. 'They drop out of sight, I drop you.'

The man froze. The pen he was carrying fell from his hand. 'Take it easy, man,' he said.

'Leave the pen. Turn round,' said Lock, advancing on the man.

The man did so, his hands up, one still clutching the clipboard. He was sporting oversized black-framed 'nerd' glasses and a hipster goatee. He shot Lock a smug smirk. 'Take it easy, brother,' the man said. 'I just want to speak to the lady.'

'She's not speaking to anyone,' said Lock.

'Then let me hear it from her, and I'll be on my way. Know what I'm saying?'

Lock grabbed his shoulder, spun him round so he was facing the wall, and jabbed the muzzle of the SIG into the back of his neck. 'What is that know-what-I'm-saying bullshit anyway?' Lock asked him. 'Is it like some kind of verbal tic?'

'Hey, hey,' the man protested. 'Chill. I'm just doing my job, Homes.'

Lock lifted the back of the man's jacket and frisked for a gun, then leaned in closer. 'Tell me to chill again, in fact say one more word to me, and I'm going to beat you so hard you'll need new kidneys. You understand me, asshole? Nod for yes.'

The man nodded.

'Paparazzo?' Lock asked.

The man nodded again.

'How did you know Tarian Griffiths was here?' Lock asked.

This guy twisted his head round.

'This time you can use words,' Lock told him.

'One of the security guys gives us tips. We usually stay outside and catch people as they leave. But we knew this lady wasn't leaving.'

Of course he does, thought Lock. 'Name?'

'No way, man. A journalist has to protect his—'

Lock slammed a fist into the guy's right side. He let out a gasp as all the air left his lungs and doubled over. Moving in, Lock spun the guy round and fished for a wallet. He found it tucked into the front pocket of his pants, flipped it open and pulled out a California driver's license. He noted the name, tucked the card back in the wallet and handed it over. 'Listen, asshole, you're not Woodward or Bernstein. Real reporters don't stalk the survivors of mass shootings on private property with a video camera, then post it on the internet. You're a douchebag paparazzo. Now, you are going to tell me the name. It's not a matter of if but when. And if you tell anyone about this, remember I just got your name and address. So you say anything, I will hunt you down. We'll have a shorter chat than we're having now, and no one will ever find your body. And while we're at it you may have adopted the lingo, but your accent tells me you're from freakin' Connecticut. Now, are we clear, homes?'

'Marco Jacks. That's the guy who told me.'

'Thank you,' said Lock, lowering his SIG and placing it back in its holster. He dug out his cell and texted Ty.

He spun the guy back round. He put one hand on his shoulder and made sure to maintain eye contact. 'Okay, listen to me. This hotel and, especially, this person are off limits now. Spread the word. If I catch you or any of your colleagues here I will cause pain. I'm not a cop. I don't have to play by the rules and I won't. Do you understand what I just told you?'

'Yeah. I understand.'

'Good,' said Lock, as the elevator doors opened and Ty strode out with his game face on. 'Tyrone, show this young man to the exit.'

Ty didn't say anything. Ty rarely had to. His mere physical presence ensured co-operation. The paparazzo went limp to the point at which Ty had to tap his face and tell him to straighten up.

He grabbed the guy's collar and navigated him past Lock, marching him back toward the elevator as Lock knocked at the door of the suite and waited for Tarian.

65

Krank's index finger ran over the contours of the map. Gretchen and Loser followed the movement from over either shoulder as he traced his way across ridges and down into the canyons around northern Malibu and beyond. He plucked a red marker pen from an empty coffee mug and began to circle the locations he'd spent months selecting. There were eighteen in total. Six per person. Together they formed a rough circle. He had scouted each one personally. He'd used online satellite maps to check for any major changes. He'd also kept an eye on things like applications for building permits.

Over his right shoulder, Gretchen sighed. He shot her a glance. 'Problem?' he asked.

She jabbed at a winding line on the map that curved its way down from the mountains to the ocean. 'What about that?'

'Don't worry. I have it covered,' he said, a hint of irritation creeping into his voice. As if he would have missed something so obvious. 'I'll need your help on it, though.'

'Of course you will,' said Gretchen.

Krank decided to ignore her tetchiness. Since the house, they were all a little more on edge. It was to be expected. Not that there had been any going back before but now everything was set in stone. All they could do was move forward and hope they reached their final objective before they were caught.

'What about you?' he asked Loser.

Loser shrugged. 'I got it. Set, move, set, move. You need any more recon?'

'No,' said Krank. 'I think we're good.'

66

A wall-mounted television beamed live coverage from outside the Hollywood Hills house where a forensics team was busy at work completing the grisly task of unearthing what the LAPD was calling 'a significant number of victims'. Tarian, still dressed in a bathrobe, had planted herself in front of the screen. From her blank expression it was hard for Lock to tell precisely how much she was taking in. In a lower corner of the screen some of the footage that had been culled from Marcus's hard drive played on an endless loop. The footage had been leaked online a few hours previously. The LAPD press office had vehemently denied it had come from them, and Lock tended to believe them. The leak had served to keep the story at the top of every bulletin.

Lock poured a cup of black coffee and took it over to Tarian. 'Here,' he said, handing it to her.

She took it from him. Her eyes never left the screen.

Lock crossed to the couch, and picked up the remote. He turned the volume down. She turned and stared at him. Her look suggested she was seeing not just him but the world for the first time, and that it was a terrifying place.

'Marcus must have helped killed those girls. Or at least he knew about it,' she said, a statement of fact that sounded like a question.

'Yes,' said Lock. 'He was involved.'

'My son,' she said.

Lock held up the remote. 'Want me to switch it off? I'm not sure watching all of this is helping you. Why don't you go take a shower and get dressed?'

She didn't answer. He tossed the remote control back onto the couch. Tarian didn't react but he knew what she was thinking. She was asking the questions that any decent person would ask under the circumstances. Was she somehow culpable? Had her parenting contributed to what had happened? Might she have done more to help her son, or at least to stop him hurting others?

Lock walked over to her. He put his arms around her and brushed a strand of hair from her face. 'The only person responsible for what Marcus did or didn't do was Marcus. You can't blame yourself.'

'But if I had—'

He cut her off. 'You did what you could. Kids grow up. They have to take responsibility for their own actions.'

Tears welled in her eyes. 'He was so angry, Ryan. Where did all the rage come from?'

'I don't know,' Lock said. In reality, he could have made a fair guess. Lock wasn't a therapist, or a shrink, but he hardly needed to be. Marcus Griffiths had grown up with a sense of entitlement that was larger than he was. Rather than make peace with the fact that he couldn't force girls to like him, he had made it about them. Then he had run into Krank, a young man who had taken Marcus's sense of unfairness and alienation and twisted it to his own ends.

When you'd seen as much of human frailty and plain old stupidity as Lock had, you understood that no amount of rationalization or amateur psychology could explain that some people were just assholes. Spoilt assholes, who lashed out when they couldn't get what they wanted. That was why they were busy pulling young women out of the ground in the hills above the Sunset Strip. But none of that helped Tarian.

'We need to move you,' Lock said to her.

'Why?' she asked.

'Someone leaked the fact you're staying here. Ty and I have found an apartment for you in the Palisades. It's not perfect but it'll do for the next few days until you decide what you want to do.'

"What about the children?" she asked.

"We can take you to see them any time, but it might be better if they stayed with Teddy's cousin for now. Just until some of the media craziness settles down," said Lock. "That decision's up to you of course. If you want them with you, we can arrange that too."

She nodded. 'Thank you. I don't how I would have coped with all this if you hadn't have been here for me.'

Lock smiled. 'All part of the service.'

His eyes snapped back to the TV screen. It had cut from their reporter outside the house. The running ticker at the bottom of the screen heralded 'Breaking News'. 'Go get in the shower. I'll pack for you,' he said to Tarian.

As she headed to the bathroom, Lock grabbed the remote from the couch. He waited until he heard the hiss of water from the shower before turning the volume back up.

The two anchors in the studio were talking breathlessly about 'new footage' that had appeared in the last few minutes on social media. Lock racked the volume up two more clicks as Ty walked into the suite. He was holding up his cell phone.

'You see this? Just appeared on YouTube,' Ty informed him. 'Already got like fifty thousand hits.'

The anchors in the studio cut to the footage. Lock recognized the face of Charles Kim filling the TV and Ty's cell screen. He was shot from the chest up. His hair was cut short and he was dressed in military fatigues. He looked a million miles distant from the one-time party animal and pick-up artist that Marcus had run into. He was reading from some kind of prepared statement in a droning monotone.

Lock turned to Ty. 'You watched this already?' he asked Ty.

Ty nodded. 'Five minutes of pure crazy.'

'Okay, give me the Cliff Notes,' said Lock.

67

Wearing Aviator sunglasses, a grey USC Trojans sweatshirt, with the hood pulled up to cover her face, Gretchen quickly ended the call she'd just made, using the code word they'd established with the LAPD that would allow them to separate official communication from some random civilian trying to crash their party. She pressed both thumbs down on either side of the back of the cell phone, and slid off the panel. She dug a long fingernail inside, pulled out the long black battery and tossed it into the trash can along with the tiny SIM chip. She got up from the bench and began to make her way slowly toward the apartment entrance.

As students milled around Cardinal Gardens, either waiting for friends or heading to and from classes at the main campus, she counted down slowly from thirty. She had guessed it would take twenty seconds for USC's TrojanAlert system to activate. Krank had gone for fifteen seconds. Loser had hedged his bets at twenty-one or over.

Out of the corner of her eye, Gretchen could see the happy couple in their usual spot. She wondered how dumb they were to be still on campus with everything that had happened. If the situation had been reversed, she would have been on a plane to Europe long before now.

The countdown had reached seventeen when she heard the first pings as the incoming text message started hitting people's cell phones. She took a moment to savor the reactions as they shifted from puzzlement to a creeping alarm. People's bodies stiffened. They began looking around. If they were walking, their pace quickened. If they had been sitting down they began to get up. A blonde co-ed was already calling someone and shrieking into her phone like a complete drama queen. Gretchen almost regretted that she was here to do a job. She would have relished the chance to give the blonde airhead something to actually scream about.

A campus security patrol car rolled past, the window down, the rent-a-cop hanging his arm out, scoping out the area. She adjusted her course so that her back was to him and all he would see was a frightened little student heading back to her dorm building as instructed.

The system was a thing of beauty. If you were in a classroom, dorm or other building you had to stay there. If you were outside you had to move inside. The rationale was obvious. Shooters roamed. If you weren't in their path, they couldn't stumble across you. If they couldn't stumble across you, you would be safe. It made sense. Unless . . .

A jock college-athlete type guy was holding the door open, shooing people inside. He wasn't taking time to check anyone's ID. He was just standing there being a good little white knight. She stopped and glanced back over her shoulder. Sure enough, Stacy and her dumb-ass frat-boy boyfriend were making a beeline toward her. She hurried through the open door and made a dash for the stairwell. She ran up the stairs until she hit the third floor, pushed out through the door and into the corridor.

She knew where Stacy's room was. She headed straight for it. A couple of students were crowded in the corridor but they were so busy chatting about the security alert that they didn't appear to see her. She swiped a cloned key card across the door handle. It clicked open. She walked inside, taking an immediate left into the bathroom. She stood behind the door and waited.

The wait wasn't a long one. Stacy and her boyfriend were obedient little sheeple, Gretchen thought. The door opened and they walked in. She had kept the bathroom door half closed, at the same angle it had been when she had walked in. The gap between the door and the frame allowed her to watch them as they walked into the tiny studio.

Stacy told the boyfriend she needed to pee. Gretchen tensed. As she walked in, Gretchen grabbed her round the neck. She made sure she could see the blade of the knife. Stacy's eyes went wide. The boyfriend must have had his earphones on because he didn't react to the slight scuffle. Gretchen had to walk Stacy back out before he realized what was going on.

He got to his feet. He raised his hands. 'What is this? What do you want?' he asked.

Stacy wriggled and Gretchen had to strengthen her choke hold. 'Sit down,' she said.

He did as he was told, then reached into his pocket and dragged out his wallet. 'Here, if it's money you want, you can take this.'

When he started pulling out credit cards like so much confetti, Gretchen poked the tip of the knife into Stacy's cheek just enough to draw blood. 'I've not come here for money.'

This seemed to shatter his worldview – as if money was the only motivation on offer in his universe. He looked up at her. 'So what do you want?'

Gretchen dug out the small handheld Flip camera and threw it over to him. He caught it one-handed. 'Your girlfriend here is going to put the record straight about Marcus Griffiths, and you're going to record it.'

Stacy began to struggle. Gretchen let her see the blade again. 'You didn't tell the whole truth, did you?' she said.

'What's this about?' he demanded.

'Just hit that red button when I'm clear,' said Gretchen, sheathing the knife and coming back up with a handgun. 'I'll ask the questions. The little princess here will answer and I'll be on my way.' She loosened her grip, and stuck her face right next to Stacy's. 'Are you ready?'

Stacy nodded. 'Yes.'

Gretchen stepped away from her and moved toward the window. She quickly closed the curtains, and raised the gun so that it was aimed at Stacy. 'Okay, so tell us about the first time you slept with Marcus Griffiths when you were dating your shit-for-brains boyfriend here. Then tell everyone how you changed your mind and told everyone he was stalking you so that everyone wouldn't see you for the little slut you truly are.'

Twenty minutes later, Gretchen slipped out of the studio-sized dorm room, and closed the door behind her. There was a slick of blood on one sleeve of her sweatshirt. Now that she was outside in the corridor it worried her. Someone was bound to notice it. She checked her watch. She was leaving a little early. The dorms, along with the rest of the campus, would still be locked down. She had time.

She wanded the card past the door and walked back in. As she passed the bathroom she could see the blood-covered bodies lying in the tub. She kept walking, opened a drawer and found a suitable replacement sweatshirt. She took off hers and put it on, making sure that she still had the Flip camera on her as she walked back out into the corridor.

It was empty. The door leading to the stairwell opened and a security guard walked through. Gretchen raised the gun and fired three shots, two at his chest, and a final shot at his head as he fell. She stepped over him and kept walking. No one came out of their room. They stayed where they were, just as they'd been instructed. This time it would save their lives. Next time would be another matter.

68

The Audi skidded to a halt between two black Dodge Chargers fitted with tell-tale parcel-shelf emergency lights that signified some serious brass had arrived to supervise the crime scene, as well as any ongoing situation. The vehicles were issued to LAPD officers of captain ranking and above. Homicide scenes demanded a visit from the on-duty captain for the division. Two high-ranking officers signified something a little more serious.

Lock got out of the Audi, pushing through the crowds of students. He headed for the walkway that led from the street into Cardinal Gardens. He had spent the last twenty minutes trying to raise Stacy and her boyfriend with no luck. His calls had gone to voicemail.

At the end of the walkway two patrol cops stood with a couple of university security officers. Lock reached them. They weren't about to let him pass. He scoped the open area behind them for any sign of the detectives he had spoken to previously but if they were anywhere it would be inside.

'Excuse me,' he said to the nearest cop. 'I'm here to collect someone.'

The cop eyed him. 'No one's leaving right now. You'll have to wait.'

The cop's partner peered over Lock's shoulder. 'That your vehicle, sir? You'd better move it before it gets towed.'

Lock stood his ground. 'I will. As soon as I've collected my friend. She's in that building over there,' he said, pointing to one of the dorm buildings where a bunch of cops stood checking the ID cards of some shaken-looking students. 'Come on, the family's worried. If I know she's okay then I can come back, but I need to know.'

The cops traded a look. Lock was pushing his luck, and he knew it.

'What's the name? I'll see if I can get you some information,' said the taller of the two cops.

As soon as he gave them the name he knew it was bad news. One of the university security guards started to say something, only to be cut off with a look from the cops.

'You're family?' they asked Lock.

'A friend of the family.'

The two cops were stony-faced. If she was a victim, then who was informed of what and when was a procedural matter. Nothing spooked cops more than procedure.

'Sir, we can't release information to anyone other than family,' said the taller cop. 'Now, I've asked you once already to move your vehicle.'

Lock decided it was best to cut his losses. He already knew the news was almost certainly not good. EMS vehicles were parked on the concourse but the paramedics were sipping coffee rather than rushing anyone out. 'Is there a number they can call?' he asked, playing his concerned-family-friend card one more time.

A security guard palmed him the USC emergency contact number on a card. Lock thanked them for their help and walked slowly back to his car.

He got in, and moved a hundred yards down the block. He thought about circling back around and trying to gain entry on the other side but decided against it. It would be the same conversation, and overly persistent civilians hanging about crime scenes tended to make cops suspicious. Suspicion got you arrested. Lock didn't have the time for that. He spun the wheel and headed back toward the freeway.

Snagged in traffic, he tried to unpick why someone would go settle an old score when Marcus was already dead. It made no apparent sense. Was it some kind of screwed-up apology for Krank and the others having killed him? That didn't follow either. None of it did. There seemed to be no logic to any of this. Yet something told Lock that this wasn't entirely random. It would have been easy to frame the events of the last few days as some Manson-Family style killing spree – an attempt to garner notoriety. There was more to it, though. He didn't know what it was but, as red lights blazed him, he sensed it hadn't yet begun. The Brentwood house, and now this? They came off like warm-ups for the main act.

69

Ty shouldered his way through the apartment door, laden with Tarian's bags. Marines travelled lighter, he thought, as Tarian followed him inside. He walked through into the bedroom and set them on the carpet.

'It's basic, but it's quiet and you'll be left alone,' he said.

The carefully choreographed journey from the hotel had passed in silence. Tarian had stared through tinted glass at the city streets, a ghost trapped among the living. Ty had known better than to try to comfort her with anything more than his presence. There was nothing he could say to make it right. If she wanted to talk, she would, and he'd listen. But she hadn't wanted to talk until now.

'Thanks for doing this,' she said, unzipping a suitcase and pulling out clothes. 'I don't know how I would have coped if it hadn't been for you and Ryan helping me.'

'Not a problem,' said Ty. He opened one of the closets and grabbed a bunch of hangers from the rail. He handed some to Tarian and began placing some of her clothes on the others.

'How long have you and Ryan worked together?' she asked him.

'Long time.'

'He seems pretty . . .' she seemed to be searching for the best phrase '. . . self-contained,' she said finally.

'Yeah, he can be.'

'Was he different before his fiancée was killed?' Tarian asked.

Ty thought about it. *Was* he different? It was hard for him to recall. So much had changed. 'I guess so. But he's always been pretty tightly wrapped. Comes with the job. You try not to be cynical about life, but it's difficult when you see some of the things we do.'

'I think I can understand that,' she said, as her eyes fell away from him.

Ty bet she could. Her worldview had changed radically and forever. Most people walked around assuming that life was broadly benevolent. Often it was. You could go weeks, months, often years and decades without anything bad happening to you. Then, from out of nowhere, Fate would strike. A car accident, a late-night knock at the door, blood in the bottom of the toilet bowl and bad news from your doctor. Or, in Tarian's case, a son trying to find the answers many searched for and falling in with a dangerous set of people in his quest to find his place in the world. And yet, thought Ty, to accept that the world was malign wasn't healthy either. The truth was, as far as he had seen, the world was indifferent.

'He got better, though,' said Ty. 'He might never get over it entirely, but he's better now than he was. You should remember that.'

She looked up again. 'I'll try.'

Ty's cell chirped. Lock's name flashed up. 'Excuse me for a moment,' he said, stepping out into the corridor to take Lock's call.

'How's she doing?' Lock asked.

'She's functional. Hasn't flipped out yet. Probably still in shock,' said Ty. 'Might get real when the bodies are released and she has to start planning the funeral. What's the deal at USC? False alarm?'

'Not quite. The call about a bomb was a bust but Stacy and her boyfriend are dead,' said Lock.

'Damn. They have anyone?' Ty asked.

'Not yet, but from the rumors that are flying around I think it was the girl, Gretchen. Looks like she snuck into their dorm and offed them while everyone else was running around looking for a bomb or a live shooter or both,' said Lock.

'Think I should tell Tarian?' said Ty.

'No, she has enough to deal with right now, but I think we need to see if we can do some more digging on this Gretchen chick. I'm starting to think that perhaps Charles Kim isn't the biggest bad ass among this crew.'

70

Krank used a crowbar to wedge open the wooden container. Inside were three specially modified .223 caliber Bushmaster XM-15 E2S rifles. They could each take a fifty-round clip. They were semi-automatic, capable of firing at least seven hundred rounds per minute. Not that this was a capability they would use. Neither Krank nor Gretchen nor Loser planned on a strategy of spray and pray. They had something far more methodical in mind.

Krank had used the last of his cash to purchase them using converted Bitcoin currency on a completely encrypted dark web marketplace. The sale would be traced but, like everything else, it would be too late by then. The deed would have been done.

Gretchen had argued for other weapons. Krank had argued against. The use of this particular rifle was symbolic. It had been the weapon used at Sandy Hook. The media would make the connection. Sales would surge, as they had after that mass shooting when the American public had peeled every single Bushmaster XM-15 that was for sale from the walls of the nation's gun dealers.

They had discussed making their stand at an elementary school. Krank had argued that the younger the victims, the more emotive, therefore powerful, the message. But Gretchen was never going to allow it. Not because she had any moral objection, but because for her their target was personal. In the end they had agreed that volume would compensate for the reduced shock factor. Gretchen got her way. The irony of it hadn't passed Krank by – the only female calling the shots.

71

Lock tucked his cell phone back in his pocket. He'd spent the past hour trying to contact anyone who might allow him an insight into Gretchen. Her mother had hung up on him after first denying, then eventually conceding, she had a daughter. It had been the same for a list of former friends, co-workers and relations. The overriding emotion Lock detected had been fear. Gretchen scared people.

Three-quarters of an hour in, he had found someone who wasn't scared of Gretchen. A college professor who'd had a run-in with her while she was in her class. Not all college students got on with every professor, but this had been a pretty spectacular clash that had resulted in Gretchen's expulsion and a restraining order. The professor's name was Janet Cristopher. She had found the experience so upsetting that she had left her tenured position after an extended absence when she was treated for stress. She had only recently taken a new job, starting afresh in a different state.

'So where's she teach now?' Ty asked Lock, as his friend finishing bringing him up to speed.

'That's where it gets interesting. She's right here,' said Lock.

'Oh, yeah?' said Ty.

'Yup.' said Lock. 'Barnes College, private school out in Malibu. I'm going to go talk to her.'

'You sure you don't want to stay here with Tarian and I'll go check this out?' said Ty.

The bedroom door was closed. Tarian was sleeping. In a few hours, Lock had to take her downtown to get an update from the LAPD. For now, though, it was best to let her rest. She had a lot ahead of her. Funerals to plan. A million unimaginable choices to make as she planned them. Closed or open coffins? To bury her son with her husbands or separately? Decisions that, in the normal run of life and death, were hard enough but that violent death made close to unbearable.

'Appreciate the offer,' Lock told Ty. 'But I got this one.'

72

Lock took a right off Pacific Coast Highway, and drove up the winding canyon road that led to the entrance of Barnes College. The main gatehouse was manned. He pulled in behind two other vehicles and waited his turn. He hit the button to lower his window and drove forward until he was level with the gatehouse window. He handed the guard his driver's license and told him whom he was visiting.

'You usually check everyone coming in?' he asked the guard.

The guard shook his head. 'Nope, pretty laid back usually. North Malibu isn't really a crime hot spot, if you know what I mean.'

The guard made a brief call to check that Professor Cristopher was expecting him and waved him through.

Ahead of him, the road narrowed for a few hundred yards before opening back up again to reveal the clean-lined, white modernist campus buildings that were laid out on a huge flat pad with multi-million-dollar ocean views. Lock followed the directions he'd been given, parked and headed toward the main administration building.

Janet Cristopher was waiting for him in her office. She was a petite blonde in her early fifties with a pleasant manner, nothing like the 'radical' women's rights campaigner suggested in the few newspaper articles Lock had found on her after a brief online search. After he had passed on her offer of coffee, she suggested they take a walk around the grounds while they talked. 'It's a shame to be cooped up inside on a day like today,' she told him, as they stepped out into the blazing sunshine.

'You seem to have landed on your feet,' Lock said.

She shrugged. 'It was time for a change. California's not so bad. Although the Santa Anas are playing merry hell with my allergies.'

It hadn't escaped Lock's notice that the hot desert winds that whipped down through the canyons had picked up in the last couple of days.

'Anyway,' Janet continued, 'I take it you're not here to chat about the weather. You wanted to talk to me about Gretchen.'

'You remember her, then?' Lock said.

Janet smiled and swept a hand through her long white-blonde hair. 'Oh, yeah. She made my life pretty damn miserable until she was finally expelled. This news about her being caught up in these murders in Brentwood, I'd like to say I was surprised, but I really wasn't. It was only a matter of time before she really hurt someone. I didn't think it would be this exactly, but . . .' She stopped.

It was obvious to Lock that she wasn't sure whether she should say what she was thinking. 'Please, Professor, go on,' he said.

'Well, I'm supposed to be this big bleeding-heart liberal, bra-burning women's libber. Which should mean I believe that people are a product of their environment. But let me tell you, Mr Lock, I think Gretchen was just bad to the bone. I don't think I actually thought someone could be born evil until I ran across her.'

She looked at him, as if expecting him to be shocked by her outburst. 'Your secret's safe with me,' he said. 'But that still doesn't give me a sense of her.'

They had reached a grassy area.

Janet took a seat on a nearby bench. Lock sat down next to her. Students were sprawled on the grass, reading or just sunbathing. A frisbee whizzed overhead, and a young student loped past them on his way to retrieve it.

Janet folded her hands in her lap. 'Okay, where do I start? Some students are argumentative, or difficult because they're encountering a subject for the first time. Or they're idealistic. But Gretchen was just openly hostile. She'd already made her mind up that she thought women's studies was a bunch of baloney.'

Lock wasn't sure that she might not have had a point, but chose to keep his opinion to himself. 'So why'd she take it as a course?' he asked.

'Not just as a course. It was her declared major. And by the time she was kicked out, pretty much the entire faculty and most of the students were asking the same question. I guess she saw herself as taking the fight to the enemy.'

'The fight being?' Lock asked.

'Gretchen believed that feminism and equal rights have destroyed the country. She's not alone either. There's a lot of people who would agree with her. The men's rights movement has been growing over the past decade. And some of its most vocal supporters are women. They want a return to traditional values, whatever those were. Gretchen was way out on the extreme edge, though. To her, I was the Antichrist.'

'And she made that clear?' said Lock.

'At first it was just arguing with me in class, which was fine up to a point. But after a while it became personal. The tires on my car were slashed. Someone killed one of my cats and nailed it to my front door,' said Janet.

'Gretchen?' said Lock.

'She wouldn't admit it, but she dropped enough hints.' She turned so that she was facing him. 'She wanted me to know it was her. Finally, she tried to attack me one night. With a knife. I managed to lock my office door and stay inside. The college didn't want the story making the news so I agreed not to press charges if they expelled her. That was that. Until now.'

'Has she been in touch since?' said Lock.

Janet shook her head. 'I don't even know if she's aware I'm here.'

Lock got to his feet. 'For your safety, it's best if you assume she does. Make sure you have someone walk you to your car. If you think someone's following you home, call the Malibu Sheriff's Department or the LAPD. Don't take any chances.'

Janet got up. 'Let me walk you back to your car.'

'Actually, before I go, would you mind doing me one more favor? If I could, I'd like to speak to whoever runs campus security.'

Together, they went back to the main administration building. It turned out that the head of security was out of town at a conference in Arizona, but Janet arranged for Lock to meet with the deputy, a former sheriff's deputy from Ventura called Bob Dersh. Janet gave Dersh a brief rundown of why Lock was there, and left the two men to it.

Lock sat across from Dersh in his office. It was law-enforcement neat. Papers carefully filed or stacked. Everything laid out just so. No personal touches, apart from a couple of framed photographs of a wife, and grown-up kids with their spouses and Dersh's grandkids.

'So you were helping out the Griffiths family?' said Dersh.

As an opener it lacked tact. Lock let it go. 'Trying to,' he said. 'I don't think anyone saw what happened coming. I'd like to think no one here will make the same mistake. The woman that's mixed up with them, Gretchen Yorda, she and Professor Cristopher have history.'

'She's mentioned that,' said Dersh, his eyes darting back and forth to the computer screen on his desk. 'We're making sure that everyone on campus is on the lookout for anyone they don't recognize.'

'You haven't had any incidents so far, then?'

Dersh shook his head. 'Right now, I'm more concerned about this,' he said, reaching over and spinning his computer monitor around so that Lock could see the screen. 'Two wildfires up in the mountains.'

Lock stood up and took a closer look at the screen. It showed a map of the immediate North Malibu area from Trancas all the way down Cross Creek. Two pulsing red dots showed the position of the fires. They were, Lock estimated, several miles away, but wildfires were no joke in the area. The last really bad ones, back in 2007, had burned almost a million acres, and cost dozens of people their homes.

'Any word on how they started?' asked Lock.

'People get careless. Campfire. Even a glass bottle dumped in the wrong place can do it. Land out there is bone dry, and now with the winds . . . Believe me, Mr Lock, when it comes to raw destructive power, Mother Nature makes human beings look like amateurs.'

'How close do they get before you evacuate?' Lock said, noting the position of the two fires. One was on a ridge line to the immediate north-east, the other in a canyon to the south.

'Oh, we're a ways away from that. Listen, I appreciate the heads-up. Thanks for stopping by.'

Dersh tilted the computer screen back round, and started to usher Lock out of the office. Lock dug into his pocket and pulled out a photo-montage of Gretchen. He handed it to Dersh. 'Some of these pictures aren't public domain yet. You might want to have your staff take a look at them.'

Dersh took the paper and laid it on his desk. 'Sure will.'

PART THREE

Alfonso Fry figured that this just might be his lucky day. Hell, going by his usual luck with women, this might just be the event of a lifetime for him. It was turning out like one of those made-up stories in the back of a dirty magazine, or a scene from a goddamn porno movie. Except it was real and it was actually happening to him.

It had gone down like this. He had pulled into the truck stop just outside Encino to get something to eat and drink enough coffee to keep him going for another six hours on the road. He guessed he'd noticed the little lady with the long red hair and the Daisy Duke denim shorts that hugged her ass hanging around outside the gas station, a huge backpack at her feet. She was kind of hard to miss standing out there, sucking on a lollipop like it was . . . well, never mind what it was like . . . and staring at all the people putting gas in their car.

Alfonso had given her a second look, and he was damned if she hadn't actually winked at him and licked at that lollipop. He'd figured she was making fun and that her boyfriend would appear any second so he'd put his head down and made for the diner.

The waitress had come over with a menu. He'd ordered coffee and a cheeseburger plate. Next thing he knew the same little redhead had slipped into the seat across from him, grabbed the menu from the table, and said to him, 'I'm Cherry. I saw you looking at me out there. Thought I'd come say hi.'

He'd looked at her, blinking, like this couldn't actually be real. He could see that the red hair was some kind of a wig, but that didn't bother him.

'Well,' she'd said, 'are you going to tell me what's on the menu, or not?'

He must have opened his mouth without saying anything because she had reached over and pushed his chin back up. 'You're drooling,' she'd said. 'It's not a good look.'

'I don't have any cash,' he'd said. She had to be a professional. Just had to be. You found hookers hanging at truck stops and gas stations. But they usually weren't quite so brazen.

Now the waitress came back with his coffee and shot daggers at the girl. The girl just smiled sweetly and said, 'I'll take some coffee too. Separate checks, though. He's broke.'

The waitress disappeared. Alfonso was slowly regaining his composure. 'I didn't mean to be rude,' he said. 'It's just I assumed . . .'

'Well,' the redhead said, 'you assumed wrong. I need a lift, and I figured with that big load of wood you're hauling you might be just the man to give me one.'

Alfonso spat out the sip of coffee he'd taken and began to cough. Cherry grabbed some paper napkins and handed them to him. It was the way she'd said it. With the emphasis on the word 'wood'. Goddamn, thought Alfonso, this was just plain crazy. Pure porn movie.

'So?' said Cherry. 'Can you give me a ride, or not?' She made a big show of looking around for another prospect before batting her eyelids at him one more time. 'I'll make it worth your while.'

'How old are you anyway?' he said, feeling better about himself now that he'd actually regained his composure sufficiently to ask a question.

'Old enough,' she'd said. 'Now, is it a yes? Or should I find myself a real gentleman?'

He grabbed another menu from the stack in the metal holder and handed it to her. 'Pick anything you like. On me.'

She smiled at him, and it suddenly seemed real.

She rubbed at his crotch as he settled back into the cab. He rolled a kink out of his neck. He'd decided to go with it, whatever it was. Maybe he wasn't the fifty-something slob that he saw in the mirror. Perhaps other people saw a different man.

'So where we headed?' said Cherry.

'Baja, California. That work for you?'

'Sure,' she said, leaning over to dig inside that huge backpack she was toting. 'But maybe we can take a slight detour first?' she said, coming up with a handgun.

He felt the cold metal press against his temple and he froze. With her free hand she lifted off the wig to reveal close-cropped hair. The cute sing-song voice was gone.

'Do exactly what I say when I say it, and you'll live. Do anything that I haven't asked you to do, and I'll kill you. Do you understand me?'

Alfonso's brain scrambled frantically. *What was that saying? If something looked too good to be true, it probably was. Goddamn right. Goddamn right.*

74

Krank twisted the throttle and the red Honda Rancher quad bike bucked up the slope toward the line of sycamores. He edged it through the trees and stopped. He climbed off and dumped his pack on the ground. A little further back there were half a dozen eucalyptus trees he'd scouted previously. They would burn fast and intensely. The scrub and duff between them and the sycamores would take care of the rest. The ground was dry as a bone. Conditions could not have been better.

Opening the top of his pack, he set to work. He had just finished laying out what he needed when he heard the snap of a branch. He looked round to see a man in hiking boots, shorts and a T-shirt walking toward him. He was in his late sixties with a shock of white hair and glasses.

'Hey!' the hiker shouted. 'Are you crazy? You can't set a campfire here.'

Hunkered down with the Rancher quad bike between him and the man, Krank slipped his left hand back into the pack, feeling for his gun.

The hiker kept on coming. Krank waited until he was within ten yards before standing up.

The hiker saw the gun and stopped where he was. 'Take it easy there,' he said.

Krank saw the flicker of recognition flit across the man's face. He didn't say anything, but his body tensed, and Krank knew that he'd recognized him. The next few minutes would decide the man's fate.

'What's your name?' Krank asked.

'Look, son, take it easy.'

'Your name? I won't ask you a third time,' said Krank.

'Ben. Ben Miles,' the hiker said.

'You live round here?'

'The Palisades.'

'You live alone, or with family?' Krank asked.

Krank knew this would go one of two ways now. Either Ben, like a true beta male, would try to establish a connection, and build rapport, or he'd realize what Krank was really asking him. If he did the latter, and he lived alone, he would lie. Krank wasn't asking the hiker if he lived alone, he was asking him if anyone would miss him.

Ben Miles smiled. 'My wife passed a few years ago. I live alone.'

'That's too bad,' said Krank, walking toward him, and shooting him once in the chest from less than a yard away. He stepped aside and the hiker fell forward.

Krank left him where he lay for the coyotes to deal with and went back to the task in hand.

75

Something had been gnawing away at Bob Dersh ever since his visit from the private security consultant. More specifically he'd been thinking about the pile of firecrackers that had been placed in one of the bathroom stalls not that long ago.

It was just – off. Not that the student body didn't pull the odd prank. They did. They were like any bunch of college kids. A little more laid back, perhaps, but a few of them could make life difficult for the faculty when they wanted, especially if alcohol was involved. This had been different, though. During the day. Intended to disrupt. But without there being any obvious pay-off. It had just seemed dumb and pointless.

The date and time had been logged. They still had the footage from all the security cameras on their system. Dersh pulled it up. He and his boss had already reviewed it. This time he went back a little further.

For obvious reasons the college wouldn't allow cameras in the bathrooms so the closest he could get was the corridor outside. Unfortunately the way the camera was mounted there didn't actually cover the bathroom door so he had to assume that anyone walking down the corridor was a possible suspect. He started reviewing the footage an hour before the incident.

To say it was mind-numbing was an understatement. Although the college kids liked to present themselves as individuals, they all pretty much dressed alike. It would have been easy enough for someone to blend. He got to the point where the firecrackers went off and people began running down the corridor. He hadn't picked out a single person from the crowd.

There was a camera positioned at the entrance to that particular building. He repeated the process with the footage uploaded from that position. Forty minutes in, he stopped. He pulled the footage back. She was shortish, slim build, white, wearing a cap and keeping her head down so that her face was obscured by the brim. But just before she passed beyond the gaze of the camera, she looked around.

Dersh pulled the sheet of pictures Lock had given him from the in-tray on his desk and smoothed them out flat on his desk. He clicked the mouse, pulling the footage back one more time, and hit play. As the young woman turned he clicked again, freezing the image. His eyes swept between the screen and the pictures.

He couldn't be a hundred percent certain, but it looked like it was Gretchen. But why? If she wanted to get her own back against Professor Cristopher, why go for such a lame prank? It made no sense. She had gained nothing from it. No one had been hurt. Professor Cristopher hadn't even known about it.

76

Lock drove. Ty rode shotgun up front while Tarian sat in back. She had showered, dressed, put on make-up and, thanks to Lock's persistence, had had something to eat before they'd left the apartment. At this stage, Lock knew, the key to having some chance of recovery from this type of sudden trauma was to stick to the basics. It was easy to go days without bathing or changing clothes or eating. The hours folded in on themselves, and a person could slowly sink into a hole it became impossible to climb out of.

They were heading downtown for a briefing from the LAPD. Not that Lock expected anything new. Everyone was doing their best but already the media's focus had begun to shift incrementally away from the manhunt. It hadn't taken much. The world's attention span was increasingly brief.

There were still multiple sightings each day of Krank, Gretchen and the other suspect, but none of them had checked out. The only thing that would ratchet interest back up was freshly spilled blood, and that hadn't been any. Already there was speculation that California's most wanted had left the country, slipping across the border into Mexico.

It was a nice thought, which was precisely why Lock didn't believe it for a second.

His cell phone rang. He hit the answer button. 'Ryan Lock.'

'Mr Lock, it's Bob Dersh here from Barnes College. I found something you might want to take a look at. I don't know what it means, if anything, but I thought I'd let you know in any case.'

77

Alfonso Fry was alone in the cab of his truck, but he was more frightened now than he had been with a gun pointed at him. A gunshot would have been clean. Done right, it might have been quick too. He wouldn't have known much about it. But this was different.

A trickle of sweat ran down his back into the crack of his ass. He wanted more than anything to reach back and scratch but he couldn't move his right hand. It had been duct-taped to the steering wheel. He didn't dare move his left hand either. He had been warned about what would happen if he did. The list of what he could and couldn't do was a long one.

And to make sure that he complied, the collar was around his neck. It was grey and padded and looked like a cross between the squishy travel pillows they sold at airports and the kind of collar a vet fitted around a dog's neck to stop it worrying at a wound and tearing out stitches.

Attached to the dash were two other devices. The first was a satellite navigation system. It showed a pre-programmed route, which, as of right now, was taking him down Pacific Coast Highway toward Santa Monica. The second was a smartphone running a Skype-type phone and video application. It relayed a live feed of Alfonso as he drove. From time to time someone would come on the line to check on him, and relay additional instructions.

There was one other piece of equipment. A clear plastic tube attached to a catheter dangled from his zipper, dead-ending in a plastic jug on the floor of his cab.

The voice came back. It was the male this time.

'How are you, Alfonso?' it said.

What a question, he thought. He was terrified. He was convinced he was going to die, one way or another.

'I'm fine,' he said. What else could he say?

'That's good,' said the voice. 'Now, I need you to slow up a little. Take your speed down to thirty-five until told otherwise. We don't want you getting you there too early.'

'Where am I going?' Alfonso asked.

He got no answer. They were already gone. He looked at the phone as it blinked red, capturing his every move. The collar seemed to tighten, a noose ready to choke him to death.

78

Wearing a blonde wig, Gretchen stared wide-eyed at the two-hundred-pound truck driver, his gut spilling over his belt as he waddled back toward his rig.

'Can I help you?' he asked. He sipped at a Big Gulp soda. She could tell that she might have better luck if she was dressed as a hot dog. He seemed skeptical.

Her cell phone rang. She struggled to contain her anger. She picked up her pack and moved off to one side as the trucker started to get back into his cab.

At the other end of the line, Krank said: 'What's going on? You done yet?'

'Last one,' she said.

'We're on the clock with this,' he said.

'I know. So quit bugging me.'

She killed the call and hopped up next to the cab. 'Could you give me a ride?'

The driver burped loudly. She could smell the stink of bologna and mustard on his breath wafting toward her. 'What's in it for me, sweet cheeks?' he asked, staring at her breasts.

'An experience you'll never forget,' said Gretchen.

79

Lock's fingers drummed out a beat on the steering wheel of the Audi as he came to a halt on the 10 freeway a mile short of the McClure tunnel that would take them back onto PCH. He had left Ty with Tarian at the LAPD's administration building, and decided to head back to Barnes College to speak to Bob Dersh. Tucked into its cradle, his cell phone's navigation system chimed with a traffic alert. He threw his hands up as all around him vehicles ground to a complete halt.

His phone rang. It was Ty. 'You seen the news?' said Ty.

'No, I'm in the car. Why?'

'Some crazy shit on PCH. Truck's blocking every lane north of the Palisades,' said Ty. 'LAPD just declared a major incident.'

'For a truck wreck?' said Lock.

'Turn on your radio,' said Ty. 'Driver claims he's being held hostage.'

'What do you mean "claims"?' said Lock. 'Either he is or he isn't.'

'Well, that's what he's saying, but he's the only person inside. Anyway, if you want to get to the college, you ain't using PCH to get there. No one is.'

Lock spun the wheel, cutting up the person in the next lane as he bullied his way toward the exit that would take him onto Lincoln Boulevard. He'd have to work his way back around. 'Thanks for the heads-up,' he said to Ty.

'You got it.'

The call ended, Lock flipped on his radio and hunted for a news channel covering the story. It didn't take him long to find one.

80

Alfonso Fry closed his eyes. Over the course of a few hours what had begun as some kind of feverish adolescent wet dream had transformed into a nightmare. Like a dream, the points of transition had been striking in their abruptness. One moment he had been primed to have sex with a nubile nymphomaniac hitchhiker, the next he had a gun to his head. Hours later, he had been admiring the sun sinking into the ocean and pondering his own mortality, the next second the screen had blinked and he'd been instructed to turn his truck so that it was straddling the Pacific Coast Highway. Perhaps if he opened his eyes he would be back at home, lying in his bedroom in the house where he lived in Bakersfield.

He counted to three and opened his eyes. The splash of a helicopter searchlight dazzled him for a moment. He blinked to clear his vision. He wished he had kept his eyes closed. Police cars surrounded the truck. He counted off three law-enforcement agencies; Malibu Sheriff's Department, California Highway Patrol, and LAPD.

Everywhere he looked there were cops, their guns pointed at him. A police German Shepherd strained at its leash, furiously biting the air. A couple of SWAT team officers decked out in full combat gear edged toward the back of his truck. A few hundred yards down, a solid block of gridlocked traffic stretched into the far distance.

Alfonso looked at the dash. 'Okay, so what do you want me to do now?' he said to the cell phone.

No one answered. The screen had gone entirely blank. He thought about trying to unpeel his hand from the steering wheel. He reached up with his free hand and felt the edge of the collar that had been strapped around his neck. The idea of escape melted away as his fingertips brushed what felt like a wire.

He closed his eyes again. This time, he prayed.

81

With Pacific Coast Highway closed a half-mile north of Sunset Boulevard, Lock turned onto 26th Street, heading for Wilshire Boulevard. From there he could pick up the 10 to the 405 and throw a big loop through the San Fernando Valley before driving down one of the canyons to the college. Reports were hitting the airwaves of a number of new wildfires sweeping Malibu. First it was three that had been burning since earlier in the day. Five minutes later the number doubled. Ten minutes after that, it tripled.

One radio report said that a spokesman for the Malibu Fire Department had confirmed that they were already seeking assistance from nearby fire departments to cope with the unprecedented strain on their resources. The mayor of Los Angeles had scheduled a press conference for one hour's time. No one was linking the fires to the hijacked truck, at least not officially. Lock understood the reasoning. The last thing you wanted to create in the middle of a 'natural' disaster was a sense of panic among the civilian population. Panic could only make things worse.

Amid the news of more wildfires, word began to filter through of a suspected second hijacked truck blocking

PCH north of Trancas. The report was officially unconfirmed. What was confirmed was that southbound traffic from north of whatever was happening at that point on PCH was stopped.

As he drove, he called Ty.

'You seeing all this?' he asked his partner.

'Can't miss it, baby,' said Ty.

'What do you think?' Lock asked. 'Coincidence?'

Ty gave a deep chuckle. 'You need to ask?'

'Did any of the stuff we have on Charles Kim or the girl mention arson?'

'Not that I can remember,' said Ty.

That was what Lock had thought. Not that it meant much. Arson was a fairly rudimentary skill at the best of times, especially if you didn't care whether you were caught or not.

Up ahead, traffic was beginning to slow. Lock moved over into the car-pool lane. Right now, he doubted whether a fine for violation of car-pool lane rules would make much difference. If his suspicions were correct about what was about to go down in Malibu, he and everyone else had bigger problems.

He buried the gas pedal, sweeping past the grinding traffic.

82

Ty paced the living room. Tarian was on the couch. He had tried to dissuade her from watching the rolling coverage unfolding live on the TV screen. She had insisted on watching it.

Tarian looked at him. 'I'll be fine here if you want to go.'

Lock would not be happy if he left, Ty knew. Then again, how would he live with himself if he didn't at least try to help his partner?

'Are you sure?' he said to Tarian.

She nodded at the screen. 'They're obviously busy doing whatever they're doing. They're not going to be coming after me. I doubt they care about witnesses anymore.'

Tarian had a point. Ty doubted that a court room or a prison cell was factored into whatever insane plan or grab for immortality was being played out now at the college. Career criminals tried to avoid coast-to-coast news coverage. These people had done everything they could to guarantee it.

'Okay,' Ty said. 'But we have to have some ground rules.'

He picked up a black canvas bag, which was lying next to the couch. 'You buzz no one into the building. You do not open the door to anyone apart from either myself or Lock. If someone turns up you call nine-one-one and request immediate assistance.'

He unzipped the canvas bag and took out a hard black case. 'You know how to use a handgun?' he asked her.

Tarian nodded. He flipped open the case to reveal a .38 Special double-action revolver. 'It's already loaded. You use a revolver before?'

'Couple of times. Teddy was big into his guns,' she said, her voice catching a little on his name. 'He used to take me to the range. He never drank when we did that so I encouraged it.'

Ty grabbed his jacket from the back of the couch. 'Okay. You shouldn't need it. I'll be back with Ryan as soon as we can.'

He began to head for the door. She called after him, 'Be careful.'

He stopped and turned. 'We'll be fine. Just sit tight.'

The rearview mirror of Ryan Lock's Audi was a whirling rectangle of red light. A California Highway Patrol car was tucked in tight behind him. It had been there for the past half-mile, sticking tight to his rear bumper.

The trooper wasn't giving up the pursuit. Lock had no plan to pull over. The lights and sirens on his rear bumper were a good way of clearing the path ahead. As long as no concerned citizen slowed down ahead of him, he was golden.

Lock and his highway convoy buddy were coming up on the exit. From there he could drop down into Malibu Decker Canyon. The road would take him to within less than a half-mile of Barnes College – closer if he took one of the side roads that ran across the canyons.

The latest reports coming in were of shots fired. With access from the main artery into Malibu blocked north and south, and fires that looked like arson, it didn't take a genius.

Glancing across the three lanes of traffic that blocked him from the exit, Lock picked out his path. He accelerated and moved across, forcing a gap. The highway patrol tried to follow but Lock's maneuver had already forced the traffic behind to concertina up.

Lock kept moving, using the lightning force of the Audi's engine to force his way to the exit. The highway patrol car was making moves, but too late. A quick glance saw it roll past as Lock powered down the on-ramp. At the bottom, he kept moving, ignoring the filter light, and hanging an abrupt left as car horns sounded their fury all around him.

Dersh was down at the main entrance into the college, waiting for reinforcements from the Malibu Sheriff's Department when he saw the truck. It had turned off Pacific Coast Highway and was heading straight for him. The driver was sporting a beard, and a John Deere cap. His arms gripped the wheel. Around his neck it looked like he was wearing some kind of physiotherapy support collar.

At first it didn't look like he was going to stop. It just kept rolling, looming closer with every second that passed. Dersh glanced over to the terrified security guard who was still jockeying the booth. Dersh had spent the last two minutes trying to persuade the guard to stay where he was. Procedure demanded that no one else, other than authorized law enforcement or other emergency personnel, get past the main gate. The truck bearing down on them didn't appear to have got the memo.

Dersh pulled his gun from his holster, and raised it. The driver raised one hand from the steering wheel. The truck slowed. Dersh stepped back, falling into a shooting stance. He needed to make sure the driver knew he wasn't bluffing.

The truck was slowing right down. The driver was waving his hand frantically at Dersh. He seemed to be pointing back up the hill toward the college. Dersh wasn't falling for it. He glanced back round as the big rig's engine roared and it kept coming. Dersh took aim at the driver's chest.

The driver was still waving at him as the bullet slammed into Dersh's back. His body twisted with the force of impact. There was the crack of a second shot and he saw the booth guard's face explode.

He stumbled forward. He looked down to see a huge hole in his lower torso. His guts were hanging out over his belt. There was blood everywhere. His knees gave way. The life was draining from him fast. He could hear pounding in his ears like the steady beat of waves rolling in on a beach.

One moment everything around him had been black smoke and the lick of distant flames sweeping down from the hills. Now there was only a black void. His face hit the ground. He found the energy to raise his head and see that the truck was turning. A second later, he was gone.

Inside the cab, the driver brought the truck to a halt. It was pulled straight across the entrance, blocking all four lanes. He had done what he had been asked. He had almost just been shot but he'd done it. Now what? he wondered. The cell-phone screen was blank. Not that he could make much out. He was sweating so heavily that his eyes stinging from the salt. Slowly, he raised one hand to swipe the moisture away.

The collar felt tight around him. He could see the wires poking out where it fastened. All he could do was sit tight and pray he didn't meet the same fate of the two men outside.

84

The fire ripped down a stand of trees that ran along the edge of Solstice Canyon toward the college. A freshly chain-sawed sycamore lay across the road, temporarily blocking access from the east. On the other side, a carpet of fire swept north to south, turning bone-dry grass and underbrush to flame. Smoke rose in thick plumes from half a dozen other sites to the east, north and south.

The whoop and wail of sirens in the far distance came close to being eclipsed by the pop and spit of the fires. A deer dove from the bushes, wild-eyed, as it searched for an escape route. It took off for a dense thicket of brush, only to reappear a moment later as fresh flames punched their way out from the route it had just taken. It stumbled uncertainly down the road, heading oceanwards, as the wind shifted, driving white-grey smoke ahead of the flames.

Beyond the sycamore, a lone figure dressed in full body armor, with a red handkerchief pulled across his mouth, sat alone on a Honda quad bike. The barrel of a Bushmaster assault rifle poked out of the top of the backpack hanging heavy from his shoulders.

His cell phone trilled a message alert. He pulled it from a pocket, read the message and put it back. He gunned the engine of the four-wheeler and turned off the road, heading for the rear chain-link of the college.

Clambering off the quad bike, he ripped at the fence with gloved hands, peeling back a section that had been cut the night before to allow direct access. He got back onto the quad bike and trundled through as quietly as the engine would allow.

Pulling his handkerchief down for a moment, Loser stared back up the hill, in awe of the raw power of the fires that blazed, ripped and skipped down the slopes behind him. He dismounted once more, took off his pack and pulled out the Bushmaster.

He put his pack back on, and began the walk down the slope toward the rear of the first student accommodation block. It had forty-six student suites. Each was a double. Ninety-two young women, minus those who were off-campus. Being generous, he calculated that would mean a minimum of eighty. Two fifty-round clips if his shooting was close to perfect and he could dispatch each victim with a single shot. Allowing for how it would really go down, he figured it was a three-clip job, maybe four.

He felt sharp and alert. Krank had given them all Modafinil to take about an hour before this point. It was a drug prescribed for narcolepsy but used off-label by Wall Street warriors and students cramming at the last minute for exams. It was like ten shots of espresso in one little pill but without the shakes. Krank had told them it would help their focus. It seemed to be kicking in because Loser had never felt more alive or in the moment than he did right now. The late-night hunts had been good. But this? This was like stepping into a whole different world entirely.

He shouldered the rifle, and clicked it to single shot, as someone rounded the corner of the building. It was a white girl in her twenties, with thick black hair pulled back into a ponytail. She saw Loser and froze. Twenty yards between them, she turned and started to run back to the building.

Loser fired a single shot. It hit her square in the back. Her own momentum and the force of the bullet threw her forward. She stumbled, and fell to the ground, her arms windmilling outwards.

Jogging down the hill, Loser hunkered down next to her and turned her over. The bullet might not have looked like much going in but the girl's chest was a different story.

The exit wound was about eight inches wide. She was dead and then some.

Loser stepped around her and kept moving. All the dorm rooms had windows, which faced out onto every side of the building.

He watched as a tall Asian girl stepped into view in one of the rooms. She grabbed at the blind cord and closed them. The smoke billowing down the hill must have provided some form of cover because she didn't appear to see him. The blinds closed and she was out of his sight.

He smiled to himself as more and more blinds were closed. This was part of the college's procedure. Shots fired meant students were to stay where they were until further notice. Doors were to be locked, and barricaded where they could be. Blinds, curtains and drapes were to be closed.

The idea was simple: it was harder for a gunman to catch someone they couldn't actually see in their scope. Krank had explained the flaw in the plan. If the blinds were closed, you knew you had someone inside.

Loser walked to the first window and used the stock of the Bushmaster to smash the glass. It was tougher than it seemed. It took him a good twelve seconds to punch it all out. He could hear whimpering and whispering inside. In the distance he could hear more gunfire. Single shots, spaced evenly apart. He guessed that either Krank, Gretchen or both of them had reached the classrooms and lecture halls.

Pop. Pop. Pop.

Loser reached in through the window and ripped the blind away. The two young women hiding inside were backed up against the door, hunkered down in a fetal position. He raised his rifle and took aim as they begged for their lives.

85

Tufts of grey-black smoke whipped across the Audi's windshield. Lock could barely see the narrow, twisting canyon road. He moved forward, hunched over the wheel, and clinging to the white center line. On one side the road fell away into a ravine.

For once, he had defaulted to using the Audi's GPS system. The blinking dot on the map told him he was within touching distance of the Barnes College campus. He kept driving.

A further hundred yards down the road he braked hard as he came up fast on a fire truck and a couple of pick-ups. He pulled in behind the truck, switched his hazard lights on and got out. The truck crew were gathered in a huddle. Lock walked over to them, the gun on his hip clearly visible.

'What's going on?' he asked.

One of the firefighters turned to him. 'Who the hell are you?'

'Ryan Lock. Work out of Sherman Oaks. My daughter's down there,' he said, with a wave down the burning slope toward the rear of the college buildings.

The firefighters traded a look. Lock guessed it wasn't a million miles away from the look they gave each other when a relative arrived at a smoldering damped-down blaze when they hadn't been able to get everyone out.

'You spoken to her?' the firefighter said. 'Is she definitely down there?'

Lock nodded. 'Think so. I'm going to go take a look anyway.'

The firefighter put his arm across Lock's chest. 'You might want to stay here.'

Lock stared at the man's arm. He dropped it back down. 'What's my best route to get down there?' he asked.

'You want to get yourself shot, be my guest,' said the firefighter. He pointed to their immediate left. 'That gully over there will give you some cover.' He swept his hand back up the slope to a stand of sycamores that, so far, had gone untouched by the fire. 'But the wind changes, and they catch . . . you won't have to worry about catching a bullet.'

'Thanks,' said Lock.

There was the sound of more live fire from the campus below. A police car was rolling down the road toward them. If Lock wanted to go it would have to be now. No cop in their right mind was going to allow a civilian to wander into the middle of the shit storm. They also weren't about to fall for some vague working-out-of line. They'd want to see a badge.

He yanked the top of his shirt up over his mouth and headed for the gully. It was about a ten-foot drop. He scrambled over the side. At the bottom was stony ground. It must have been a stream or culvert that had long since dried up in the months of dry, hot weather. It offered some protection from the fire. But if the trees and bushes that ran alongside it caught, he would be trapped with no exit.

Lock put his head down, and began to scramble over the loose rocks and stones. Staying on his feet was harder than it looked. Even in boots, and watching every step, he slipped a couple of times. The final time, he went down hard, banging his left knee against the edge of a boulder. The smoke in the air made breathing hard. His eyes stung to the point where they teared up.

Glancing back, he saw the fire jump suddenly to catch one of the furthest trees. At first nothing happened. Then one of the higher branches caught. Even if he'd wanted to, going back was no longer an option. His route to where the firefighters were on the road would be blocked by the flames.

Lock jogged along a ridge that ran parallel to the rear of the college. The wind had changed temporarily, pushing some of the fires back up the hills. Down below, beyond the college buildings, he could see a couple of Malibu fire trucks parked at the entrance, their entry blocked by a truck. A couple of Sheriff's Department cars were parked next to them. The deputies had their weapons pointed at the driver. He wasn't making any moves to exit the vehicle.

With the truck parked there, the fire trucks had no way of getting into campus. It was also blocking any evacuation. If students and staff were to get out, they would have to do it on foot. Right now, with gunfire still crackling through the air at regular intervals, that was a high-risk strategy. Any sniper worth their salt would just find high ground and pick off anyone fleeing one by one.

Lock could go after the shooters. But that would take time. And with every second that passed, the fires were drawing closer.

There was no good option available. Only a series of bad options. Lock guessed that was part of the plan.

86

Janet Cristopher unlocked her office door and stepped out into the corridor. It was empty. Every door was closed. She knew there were people in some of the offices and classrooms because she could hear the ping of incoming text messages and muttered conversations.

The gunfire had been steady. At first it had been distant. It sounded like the shots were being fired in or near the student residences. But over the past five minutes it had seemed to move closer to the main teaching and administration area of the campus.

Janet walked to the end of the corridor. She could hear sirens. Finally. Although perhaps only a half-hour had passed since her cell had buzzed with the text message alerting her to an 'incident' on campus, it had seemed like eternity.

Ahead of her was a door that led outside. It was clear glass. Looking through she could smoke rising from the hills overlooking the campus. The whole area was ablaze. The door itself was locked. That was part of the security procedures.

There was a button next to it. If she pushed it, the door would unlock for a few seconds. She could open it and step outside. But once she was outside the only way she could get back in was for someone to buzz her in. That was unlikely. Procedure said that no one was to allow anyone inside a building once it had been locked down. If she stepped outside, that would be it.

She took a deep breath, opened the door and stepped outside. It closed behind her. A second later she heard it click. There was no going back.

She walked down a pathway. She was out in the open. There was no one about. No sign of life.

Janet kept walking. There was a sudden staccato burst of gunfire from the administration building on her left. For a moment, Janet froze. Several seconds passed. She started walking toward the sound of the gunfire.

87

His SIG Sauer 226 punched out in front of him, Ryan Lock rounded the corner of the building. He'd followed the sound of shooting to this location. He held his breath as the wind changed again and a fresh wave of smoke swept toward him. Red hot cinders stung his face. His eyes watered. He swiped the tears away with the back of his sleeve and hunkered down to find some fresher air.

Visibility was maybe twenty feet. From the design of the building he was fairly certain that it was one of several dorms. In military terms it was what would be termed a 'target-rich environment'. From the number of rounds he'd heard fired, and the pattern of their timing, he guessed that a number of those targets had already been dispatched.

With his back to the wall, Lock skirted it. Blinds fluttered through the first window he came to. Here goes, he thought, pushing them to one side and stepping through the window. Glass crunched over his boots. It took a second for his eyes to adjust to the gloom.

It was a standard two-person dorm room. The kind that you'd find on campuses across the country. A single bed either side of the window. Two small desk/study areas. An open cupboard with rails and drawers for clothes. A cell phone buzzed on one of the desks, still attached to its charger.

Lock crossed to it. The display read: 'Mom'. The three letters and what it held caught him unawares for a split second. He focused, pushing his emotions away from him. Now was not a time for reflection.

He reached over and flicked on a light. As he did so, the toe of his boot hit something. He looked down to see a young woman lying in a fetal position next to the door. Her hands were up over her head. That hadn't stopped someone shooting through them and into the back of her head. Her roommate lay next to her, her body position more open, her legs twisted over each other. She had been shot in the back. They were both dead.

Reaching down, Lock had to drag them out of the way to get to the door. He did it as quickly as he could. He didn't look at their faces, just hauled them out of the way. As he unlocked the door, the cell phone on the desk rang once more. He didn't look back. A cold rage had welled in him. He tamped it down, and stepped out into the corridor.

He walked along the corridor to find doors kicked or shot off their hinges. Some victims were still lying against the doors where they had tried to stop the shooter forcing their way in. Others were inside. He reached a communal bathroom. He pushed the door open. It was a slaughterhouse. Blood coated the floor and walls. He counted six young women, all dead. A couple had been shot multiple times. Three had died huddled together, arms around each other for comfort.

Pushing his way back out of the bathroom, he called 911, using a Bluetooth headset to ensure his hands were free for his weapon. In the corridor he heard fresh gunfire. It was close in, maybe on the second floor, but the echo told him it was inside the building. He heard a woman scream.

Lock ran down the corridor, pushing through double doors into a communal living area. There were two bodies here, one behind a sofa, the other just lying on the floor.

Another scream. Lock hit the stairs. He took them two at a time, racing up them. He heard a fresh shot. The shooter was definitely up here, roaming this corridor, picking out his victims.

At the top of the stairs, Lock stopped for the briefest of moments. He had just connected to a dispatcher. Bad timing. He couldn't start talking and risk giving away his presence. He was almost certain that the shooter was toting more than a handgun. If they had any sense, they'd also be wearing body armor. All Lock had was his SIG and regular clothes. If it came down to a gunfight at distance, he was toast. Surprise was what he needed, and even that might not be enough.

He reached up with his left hand and killed the 911 call. On tiptoe, he pushed through the door and into the corridor. The scene that greeted him was a mirror image of the downstairs corridor. Doors forced open. Bodies lying everywhere. But it wasn't an exact copy.

Peeking round the corner, Lock could see at least a half-dozen doors at the far end of the corridor that were still closed and intact. He ducked back as he saw a flash of movement. The shooter strolled out of a dorm room. Lock's guess had been correct. He had an assault rifle in his hands. He was wearing body armor. He had a handgun on either hip and what looked like spare mags dangling on a clip from his belt.

The shooter was white and male, which ruled out Gretchen and Krank. He stood about five ten. He was early twenties. He moved with purpose.

For Lock to step out now, and offer his whole body as a target would be suicide. A three-round burst would end it before it had begun.

Situations like this were close to triage. Calculations had to be made in order to minimize the loss of life. Like triage, sometimes saving the most lives entailed sacrificing others. It sucked. But it was the reality. It was where military training truly separated men like him from anyone else.

He waited. He could hear screams from behind a door. The shooter was shouting for the people or person on the other side to open up. When they didn't, Lock heard him kick out at the door.

There was the sound of wood splintering followed by another kick. Lock counted to three and took another peek. He was just in time to see the shooter push his way in through the door, the rifle raised.

That was Lock's cue to dash for the door. As he reached it, he heard someone inside the room reciting the Lord's Prayer between sobs.

'Our Father, who art in Heaven, thy kingdom come, thy will be do—'

The *thwump* of a round hitting flesh. A scream close by. The prayer continued, the crying sharper and higher-pitched. The shooter must have just killed the room mate. The person speaking was number two.

Lock conjured the dorm room in his mind. The victims must have hidden at the far end, close to the window, away from the door. If Lock pivoted in now, he'd have the same problem he would have had confronting the shooter in the corridor, only at a shorter distance.

He said his own prayer, asking whoever was up there for forgiveness. He closed his eyes for a split second and waited for the shot. When it came and the praying stopped, he opened his eyes. God forgive me, he thought.

He was already positioned so that he was on the side of the door that was opposite to the shooter's direction of travel. Eyes open, he raised his gun, his finger on the trigger. Using the SIG for years gave him intimate knowledge of the trigger pressure. He squeezed, stopping just short of firing.

The next part was a blur. The shooter stepped out. Lock leveled the SIG at point-blank range to the back of the shooter's head. The inner pad of his index finger travelled the last fraction. The gun fired. A single shot. Straight into the back of the shooter's head.

One shot.
One down.

More to go.

Lock reached down to check the asshole was dead. He was. Satisfied, Lock took his rifle and the clips. He hit the call button on his Bluetooth, and waited for a fresh 911 connection.

88

Janet Cristopher felt the rifle jam painfully into the small of her back. She was trying her best to contain her fear. It was a losing battle. She knew she was going to die. She had figured that by confronting Gretchen she could buy her students and colleagues some extra time, and perhaps the chance to escape. It was a noble act. She now realized that noble acts didn't take the edge off the thought of a painful death. Part of her wished that she had done the selfish thing and made a run for it into the hills and taken her chances with the fires.

The pressure in her back relented. Behind her, she heard Gretchen say, 'Okay, you can stop now.'

They were standing at the front of the college's main auditorium.

'Turn around,' said Gretchen.

Janet faced the hundreds of empty seats. Gretchen had retreated to the front row. She was completely composed, in the way that only a true psychopath could be. Even with the intense heat from the fires her body didn't betray even a single bead of sweat.

'Now what?' Janet asked her.

Gretchen reached into the pouch of her flak jacket and pulled out a small handheld video camera. 'Now you are going to apologize to the world for the damage that you're ideology has done.'

To emphasize her point, Gretchen laid the rifle down flat on the desk in front of her, and pulled out a handgun. She pointed it at Janet.

Janet was about to tell her to go to Hell. Then she remembered why she was there. If an apology would buy time, then who cared? Let her have her apology. Even if it was released at a later date, the world would know that it had been given under duress. Did anyone watch some poor hostage of Islamic militants and believe a word of their denunciations of Western depravity? If Gretchen wanted an apology, she could have one.

Standing there, trying to think of how to begin, Janet's heart almost stopped beating as she saw one of the doors at the very top of the auditorium begin to open. She couldn't see anyone, just the door slowly opening, half an inch at a time. She looked back at Gretchen, who was staring at her expectantly.

'Do you want a general apology or one for how I treated you?' she said to Gretchen.

Gretchen smirked. She was clearly reveling in having the upper hand. 'However you want to begin.'

Janet cleared her throat as the door slowly swung shut. Gretchen's head whipped round. There was no one there.

'Did you hear that?' Gretchen said.

Janet shrugged it off. 'What?'

Gretchen turned back round.

Ryan Lock crawled on hands and knees along the back of the auditorium. As he'd been walking from the dorms he'd caught a glimpse of Janet being forced at gunpoint into the building by Gretchen. He'd already briefed LAPD dispatch about what he knew, and alerted them to the fact that he was also wandering campus with a Bushmaster assault rifle. The captain he'd spoken to had ordered him to drop the weapon and make his way out unarmed. Lock had politely declined. He had the feeling that, even if he survived this, Los Angeles might be off his list of places to stay for a while.

Following Janet and Gretchen, and with no clear shot, he'd circled around, and found a way in through the rear entrance. At least this time he wasn't outgunned.

With the rifle in his hands, he crawled to the far end of the auditorium. The floor was carpeted, which cut down on the noise. He reached the far end. Ahead of him lay about twenty-five steps leading down. He scooted forward, and slowly began to crawl down.

The rifle made it hard work. He had to use the edge of his hands, and his upper body and leg strength to stop himself losing control and tumbling forward.

A short distance away now, he could hear Janet talking. From time to time Gretchen would interrupt her. It seemed to be some kind of enforced *mea culpa*.

He tuned out the words and kept moving. He could hear the periodic crack of single shots from somewhere outside. He figured Krank, or someone else, was still out there wreaking havoc. He wanted to deal with Gretchen and get back out there. Though, from what the LAPD was saying, SWAT teams were close if not already on site, so maybe he'd be able to leave the mopping up to someone else.

The decibel level between Janet and Gretchen began to rise. Lock tuned back in.

'You really think this will change anything?' Janet said.

'You think I'd be doing this if I didn't?' Gretchen fired back.

As they argued, Lock was reaching the front row. He stopped climbing down. He twisted his hips so that his body was lying directly across the step. He figured that if he moved fast enough he could have his rifle trained on Gretchen before she got to hers. He took a quick look, peering round the edge of the seating without putting his head over the top where he might be seen. Gretchen's hands were at her sides. The rifle was lying on the desk.

Moving into a squat, Lock held the rifle, ready to fire if he absolutely had to. He counted down in his head from three. As he counted he flicked the weapon to a three-round burst.

On one, he stood up, swinging the barrel of the Bushmaster fractionally so that it was pointed it at her upper torso and head. Even with body armor, being hit at such close range would dump her on her ass.

'Don't move!' he screamed.

Janet started more than Gretchen did. While Janet let out an involuntary 'Oh', Gretchen stared at him, as if she had been expecting this sudden intervention all along.

There was a long moment of silence. It was about to settle between them when Gretchen broke it: 'What you gonna do if I move?' she asked Lock.

'Shoot you,' he said, his tone completely flat. He wasn't playing games. It was a statement of fact. 'Raise your hands.'

Gretchen turned her attention from Lock back to Janet. 'This is on you, Professor,' said Gretchen, as she reached down for the rifle.

With the Bushmaster at his shoulder, Lock studied her face through the scope. 'Don't do it,' he shouted at her.

She picked up the rifle. Lock fired.

89

In the skies above Barnes College, several helicopters circled over the scene. The big rig truck was still parked at the bottom of the hill, completely blocking the main access to the college. Dersh's dead body lay to one side of the cab. A Malibu sheriff's deputy was talking to the driver, trying to keep him calm as they waited for a trained LAPD negotiator to arrive and take over supervision of the scene. Meanwhile, a small convoy of medical, firefighting and law-enforcement vehicles sat in a bottleneck, waiting.

There was not only the matter of the explosives collar around the driver's neck. The last person who had tried to approach the cab had been taken down by a sniper who had since fallen silent. Members of an LAPD SWAT team scoured the nearby hills with field glasses, trying to get a glimpse of the sniper, but the smoke and fire made it a thankless task.

A hulking African-American man was shouldering his way through the crowd. Dressed in jeans, boots, a black tactical vest and a light jacket, he pushed his way to the front.

Moments later, he was walking toward the cab of the truck. A couple of deputies screamed at him to stop. Eyes shielded by Oakley sunglasses, he dutifully ignored them as he hopped up onto the running board of the cab. One of the deputies ran after him.

Ty Johnson stopped and looked at him. The sweep of his gaze took in the deputy and everything around him.

The deputy flipped open a pouch and took out his Taser. 'I told you to stop,' he barked.

Ty lowered his Oakleys. He peered over the top of them with the look of a weary college professor. 'Officer, this here's Malibu not Missouri. You shoot a black man here, the *white* folks will lynch you. And, in any case, I'm about to save your ass. Now why don't you put away that little stun gun and help me move this thing so we can get those kids up there out before they burn to death?'

The deputy lowered the Taser. 'We can't move it. The driver's booby-trapped.'

'I seriously doubt those are explosives, but it ain't my head about to get blown off so let's err on the side of caution,' Ty said. He waved one huge hand toward the big rig. 'This here is a tractor-trailer. Correct? Clue's in the freaking name.'

Ty opened the cab door.

Quickly taking in the jerry-rigged nature of the cell phone taped to the dash, the explosives collar confirmed his first thought. There was no way this was a credible IED. He'd seen enough of them overseas to know. But law enforcement couldn't risk it. Ty wasn't law enforcement.

Judging by the state of the driver, ripping the collar straight off might kill him with a heart attack, even if the collar didn't blow his head from his shoulders.

'Take it easy,' he said to the driver. 'Don't move. Don't do shit unless I tell you. You're going to be fine. And if you ain't then I'm going with you. You feel me?'

The driver, who looked on the point of collapse, nodded.

'What's your name, partner?' Ty asked.

'Bill.'

'Okay, Bill. My name's Tyrone. Now, first step, I want you to look at me.'

The driver turned his head to look at Ty. Ty could see a couple of wires poking out from the padding of the collar. Two straps were keeping it in place.

'Bill, do I look like a man with a death wish?' Ty said.

'You're in here,' said Bill.

Ty smiled. 'That's good. You have a sense of humor. That's an excellent start. But, let me tell you, I have absolutely no desire to die today. You don't either. But if we can't move this big rig and let these good folks through properly then a lot of kids up on that hill there aren't going to see tomorrow.'

Ty reached a hand up and started to loosen one of the straps.

'What are you doing?' said Bill. He reached his free hand over to push Ty away. It didn't work. Ty was solid muscle.

'Bill, I'm doing what the cops can't,' said Ty, working on the second strap. 'I don't think there are any explosives here.'

He freed the second strap. The collar was loose around the driver's neck. Ty reached both hands up to pull it apart. If it was going to go, it would probably be now.

Either end of the collar was separated. As gently as he could, he began to lift it away from around Bill's neck. Bill had closed his eyes.

Ty held the collar in his hands. He looked down at it. So far, so good. He reached over and laid it on the seat next to Bill. Digging out his Gerber knife, he set to work freeing the driver's hand, which had been duct-taped to the wheel.

Bill had opened his eyes. His body was still rigid with fear. Ty finished stripping out the tape. He reached back over and picked up the collar. 'Okay,' he said. 'I'm going to take this outside, and when I'm a hundred yards away, I need you to move this big rig so that the road's clear. Think you can do that for me?'

'Yes, sir,' said Bill, his eyes still focused on the collar.

'Attaboy,' said Ty. He pushed the cab door open with one foot. Holding the collar in both hands, like it was a precious Ming vase, he slowly began to climb out.

His feet hit the running board. He stepped back down, the collar in his hands. He could see that the cops surrounding the big rig had lowered their weapons. It was a small mercy.

One step at a time, Ty began to walk toward the grassy slope. Behind him he could hear the rumble of the big rig's engine turn over.

As he walked, he counted out his steps. When he hit eighty, he squatted down, and laid the collar gently on the grass in front of him. He turned to see the big rig back up, and swing round.

Ty stood up and walked back toward the nearest patrol car, his hands raised, palms open. He had just reached it when there was an explosion behind him. The blast wave pushed him forward onto the hood of the patrol car. Dirt and debris flew into the air. Ty rolled over the hood. He came to rest, face down, kissing the blacktop.

Getting back to his feet, he did a quick visual inspection. Everything was there. Arms and legs were all accounted for. He didn't appear to be bleeding. His left knee was sore, but that was about it.

The explosion had punched a hole in the side of the trailer. Deputies ran toward it, helping the driver down from the cab. One of them took over, inching the big rig away.

Ty stood up, a little shaky on his feet. He looked at the hole in the ground where the collar had been. Where, only a few moments ago, he'd been standing. There was a ringing in his ears from the explosion. His legs felt shaky. He kept staring at the hole. After another few seconds he opened his mouth to speak: 'Motherfu—'

Krank stalked down the wide, carpeted corridor. A sudden flash of movement in a doorway stopped him cold. He brought the Bushmaster, freshly reloaded with a new clip, to his shoulder. His finger settled on the trigger.

He had lost contact with Loser and Gretchen. He assumed they were dead. That left him as the last man standing. It felt good, though he had yet to meet any real resistance. In one classroom a male professor, a man in his sixties, had charged at him with a pocket knife. The old guy had balls. Krank admired him. But when the moment came, he still shot him dead. Then he had killed the half-dozen young women hiding in a supply cupboard at the back of the class.

Edging slowly down the corridor, Krank listened carefully for sounds of movement behind the door. It was rare that he had entered a completely silent room. There was usually at least one person whispering into their cell phone, or just plain crying.

He reached the door where he thought he had seen someone a few moments before. It was partially open. He took a step back, raised his foot and kicked it.

The room was smaller than the other classrooms. It held four low tables arranged in a rectangle. There was an electronic whiteboard and a desk at the front. He didn't see anyone at first. Then, as he walked in and looked round, he saw someone's leg poking out from behind the desk.

Krank walked slowly to the other side of the desk. A young African-American woman with corn-rows was lying behind it with another young woman. The other woman had sandy-blonde hair that was cut short and spiked with gel.

Pointing the gun at them, Krank ordered them to stand up. They looked at him blankly. Fear seemed to have paralyzed them. It didn't look like willful disobedience but, as far as he was concerned, the result was the same.

He took aim and shot the white girl with the short blonde hair in the chest. The African-American girl screamed. The blood spattered across her face. From nowhere, she launched herself at him.

Before he had a chance to react, her long nails had raked across his face, almost catching one of his eyes. He jabbed the barrel of the gun forward as hard as he could. It hit her in the throat. She stumbled backwards, choking and gasping for air.

Krank flipped the rifle around, and hit her in the face with the butt. He heard a crunch as the blow fractured her cheekbone. She fell to her knees.

He was still holding the hot end of the gun with gloved hands as a figure appeared in the doorway. The man standing there was white, a little over six feet, with a muscular build. Unlike everyone else Krank had encountered, he didn't look scared – far from it. He was staring at Krank with a cold, calculating hunger. In his hands, he held the exact same Bushmaster rifle that Krank had. He raised it, and aimed straight at Krank.

Krank ducked down. He heard the bullet whizz over his head and smash the window behind him. Glass flew everywhere.

Raising the rifle above his head, Krank fired blind toward the doorway. The covering fire gave him enough time to drop onto all fours and start to crawl toward the girl he'd just hit with the rifle.

Reaching her, he grabbed her hair, and dragged her back toward him. She screamed in pain. His hand tightened around her hair and he pulled her on top of him. He dropped his rifle onto the ground, and went for his Glock.

He unholstered it, and pressed the barrel into the side of her head as the man in the doorway appeared again. The man walked toward them. He stopped when he saw the gun pressed to the girl's temple.

'Back off,' said Krank.

The man lowered the barrel of his rifle. His finger stayed on the trigger. He stepped off to one side. He was closing the angle between them, making it hard for Krank to whip round and take him out with the Glock.

'Further than that,' said Krank. 'And put that rifle down on the floor.'

The man stared at him. Krank didn't think he had blinked since they had first made eye contact. The one person Krank could recall with the ability to look at someone like that was Gretchen. There were chips of blue ice in the man's eyes.

'Okay,' said the man. 'I'll step out into the corridor and then I'll slide the rifle back through the doorway. I'll let you get out of here, and I won't fire. You have my word.'

'How do I know I can trust you?' Krank asked.

'You don't,' said the man. 'But the longer you sit here the less chance you have of getting out. The more cops arrive, the lower your odds. The fires and the general mayhem actually give you a pretty good chance. Better than most shooters have had. What's the point of making history if you don't have a while to enjoy it?'

Escape was not something that Krank had countenanced before. It had never been discussed. But with the others probably dead, it suddenly held an appeal. Even if Krank didn't escape properly, he could spend years in the prison system. There would be intense media interest. He would be famous. That much was true.

'Okay,' he said. 'Back out. Push the rifle and whatever else you got through.'

The man nodded. 'You got it.'

'But I'm taking her with me,' he said, pressing the barrel into her temple hard enough to make the girl squeal with pain.

'Understood,' said the man.

'Okay,' said Krank. 'Let's do this.'

Still facing Krank, the man backed away to the door. He disappeared into the corridor. A few moments later, the rifle skidded its way across the floor, minus the clip.

As a show of trust, it was good enough. Tightening his grip on the girl, Krank pushed her to the door. Despite her earlier resistance, she was too terrified to struggle.

They reached the doorway. Krank made sure she was ahead of him as they inched out. He looked in both directions, expecting to see the man, but the corridor was empty.

Ryan Lock stood inside a room three doors down from the classroom where he had found Krank. If he had been Krank, his first move after exiting the room would have been simple – use the girl for cover. Shoot Lock dead. Lock had something different in mind.

He flattened himself against the hinge side of the door. He listened for Krank to exit the room with his hostage.

Under ten seconds later, he heard movement. The girl was gasping for air. It sounded to Lock more like she was hyperventilating than being choked. Through the gap between the hinges and the door frame, he watched as Krank pushed her ahead of him to a fire-exit door. At the end of the corridor.

Lock stayed where he was. Right now saving the girl with the corn-rows trumped his desire to kill Krank. Not that he didn't want to kill him. He did. More than he'd wanted to kill many people who were already dead at his hand.

That changed rapidly as Krank let go of the girl. He pushed her off to one side. She fell against the corridor wall. She slid down the wall, her hands covering her head.

Krank raised his Glock and pointed it at her.

91

Lock moved around the door, his SIG up, his finger already on the trigger. Sweeping round the edge of the door, he fired a single shot in Krank's direction.

It went wide, slamming into the fire door. Krank spun round without firing at the girl. Lock held his position. His head and upper body were visible from around the door frame so that he would draw fire.

Krank took aim. Lock ducked back inside, almost losing his balance as he moved his foot back. A shot slammed into the wooden door, blowing a six-inch hole in the center.

Retaining cover, Lock punched his gun hand out into the corridor and fired. His aim was way right to avoid any chance of hitting the girl.

Krank fired again. Then again. Two shots in quick succession. As the shots came in, sending wood and plaster everywhere, Lock dove for the floor. Lying flat on his stomach, he inched back round the door. Krank would be expecting him to reappear at standing level. He would be mistaken.

Lock took aim. He squeezed off two shots at Krank. Krank fired back but his shots went high. Lock's first shot missed left by a few inches. His second hit Krank's side. His body armor took the hit but the force of contact pushed him back, sending him off balance.

A slow-motion second passed between them. Lock could almost see the cogs turning as Krank decided what to do next. Whether he stood his ground, took another shot or fled, the girl was out of the equation for now. She was a number. Lock was a threat. A threat always trumped a notch on someone's belt.

The rifle still raised, Krank backed toward the door. He lifted his foot and kicked back with his heel. Then he was gone.

Slowly, Lock got to his feet. Gun facing the fire door, he moved down the corridor toward the girl. He hunkered down next to her, his SIG aimed at the fire door lest Krank made another appearance.

'You hit?' Lock asked the girl.

'No,' she said. 'I don't think so.'

'Let me look, real quick.'

She made no move. Lock peeled her hands from her head, then checked her skull and neck for blood or signs of shrapnel. He helped her to her feet. She was banged up. In shock. She'd live.

He led her back to the nearest room and sat her down. He handed her his cell phone. He told her the number to call and what to say. He made her repeat it all back to him.

Back in the corridor, Lock exploded through the fire exit, gun drawn. He looked around. The fire had taken hold of one of the nearby buildings. Smoke poured thick and black from several windows. He could hear screaming overlaid with gunfire.

Lock pivoted around, eyes narrowed, his focus intense. That was when he saw it. A red Honda quad bike. Krank was swinging a leg over it.

Raising his SIG, Lock took aim. Too late. Krank gunned the engine and took off for the far side of the campus.

Lock tore after him as fire surged on all sides.

92

The big rig lay on a piece of ground to the side of the road as emergency vehicles poured through the barriered college entrance. The remainder of the LAPD SWAT team who hadn't already moved through on foot led the way. Behind them came Malibu Sheriff's Department and LA County Sheriff vehicles.

Further back there were more fire trucks, of six different fire departments from as close as Malibu and as far afield as Ventura, and Emergency Medical Support vehicles. Some of the fire crews had already set to work on either side of the entrance, beating back the flames to make sure the route to the Pacific Coast Highway would remain clear for the evacuation.

On the highway, ambulances were stacked up, awaiting the signal to head into campus to treat the wounded. Most of those were individuals suffering from the effects of smoke inhalation, as well as shock. First reports crackling over the radios spoke of few survivors from the actual shooting. Students who had been shot by one of the gunmen hadn't made it.

Wearing a hastily borrowed blue windbreaker with 'POLICE' emblazoned on the back in yellow letters, Ty ran toward the center of the campus. He'd lost contact with Lock some time ago. It was not a good sign. He had a sick feeling in his stomach as he did his best to get one step ahead of the cops, who were swarming in every direction.

Running in the smoke and heat was hard. Seeing anyone, never mind a suspect fleeing on a quad bike, was harder. At any moment Lock expected to take a bullet from one of the SWAT team members he could hear moving through some of the nearby buildings, clearing and securing as they went to allow the paramedics and other medical personnel in to do their work. Most of the talk was about bodies found. From what he could tell from the shouting and crackle of radios there seemed to be few survivors.

He stopped for a moment. He hunkered down so that he was closer to the ground. He tried to catch his breath. While he did that, he thought about Krank. If he had wanted to make a final stand he would have done it. But as soon as Lock had given him an out, and a rationale for taking it, he had jumped at it. He was committed to escape. Unless he was cornered, of course.

The scale and nature of the attack told Lock that it hadn't been arbitrary. It had been a while in the planning. The fires had been carefully set to encircle the campus, minimizing any possible escape route. Or, at least, an obvious one. But the study that would have required must have given Krank an intimate knowledge of the landscape.

That left Lock with one question. If he was Krank, and he wanted to escape, what path would he take?

Lock got back to his feet, and set a new course. He headed north and east, taking a wide loop round the dorm buildings. To his immediate left the grass was ablaze. But further up the fire had begun to burn out.

He kept moving. He could feel the heat through the soles of his boots. If the world ended, he had a feeling this was what witnessing it would be like. Black-charred earth, and a planet with barely enough air to sustain life.

Hitting a rise, he stopped. He could hear voices behind him. He couldn't make out what was being said. He decided against turning back. To emerge from the smoke carrying a gun and no uniform would not have been the best of ideas. In any case, he had come this far. Now that he had gun-faced Krank, it seemed suddenly personal. When someone shot at you, no matter what anyone told you, it became about the two of you.

Lock's left hand dropped to his thigh. He pushed down, forcing his body upwards and onwards. The smoke cleared for a fraction of a second and he saw a flash of red.

By the time he took a closer look it was gone, taken by the glare of freshly ignited scrub as it raced toward the ocean, driven hard by the Santa Ana wind.

Looking behind him, Lock saw that even if he wanted to go back his path would be hard to navigate through the fires. He had climbed too high. His only hope now was to get to the highway and the man-made sliver of a fire break that the black top might offer.

That was when he saw the red flash for a second time. Except this time he could make out that the red was the quad bike Krank was riding, the Bushmaster slung over his shoulder. The engine was making a high-pitched whining noise. As Krank twisted the throttle, it inched forward. Looking at the tires, Lock could see that the treads had begun to melt in on themselves, making grip harder.

Krank was too busy struggling with the machine to notice that Lock was standing less than a hundred yards behind him. Lock stayed low and started toward him, ignoring the intense heat that was ripping up through the soles of his boots. He stopped. He drew his SIG, and took aim at the back of Krank's head.

Some kind of sixth sense must have taken over for Krank. He gunned the quad bike. This time it did respond. It lurched forward enough that Lock's shot, at the edge of his accurate range with a handgun, went wide. He had to duck for cover as Krank spun round, shouldering the rifle, and fired a burst of shots. The slope of the ground saved Lock from the bullets, but he could feel his clothes burning. It was like lying face down on a giant hotplate.

He rolled over, staying on his back for a second, before moving back onto his front. He saw Krank lower the rifle. Through the smoke, Lock was pretty sure he recognized the curve of the highway he'd come down.

That meant the culvert he'd used to get onto the campus was about fifty yards ahead and to the left of Krank's current position. Quad bikes and culverts were a bad combo, especially culverts obscured by smoke.

Scrambling to his feet, Lock made a charge toward Krank. Krank twisted the throttle and took off as Lock ran in a wide loop, trying to force him left.

As he ran, Lock fired until his clip was empty. He ditched it and jammed in a fresh one, trying to stay on the move as he did so. He was fading. He could feel the heat and the smoke really starting to take a grip. His lungs felt squashed down into his chest cavity. Every breath was painful. He choked and coughed as he ran.

Krank was drawing clear. Lock dropped to his knee and fired three shots in quick succession to Krank's right. Krank would be able to see the highway now. There were no flashing lights, no police vehicles. It looked to all the world like a clear route north up into the canyon.

Lock fired another two shots wide on Krank's right. It had the desired effect. Krank kept bearing left. Lock continued to move as Krank drew away.

The next second the front wheels of the quad bike must have hit the edge of the culvert. It tipped forward. The momentum took Krank head first over the handlebars. There was a loud crash of metal and stone. Both the bike and Krank disappeared.

From behind him, Lock heard a man's voice. 'Police! Do not move!'

Lock froze. He didn't move a muscle. In any case, he wasn't sure that he had anything left in the tank.

'Okay,' said the voice. 'That's good. Now drop your weapon.'

Lock kept his SIG by his side. He squatted down and laid it slowly on the burning ground, careful to point the hot end facing up the slope toward Krank and away from the cops behind him. He was betting they had to be cops. He figured that if they weren't, if there was a fourth shooter, they would have shot him in the back by now.

Behind him, he could hear people rushing up behind him. To one side he caught flashes of black. SWAT officers wearing breathing equipment. Properly equipped. Unlike him.

He followed the rest of the instructions. He laced his hands behind his head and knelt down. The burning pain on his kneecaps was intense. But less intense than being shot at close range multiple times.

He felt the snap of cuffs. He was hauled to his feet. It was a blessed relief.

A fresh wave of fire was sweeping down toward the culvert. Since the bike had gone over the edge he had heard nothing. The SWAT team had obviously missed it.

'Is it just you up here?' one of the officers asked him.

The fire had reached the edge of the culvert near to where Krank must be lying. There would be no oxygen left in a few seconds. Assuming Krank was still alive. Lock thought it over. Krank might be dead. He might be alive. Right now he was the proverbial cat in a box, alive and dead. If he lived, and survived, he would be a living reminder of what Lock guessed was the nation's biggest mass shooting. The survivors didn't need that.

On the other hand, Lock wasn't the law. Decision time. Lock closed his eyes. He did his best to clear his mind as a hand reached round and placed a breathing mask around him. He sucked in the first clean air he'd had in what seemed like years.

He nodded forward, indicating that he had something to say. The mask was lifted from his mouth and nose. With the air had come his answer. To hell with the asshole lying down there. He had shown no mercy to innocent people whose only crime was some imagined slight constructed in his sick mind.

'No,' said Lock. 'It's just me. I was going after the last shooter, but I lost him.'

94

Lock kept his hands steady as the Malibu sheriff's deputy uncuffed them from behind his back. He rolled his neck. He guessed that the rear bench seat of a cop car had not been ergonomically designed for comfort. They tended to focus more on functionality so that, among other things, they could be wiped clean with a damp cloth and bleach.

In the hills above the college, the fires were still blazing. The northernmost tip of the wildfire had raced up the coast a mile. A state of emergency was in full effect, and already the politicians had set to work on advancing their particular agenda.

From behind the patrol car he had just stepped out of he heard a long, low, throaty laugh. He knew who it was without having to turn around.

'What's so amusing, Tyrone?' Lock asked.

Ty stepped in front of him. He held his cell phone in the palm of one hand. On the screen was a picture of Lock cuffed in back. He had to admit he looked none too pleased.

'So?' said Lock.

'Brother,' Ty began, 'if you can't see the humor in you sitting in the back of a black and white while I'm strolling round in a jacket with "police" on the back, you don't understand America.'

Lock held up his right fist, knuckles facing Ty, and used his left hand to slow-crank his middle finger up. Ty didn't miss the opportunity to take another quick snap as his laughter threatened to overwhelm him. 'Oh, man, Ryan, you kill me.'

A female LAPD patrol officer who was passing by shot Ty a dirty look. He ignored her. Lock didn't blame him. He knew as well as Ty did that humor was what got you through stuff like this. The darker the event, the blacker the jokes.

Up on the hill above them, dozens of young people, most of them women, lay dead. Dozens more were injured. Those who hadn't been physically injured would carry other scars. Scars that could run deeper, and prove more difficult to recover from, than a broken arm or even a gunshot wound.

After a time, Ty gathered himself. 'What you want to do now?'

Lock nodded back toward the massed ranks of LAPD brass that had descended. 'They're going to want to talk to us.'

'He would have killed more if you hadn't been here,' said Ty.

Lock smiled. 'Maybe.' He sure as hell wasn't going to play that angle – with the cops or anyone else for that matter.

He would happily allow the authorities to take whatever credit they wanted. His only aim now was to duck the media. He had no interest in celebrity. His eyes narrowed as he took a final look back toward the blackened hills. The love of celebrity. The world's unending need for fame and ego gratification had done enough damage already.

Epilogue

Two months later

Her eyes hidden behind oversized Jackie Onassis sunglasses, Tarian Griffiths smiled at Lock as he took a seat opposite her. They had seen each other since the events at the college. Lock and Ty had both attended the funerals of Peter, Teddy, and Marcus as a way of offering moral support. This was Lock's goodbye. At least for a while.

The waiter came over and offered him a menu. Lock thanked him, but declined. He looked at Tarian and smiled. 'It's good to see you.'

She took off her sunglasses and laid them on the gleaming white tablecloth. Behind her, the sun glistened off the equally gleaming boats moored in the marina. 'You can't stay for lunch?'

Lock stared into her eyes, getting lost for a moment. 'Ty and I have an operation in Europe this weekend.'

'Top secret?' she said, teasing.

'Something like that.'

Her smile faded a little. He could see the sadness in her eyes that she would likely always carry now. 'Just be careful,' she said. 'I don't think I could take losing one more person I cared about.'

'This should be pretty straightforward,' he said. 'Fly somewhere, collect something, bring it back Stateside.' He looked at the empty place setting in front of her. 'You're not eating either?'

Tarian glanced across to a nearby table of glamorous young twenty-something women. They were all preened to within an inch of their lives. 'Competition's pretty intense here. Have to keep myself in shape. Although grief is pretty amazing for weight loss.'

Lock followed her gaze, then looked back at her. 'I'd say you're in a league of your own.'

'Can I see you when you're next in town?' asked Tarian.

Lock rose from his chair. He leaned in and kissed her cheek. She moved her head so that their lips brushed. He could smell her perfume. Part of him wanted to cancel his weekend job. He drew back. His hand fell to hers. His fingers closed around it. 'I'd like that.'

Ty was waiting for him in the car. The R6 was parked in the spot closest to the door. Face out. Engine running. Ready to go. Lock opened the driver's door, and handed Ty a manila folder that held a couple dozen sheets of paper. 'LAX to London. London to Budapest. One night in Budapest, then back to London with the asset on Sunday,' he said to Ty. 'We deal with the exchange and we're back Stateside by Tuesday morning.'

Ty took the folder and began flicking through. 'As romantic weekend getaways go, this sucks.'

Lock pulled out of the parking lot and took a right onto Admiralty Way, heading for the airport. 'Go to the last page. Check the fee.'

Ty did so, and let out a low whistle. 'Perhaps romance really is overrated.'

THE END

Ryan Lock Books

Lockdown (Ryan Lock 1)
Deadlock (Ryan Lock 2)
Gridlock (Ryan Lock 3)
Lock & Load (Short)
The Devil's Bounty (Ryan Lock 4)
The Innocent (Ryan Lock 5)

Other Books

Post: (Byron Tibor 1)

Printed in Great Britain
by Amazon.co.uk, Ltd.,
Marston Gate.